CONSUMING

THE

SOUL

Enjoy!

Ellen H Reed

Also by Ellen Reed

The Gangster's Gold

The Ghost of Barred Owl Farm

CONSUMING
THE SOUL

BY
ELLEN H REED

Consuming the Soul

Cover Design: Amanda Stacey of Hops Designs

KDP Publishing

Printed in the United Stat

CHAPTER ONE

Vampires. What does the word conjure? Bela Lugosi clothed in a flowing black cape declaring he wants to suck your blood? *Twilight's* sparkling Edward Cullen romancing the lovely Bella Swan, foreswearing his bloodlust? Or can it mean something entirely different? The summer my family spent in northern New Hampshire when I was fourteen showed me that a simple word can have many meanings, and in this case, none of them good. There was not a sparkle or a flowing cape to be found. Just death.

My dad, Roger Whelan, is a paleontologist. He studies dinosaurs during the summer. The rest of the year he teaches biology at this little no-name college that's so exclusive, parents will do practically anything to get their kids enrolled. He loves dinosaurs. He will talk about nothing but dinosaurs. Throughout our house, we have models and bones and skulls and casts of giant footprints and well, you get the idea. He tried to convince me that dinosaurs were really interesting and took me to one of his digs out in Montana one summer. Worst two weeks of my life. I'm sorry, but sitting in the dirt, brushing away one grain of sand at a time from some glorified rock with a paintbrush for hours on end is not my idea of a good time.

However, Dad seems like the king of Normal Guys compared to my mom, Lina. Mom is convinced she is descended from Gypsy psychics. Granted, Grandma Ludmilla was kind of freaky. Once she'd looked at me with those beady little eyes buried in her wrinkly face, pointed her bony finger at me and said, "Don't go to the mall tomorrow. There is danger." Next day, the roof of the mall caved in during a big rainstorm. She also talked to ghosts she claimed were sitting next to you on the couch. Spooky.

Anyway, Mom believes she has inherited this so-called 'gift' and is always 'communing with the spirits'. Right. She is so convinced of this power of hers that she became an online and phone psychic. These pathetically stupid people call her at all hours wanting to know if they should break up with their ex-con boyfriend or move to Gnawbone, Indiana to take a job. My personal favorite was the moron who called when someone was breaking into his house. He wanted Mom to tell him if she could see who it was. Jeeze. At least Mom had the sense to tell him to hang up and call the cops. The guy was definitely from the shallow end of the gene pool.

So, it's Mom, Dad, and me. That's it. Just me. Well, in a perfect world it should have been just me, but I do have a sister. Maya. She's about to turn seventeen and reminds me of that constantly. She's a lot like Dad. Much more into science and math. She's been taking college classes since she was my age. Again, she never hesitates to bring that up whenever possible.

Despite my know-it-all sister, who I manage to avoid most of the time, I was reasonably happy spending my days reading, writing stories, watching movies, and occasionally doing homeschool work. Then Dad dropped the bomb. The one that moved my life from merely tedious into a recurring nightmare.

As long as I've known him, Dad has been writing some book about dinosaurs. I don't know what it's about. What they eat, maybe? Frankly, I always thought they just ate each other, or maybe lawyers if *Jurassic Park* is anything to go by, but Dad seems to think he's got enough new information on dino dining habits to write an entire book. This summer, he decided we're all going from our nice little house in Manchester, New Hampshire to some cabin up in boonies of the White Mountains so he can write this long-awaited book. Why he doesn't just go by himself is beyond me. I mean, if he wants privacy, he could just leave me, Maya, and the Psychic Queen here. Actually, I think that might have been his plan all along, but Mom claimed the stars were in a bad position, and we should all stick together. Figures.

I'm not exactly the outdoorsy type. I guess my complexion could be described as "whale belly white". I don't even need to apply makeup to achieve that pale look. Add my naturally black hair and voila: instant Goth. Jenna, my very best friend, on the other hand, looks like a model with her perfect peachy skin, azure blue eyes, and glorious blonde hair. She's gorgeous.

Well, she is when she isn't dying her hair chartreuse or whatever. Anyway, I digress.

I don't like the outdoors. There are bugs outside. Nasty bugs like ticks and mosquitoes and black flies. Things that bite. Maybe poisonous snakes. I'd have to check on that one. All I know is that spending the summer in the Great Outdoors in a dumpy little cabin with nobody but Mr. and Mrs. Bizarro and the Know-it-all would be a fate worse than death. Plus, this was the summer Jenna and I had planned to try and get into the summer writing program at the college.

"You're going to love it up there," Dad assured me. "The original part of the house was built in 1720. It's situated on a lake and very private. We can go fishing right outside the front door! Believe it or not, your mom's dad's family came from the area."

I just stared at him. I hate fishing. It involves touching disgusting worms and even more disgusting fish. And Grandpa Parson's family was as weird as they come. Is that the best he could come up with?

"I think it sounds like a fantastic idea," chimed in Maya in that smug way of hers. "I can do some research on the benthic zone of the lake for the advanced ecology class I'll be taking next fall. They always assign an in-depth research project so this will give me a head start." I rolled my eyes. What a brown-noser.

Mom came and sat beside me, staring deep into my eyes. I really hate it when she does that. "Sophia, darling," she said in her deep voice, "It is very important we all stay together this summer. I did your horoscope, and you have a great challenge ahead of you. In fact, we all have challenges we must overcome. We will need each other for support to get through the difficult days ahead."

I rolled my eyes again. I'm very good at it. I've had fourteen years to practice. "If it's so terrible, then why are we going? What will happen if we stay here?"

Mom patted my hand. "We are destined to go on this journey, but there will be danger. In the end, we will all be stronger for the experience." I glanced over at Dad who was studiously ignoring all this. He was a scientist through and through, but he tolerated Mom and her quirks. I don't think he really believes Mom has psychic talent, but he'd been just as spooked by Grandma Ludmilla as I'd been. So, who knows, maybe Mom does have some smidgen of psychic power under all those gauzy skirts and beads.

I just sighed. I knew when I was beat. When Mom decided that we were "destined" to do something, there was no arguing with her. "So, when are we leaving?" I grumbled.

"Next week," replied Dad looking happier now that I'd surrendered to the inevitable. "After the semester ends." He looked at me thoughtfully. A look that usually did not bode well. "I think we'll need to come up with some project for you. You don't want to waste your entire summer writing *Phantom of the Opera* stories."

I felt my face flush. Writing fan fiction stories was my one big joy in life. I loved losing myself in the lives of my favorite characters from books, TV, movies, whatever. I could write a story, put it online and get instant feedback. My author persona, writerchick333, was renowned in some genres. I want to be a writer, which is why I've been hoping to get into the college summer program. But Dad didn't get it. He thought fanfiction was a total waste of time. In theory, he was supposed to be in charge of my homeschooling, and although he was strict about the math and science, I pretty much chose whatever else I wanted to study. However, every now and then, he'd get it into his head he needed to give me special assignments. Looked like this summer was going to be another one of those times.

"What kind of project?" I mumbled suspiciously as I glanced at Maya. So help me, if it had to do with benthic zones, whatever those were, I'd go right outside and throw myself in front of the next Mack truck that came along.

"I'm not sure." Dad tapped his chin. "Something to do with history. We'll have to wait until we get up there, but I'm sure we'll think of something. New Hampshire is brimming with history. No doubt we can figure out some project you'll find interesting."

I tried not to groan. Dad and I did not often see eye to eye on what I considered interesting. If I knew him, he'd have me searching for fossils in the woods or analyzing tree fungus to see if dinosaurs might have eaten it. I'd rather shoot myself in the head. However, if we could come up with something more historical, possibly even supernatural in nature, well, then we might be getting somewhere. All I can say in hindsight is be careful what you wish for.

CHAPTER TWO

We arrived in Parsons Corners, this infinitesimal town in the middle of the White Mountains, on a Friday. We turned off the highway onto a narrow winding road that changed from asphalt to gravel to dirt. It's a good thing our SUV has four-wheel drive, or we never would have made it. Finally, I spotted the modest, brown farmhouse perched on the edge of a beautiful lake. I have to hand it to Dad; the location was stunning. Even I appreciated it. The old clapboard house had an inviting porch attached to the front and faced the shoreline.

Upstairs were four bedrooms, and on the main level, a big kitchen, a small living room, and a dining room. Fortunately, the owners had installed a couple of bathrooms, so no outhouse. I claimed the smallest bedroom in the front corner; Maya the one next door. Mom and Dad took the biggest at the other end of the house. Dad would use the fourth for his study. And Mom could do her psychic schtick from anywhere as long as she had a phone. I was just relieved that although we didn't have TV, we did have internet access. I could talk to my friends online at least. I hoped they were up to listening to some major griping.

Mom and Dad disappeared downstairs to check out the kitchen while I decided to examine my new digs. The space was a little bigger than my room back home which was a plus, and the window looked out over the lake. I stared outside and smiled at the rippling expanse of water, loving its pristine beauty. I spotted ducks swimming out on the water dunking their heads every so often. Very picturesque.

The plaster walls of the room were painted a ho-hum white and the floor consisted of wide pinewood planks covered by a worn blue and green braided rug. The wooden bed had four tall posts, which were a nice historic touch. I liked old things like that. Beside the bed stood a small table with an electric lamp made from an old lantern and against the wall leaned a tall dresser. Hmm. No desk. I would have to talk to Dad about that. Despite what he said, I still planned on doing a lot of writing this summer.

I dragged my suitcase up onto the bed to unpack, throwing my shorts and underwear into the dresser. I looked around and spied a small closet on the far side of the room. A good place to hang my shirts, assuming there were any hangers. As I opened the door, the screech of the rusty hinges made the hair on the back of my neck stand up. Sounded like something out of a horror movie. Now is the time the madman in the closet should jump out and slice and dice his hapless victim with a bloody axe. I'll admit, a slight chill rippled down my spine.

I was happy to see that although no deranged axe murderer lurked behind the door, there were some hangers. As I reached in to get them, I made out a small door in the back of the closet. That was weird.

Why was there a door in a closet? I stood there for like a minute trying to decide what to do. A normal person would just walk in and open the door. I mean, what did I think would happen? I gave a short laugh as I recalled one night when I was about eight. My babysitter was watching an old horror movie called *The House on Haunted Hill*. She didn't know I'd snuck downstairs to watch. Well, at one point these stupid people are searching the basement of an obviously haunted house. They go in this one little room and a horrible witch leaps out of the wall. I screamed. Carla screamed. We both stood there screaming for like five minutes. It's pretty funny now, but I was hysterical for the rest of the night and had nightmares for weeks. Poor Carla wasn't much better. That's what ran through my head as I stared at the door.

"Sophia," I muttered to myself, "Quit being an idiot. You're not a baby, for god's sake. You're almost fifteen years old. Get a grip! There is no creepy witch waiting to jump out at you." I took a deep breath, stepped forward and yanked opened the door. I had no trouble making out a set of steps leading upwards into the shadows. I sighed. It was nothing spookier than access to the attic. I shook my head. What an idiot. I stuck my head in the little doorway but couldn't see a light switch or anything. I'd have to wait until I located a flashlight. Maybe I'd find something interesting up there. Maybe even something that would work for my project. It would be infinitely better if I managed to find a project for myself than wait for Dad. Anyway, it was definitely worth investigating.

I finished hanging up my clothes then headed downstairs. Mom and Dad were organizing the stuff in the kitchen. Maya was still up in her room. I watched my parents for a few minutes. I could go in there and help them organize pots and pans, or I could go check out the lake. That was a no-brainer. I slipped out the front door and made my way to the little dock on the lake. There was a small boat tied to it. I guessed that was for fishing. I didn't have a clue how you worked the thing. I'm sure Maya would be ecstatic. I stood on the deck and inhaled the fresh pine scent of the surrounding trees. There was a cool breeze coming off the water. It felt wonderful. I found some rocks near the base of the dock and spent a good fifteen minutes trying to figure out how to skip stones. Did I mention I'm not very coordinated?

"You're not doing it right."

I whirled around to find this guy standing about ten feet from the end of the dock watching me. I have to confess, my mouth dropped open. I guessed him to be about my age, maybe a little older with light blonde hair and the bluest eyes I'd ever seen on a human being outside of a contact lens ad. I was speechless. Guys this cute don't normally acknowledge my existence, much less talk to me. A warm flush crept up my face.

"If you want, I can show you how to do it." The guy came closer. He studied me warily like I might attack him or something and smiled uncertainly. "My name is Liam MacKenzie."

I opened and closed my mouth a few times, like a dying guppy. Finally, I swallowed and tried to sound calm, cool, and collected. "Yeah, sure. Okay." Right answer. His face lit up like the sun. My stomach swooped. He was so good looking with those blue eyes and sculptured cheekbones, and when he smiled, the gods sang.

He trotted down the hill and joined me at the end of the dock. He looked at my collection of stones and frowned. "These aren't the right kind. We need some flat ones. Those work best." He returned to the shore and scoured the ground for whatever he considered the "right" kind of rocks. I could have watched him all day. He returned after a while with a handful of flat stones of various sizes. He handed me one and dumped the rest at our feet.

"Okay," he began as he took his own stone. "It's all in the wrist. You need to flick it so it hits flat. Like this." He neatly flung his stone, and I gaped in awe as it bounced five or six times across the surface of the water. He turned to me. "Now you try." He took my hand and positioned it just so. I barely heard what he said. His touch sent a jolt of electricity through me. "Remember, try to keep it flat."

I gulped, bringing myself back to the stone. Who would have thought throwing rocks could be so exciting? I nodded and awkwardly flicked the rock out across the water. It bounced once before disappearing below the surface of the lake. I squealed like a little girl and immediately blushed.

"Great job!" grinned Liam. "You're a natural."

"Thanks," I mumbled. I suddenly wanted to run back to the house and hide in my room. My few guy friends are more of the kind you'd find presiding over the local chapter of Dungeons and Dragons or hacking into CIA secure servers. They certainly don't look like Greek gods. Guys like Liam usually go for the popular girls - girls born knowing how to use mascara and dress fashionably. Me? I'm lucky if I can match my socks. The one time I tried using mascara, I got a massive eye infection. I guess I'm just not destined for beauty. Anyway, I didn't know what to say to this guy. He didn't look like the type that would spend hours reading Japanese manga.

"So, do you have a name?" He looked at me expectantly. There was nothing mocking about him. He simply looked interested.

"Um, Sophia." There I got that out at least.

"Great to meet you, Sophia." Liam smiled his brilliant smile, his neon blue eyes nearly blinding me. "It's always great to see new kids around, even if it's just for the summer. How long are you guys staying here?"

I frowned. How did he know we were renting? Well, that was stupid. If he lived up here, I'm sure he knew all the year-round residents. I shrugged, again, trying to act cool. I really suck at that. "For a couple of months. My dad is writing a book."

Liam nodded. "Lots of people do that up here. They come up during the summer to write or paint or whatever. They like the peace and quiet. What is he writing about?"

Inwardly, I cringed. "Dinosaurs." There is simply no way to make that sound cool. Or so I thought. Liam's face lit up like a six-year old's.

"Really? He studies dinosaurs? Do you think I could meet him sometime? I've always wanted to be something like an archeologist or paleontologist. I love studying the past."

Now it was my turn to be amazed. This Adonis was a science nerd? And he liked history? Well, well, well, this summer was looking up. "Yeah, I'm sure he'd love the chance to talk about dinosaurs. Mind you, he won't shut up once you get him started, so you better make sure you have plenty of time."

Liam laughed. And what a laugh. It was deep and throaty and it made my heart soar just to hear it. I shook myself. This was getting seriously weird. I never went gaga over boys. Sure, I liked them and all, but I never found they had any interest in me, so I admired them from afar and kept it at that.

"So, um, do you live around here?" I figured I really ought to find out something about this guy. I mean, if it turned out he was actually a psycho serial killer, it might be helpful to obtain some basic info to give the police.

Liam nodded as he folded his legs under him and lowered himself to the edge of the dock. I quickly followed. "Yeah, my family has lived up here for generations. We own a lodge on the lake. We're one of the few open year-round. It's me, my parents, my two brothers and my sister."

I tilted my head as I studied him. "Do you like it? Running a lodge, I mean."

He gave a little laugh and shrugged. "Depends on the day. I don't like the cleaning and that kind of thing, but I like taking visitors out fishing or hiking. That's always interesting. It does get kind of lonely though. Not many kids my age live around here."

"What about school? Don't you have friends at school?"

He grimaced. "I'm homeschooled. Since we run the lodge all year, it just works out better that way. I used to go to the village school when I was younger. but since there aren't enough older kids in Parsons Corners, I had to ride a bus for over two hours each day to get to the high school in Berlin. That got really old." Suddenly he blushed. "I bet you think homeschooling is really weird."

Now I laughed, and he stared at me. "If it is, then I'm just as weird as you are. I've been homeschooled my whole life." I shook my head. "Frankly, I think it's because my parents didn't want to deal with the rules and regulations of a school system. I honestly can't see my mother sitting through a parent/teacher conference." I tried to picture that. I'm not sure what a teacher would make of Mom when she claimed I'd failed a math test because the stars weren't properly aligned.

Now Liam definitely looked interested. "You're really homeschooled? You're just not saying that?"

I shook my head. "Nope. I'm not just saying that. I mean, I do go to some homeschool co-op classes, and in the fall, I hope to take some classes at the community college like my sister, but I've never been to a traditional school."

Liam smiled again. My heart fluttered. "Well, that's a relief. I get so tired of trying to explain to people about homeschooling. They always seem to think we're a religious cult or commune or something. They can't seem to fathom that normal people also homeschool."

I nodded sympathetically. I knew exactly what he meant. I'd run into my fair share of nutjobs who thought homeschooling should be illegal, and that it would result in nothing but a nation of unsocialized illiterates. Seemed to me a lot of the public schools already had that covered. I suddenly felt more at ease with Liam.

"You and your family are welcome to come eat at the lodge any time you want," said Liam still smiling. "First meal is on me."

"Thanks," I replied, a little puzzled. "You don't have to do that."

Liam climbed to his feet and brushed off his jeans. "It's my pleasure. I don't meet many good-looking girls who understand about homeschooling or have a dad who's a paleontologist. If it means I'll get to see you

more often, then I'll pay for your meals all summer!"
He glanced at his watch and frowned. "I need to go,
but I'll definitely be seeing you around, Sophia."
Flashing his brilliant grin once more, he hurried down
the dock back to the shore and then with a little wave,
he disappeared into the woods.

I stared at the place where he'd disappeared. My
whole being felt lighter somehow. I had a goofy grin on
my face that I just couldn't seem to shake. I turned and
headed back to the house. "Sophia," I said to myself
with a small shake of my head, "I think this summer
just got a lot more interesting!"

CHAPTER THREE

After Liam left, I had a hard time thinking about much else. Could a guy like him really be interested in a nerdy girl like me? That sounded like something out of one of those pathetic teen romance novels Jenna always reads. Only thing missing was a vampire.

I spent another fifteen minutes or so working on my rock skipping technique. I frowned as I tried to remember what Liam had told me. I did improve after a while. One stone must have skipped like ten times. Obviously, I was a rock skipping prodigy.

The sun's rays faded as it sank below the trees, casting long shadows and taking the day's warmth with it. I rubbed my arms and decided to head back towards the house. I couldn't wait to tell Jenna about my first day in the boonies. She would act thrilled, but I knew inside, she'd be fuming. I smiled at that. Usually, the boys noticed her, not me.

Mom and Dad had gotten the kitchen pretty much in order by the time I wandered in. Mom stood before the refrigerator trying to figure out what to make for dinner. I wasn't holding my breath. Cooking is not Mom's forte. She claims standing around a hot stove disrupts her aura or something. If anybody cooked, it was usually me, and to be honest, that meant a lot of microwave dinners. How did kids survive before microwaves? Maybe that should be my research project.

"Who was that boy?" asked Dad, opening a beer.

My eyebrows shot up in surprise. Who knew he noticed things like that?

"Boy? What boy? Are you telling me some guy actually talked to you, Sophia?" Maya had entered the room just in time to add her two cents. "Was it pitch dark out?"

"Shut up, Maya," I snapped. Great. Now I'd have to endure Maya's stupid remarks about liking a boy. I sighed and looked back at Dad. "His name is Liam MacKenzie. His family owns a lodge someplace on the lake. He invited us to come eat there some day and said it would be on the house."

Dad's eyes widened as he grinned at me. "You must have made quite an impression." He took a swig from his bottle. "Must be the Pine Forest Lodge. Nice place. Since you have connections, we'll definitely have to visit."

My face grew hot. Why did parents always have to make such a big deal out of everything? Okay, yeah, I wanted to see Liam again, but not with Mom and Dad in tow. And especially not with Maya. Unlike me, my sister never had trouble talking to guys. With her olive skin and dark curly hair, Maya had an exotic quality that attracted boys wherever she went. Then I remembered Liam's interest in the past. "I told Liam you're writing a book about dinosaurs. He said he'd really like to talk to you. Guess he wants to become an archeologist or paleontologist."

Dad's face lit up. "Really? That would be great. Next time he happens by, bring him on in. I'll be happy to speak to him."

"Oh, Dad," Maya turned to look at us. "Can you show me that website with all the information on this lake? I'd really like to get started on gathering some data." Maya hated not being the center of attention.

"Sure, come on." Dad and Maya disappeared up the stairs.

I turned to go up to my room when I glanced at my mother. She continued to stare into the refrigerator but had a weird, vacant look on her face. More vacant than usual, I mean. I frowned. "Mom? You okay?"

She blinked a few times, looking a little confused. A moment passed before she turned toward me. "Oh, yes. Yes, I'm fine. Just felt a bit dizzy for a minute." She looked back at the refrigerator. A chill ran down my spine.

"Why don't I find something for dinner, Mom," I said moving closer. "You've been working pretty hard today. It's the least I can do."

She smiled vaguely and nodded. "Thank you, dear. That would be great. I think I'll go lie down for a bit." I watched as she shuffled from the room. My stomach gave an odd twist. Something wasn't right. Sure, Mom often claimed she entered into psychic trances to commune with the spirits, but this was different. Her face showed little color. I didn't like it.

With a sigh, I turned to the refrigerator and pulled out a package of ground beef. I knew how to slap together some hamburgers at least. With any luck, I wouldn't burn down the house.

At dinner, Mom appeared better. She still seemed a little distracted, but the color had returned to her cheeks, and she ate well. The days leading up to the move had been pretty stressful, and she'd put in long hours on the psychic hotline to give her some time off to get things done. I suppose it all caught up with her.

Dad helped me and Maya clear away dishes and clean the kitchen. I considered saying something to him about Mom but decided to wait. I mean, she looked okay now, so I hoped it was just a one-time deal. When we finished, I headed up to my room and booted up my laptop. Normally, I would have texted Jenna, but my cell phone didn't get good reception up here, so it forced me to rely on the computer. Disappointed to see she wasn't online, I quickly typed up an email and sent it on its way. We would have to schedule times to be online so we wouldn't keep missing each other.

I shut down my computer and lay down on the bed, my brain buzzing. I couldn't help grinning like an idiot when I thought about Liam and his amazing topaz blue eyes and stellar smile. I honestly didn't expect us to be any more than friends, but a girl can dream, can't she? No boy had paid me any attention in all of my fourteen years. Well, except that kid in my co-op algebra class. He used to follow me all over the place, but at ten years old, he gave me the creeps. As I said, I had a couple of guy friends, but mostly, they showed far more interest in playing video games than meeting girls.

I shook myself. "Get over it, Sophia! You are not going to spend the entire summer mooning over some guy. I don't care how nice or gorgeous he is. You have things to do." I sighed. But he sure was cute. I'd never kissed a boy before, but I suspected kissing Liam wouldn't be half bad.

A muffled thump interrupted my romantic reverie. I blinked and sat up. Where had that come from? I frowned, staring at the closet door. I swore it came from there. Slowly rising, I approached the door. I rubbed my damp palms against my jeans. Could there be someone up there?

I put my ear to the closet door and listened. Nothing. My mouth dry, I reached out and grabbed the knob. With surprising force, I wrenched the door open, leaping back as I did so. Again, nothing. I released a long, slow breath and shook my head. Weird noises were to be expected in old houses. Maybe a raccoon lived up there. This would be a very long summer if I freaked out over every odd noise. All the same, I was sleeping with my light on. Tomorrow I vowed I would check out the attic. In the daylight.

The next morning, I awoke to the sound of rain hammering on the roof. Who on earth thought putting a metal roof on a house was a good idea? I covered my ears against the deafening roar then crawled out of bed and stumbled to the window. The sky was a dark, depressing gray, and the lake a mere shadow in the downpour. Dampness permeated everything. I sighed. Guess I wouldn't be going anywhere today.

I pulled on some clothes and headed downstairs to breakfast. No one was around. I listened to the sounds of Dad in his office. So, he was up. Mom rarely rose before noon. The loonies come out mostly at night, so she works the psychic hotline then.

I poured myself some cereal and thought about how I should spend my day. That's when I remembered the thump I'd heard the night before. I pursed my lips. Exploring the attic would be the first order of business. I would have preferred a nice sunny day, but I'd sleep better if I knew what was up there.

I rinsed out my bowl and rummaged around until I located a large electric lantern. I wanted lots of light up there, and some dinky little flashlight just wasn't going to cut it. I would have brought up high intensity spot lights if we had some.

Lantern in hand, I made my way back up the narrow stairs to my room. I tried to picture ladies in hoop skirts climbing them but had no idea how they did it. Moments later, I stood in front of the closet once more. Mouth dry, I inched the door open and peered in. There was no use trying to listen for any unusual noises. The pounding rain obliterated all other sounds. An ache settled in the back of my head. How Mom could sleep through this was beyond me.

I took a deep breath and stepped into the small space. My stomach had that weird flutter again. Other than my stuff hanging on the rod, it was empty. Empty, except that odd door.

Now, in modern movies, that door would no doubt be a portal to Hell, and if I open it, I will release the hounds of the underworld. That, of course, would spell the end of me and my family and half of Parsons Corners, thus becoming a plot for another Stephen King novel. Although, he'd have to change the locale from New Hampshire to Maine because it seemed only really creepy things happen in Maine. Or New York. If I recall that's where the Amityville Horror took place. Regardless, horror stories never seem to take place in New Hampshire. With that line of reasoning, I had no excuse to be scared. I was an idiot.

The powerful beam of my lantern cut through the murk and illuminated the narrow steps leading upwards. Feathery cobwebs dangled in front of my face. Swallowing, I put my foot on the first step. It creaked appropriately. The butterflies in my stomach threatened to burst free. Part of me wanted to turn around and get out of there as fast as my skinny little legs would carry me, but another part, the masochistic part, wanted to see what was up there. The masochist won.

Step by step, I made my way up the stairs; the ring of the pounding rain on the metal roof grew more deafening the higher I rose. The brush of the cobwebs against my skin caused me to cringe in disgust. With a sigh of relief, I finally reached the top and stepped into the attic.

It wasn't a large space as far as attics go, but was crammed with tons of ancient stuff from top to bottom. Some of it looked like it dated from the 1700s when the house was built. I flashed my beam around. We really needed an overhead light in here. My fear dissipated as my curiosity grew. What was all this junk? Old furniture, some broken, some intact, but all looking grimy and flyspecked, lay in haphazard heaps. A ton of boxes, crates, and antique trunks stood piled in every corner. A solid inch of gray dust blanketed all exposed surfaces, and the room smelled of damp and mildew. I rubbed my itchy nose. Who knew what lay hidden here? It might be a time capsule of the house's 200 plus years of existence. I was breathless with excitement.

It was possible that I'd found my project for the summer. If I unearthed enough information on the previous tenants, I could create a record of the house over the centuries. The attic was full of possibilities.

I tapped my lips considering the abysmal lighting situation. I decided to go downstairs to see if Dad knew how to rig some decent work lights. He'd be as excited as I was to learn about the house's past. He was a sucker for anything history related.

I hurried down the hall eager to get things started and called out for my father. He wasn't in his office. On my way to look downstairs, I figured I'd check on Mom just to make sure she was okay. Her odd behavior worried me.

Gently, I tapped on her bedroom door, pushed it open and peered in. The drawn curtains blanketed the room in a smothering gloom. I chewed on my lip as I pushed my hair away from my face. "Mom?" A slight movement caught my eye. "Mom?" I called again. No answer. My fingers fumbled around for the wall switch and a moment later a dingy, yellow light flooded the room.

Mom sat in the rocking chair next to the window. Her eyes were closed and seemed sunken in her bone white face. My stomach dropped. "Mom!" I yelped. I hurried over to her and took her ice-cold hand.

What should I do? I wanted to go get Dad, but my legs refused to respond. Speechless, I watched as my mother's eyes slid slowly open. She gradually turned her head until she stared directly at me. "Sophie," she rasped, her expression eerily blank. My throat was so tight no sound would emerge. Without warning, she grabbed my arm, her grip like a vise. "Whatever you do, *don't let him in!*" Then she released me, closed her eyes and slumped unconscious in the chair.

CHAPTER FOUR

The spell broken, I turned and fled the room crying out for my father. "Dad! Dad, where are you?"

"Sophia?" He stood at the bottom of the steps looking up at me, a puzzled expression on his face. "What's wrong?"

"It's Mom!" I looked back towards the darkened room. "There's something wrong with Mom." Without another word, Dad pounded up the stairs. He brushed past me and disappeared into the bedroom. I followed right behind him, feeling shaky. Maya entered a moment later.

Dad knelt next to the rocking chair, holding Mom's hand and gently calling her name. "Lina? Lina, honey, are you okay?" For a long moment, there was no response, then Mom stirred, her eyes slowly fluttered opened. She stared at my father in confusion.

"Roger?" She turned her head back and forth. "What's wrong?" Her eyes widened. "The girls! Are the girls all right?"

"The girls are fine." My dad brushed the hair from Mom's brow. I had never seen him like this, so gentle and calm. A surge of love for the man washed over me as he tended my mother. "Sophia said you weren't feeling well." I saw him taking in Mom's pale appearance and shadowed eyes.

A frown briefly crossed her face. "I'm okay," she replied, her voice a bit uncertain. "I was a little dizzy and sat down to rest. I must have fallen asleep." Then she smiled at us. "Really, I'm fine. I just need some breakfast."

Dad sighed in relief. He didn't like it when anything veered out of the ordinary and was willing to take Mom at her word. I, on the other hand, wasn't so easily fooled. I clearly recalled how spooky she looked sitting there in the dark, staring at me with that blank expression. Then I remembered the words she'd spoken: *Don't let him in.* What on earth did that mean? My throat tightened, scared by those simple words. Did Mom truly possess the Gift of Seeing and have some kind of vision? That freaked me out even more. I liked it better when I could pretend it was all a joke. I mean, what did that signify for me? My grandmother had it, and now my mother? Would I soon be noticing dead people stalking me? Uh, no thanks.

Mom got to her feet. She seemed a little unsteady, but at least she was moving under her own steam. She disappeared into the bathroom and shut the door.

I turned to Dad. "Dad, I'm telling you, there was something wrong. She was freezing cold, and she was staring right at me. It was like she was in some kind of trance."

Dad smiled at me, his brown eyes comforting. "Don't worry about it, kiddo," he said giving me a hug. "You know your mom. Occasionally she gets a little spooky. She'll be fine once she eats some food. I expect she just has low blood sugar." He stepped toward the door. "I'll go start her some eggs. And perhaps some toast..." I heard him continue to mumble to himself as he clomped down the stairs. I sighed. Why were grown-ups often so dense?

Maya stood at my side. "She did look pretty weird. Maybe she's coming down with something?"

I shook my head and crossed my arms across my chest. "Not much we can do if they won't even admit there's a problem."

A few minutes later Mom came out dressed and looking more like her usual self. She still seemed pale, despite the carefully applied rouge.

"Mom?" I stepped closer to her. She turned and smiled.

"What is it, Sophie?" She's the only one I let call me that. I much prefer Sophia.

"Mom," I began again. "Do you remember saying something right before Dad came in?"

My mother frowned and tilted her head as she studied me. "I said something? What did I say?"

I bit my lip, unsure if I should have brought this up. "Well, you looked at me and said, 'Whatever you do, don't let him in.' Who did you mean? Who shouldn't I let in?" Dad? Liam? Since we had no pets that pretty much exhausted all the 'him' possibilities I could come up with.

Mom lost what little color she had regained, the blush looking too bright against her white cheeks. "I... I don't know..." she trailed off, her eyes going distant.

She gave herself a slight shake. "Well, I wouldn't worry about it," she said with forced joviality. "C'mon. I can smell bacon. I'm sure your Dad is wondering where we are." She turned and hurried from the room.

Maya glanced at me, shrugged, and followed her out. I stood there for a few unsettled minutes. Despite my mother's words to the contrary, I found myself very much worrying about her mysterious statement.

When I got downstairs, my parents and Maya were sitting at the dining table eating breakfast. I grabbed a couple of pieces of bacon and joined them. They chatted away like nothing had happened. No one else seemed upset about Mom's odd behavior. I bit down on the crispy strip and remembered the attic.

"Dad," I began, reaching for the orange juice. "I was in the attic this morning and found all kinds of stuff up there. I was thinking, if we rigged up some decent lights, I could go through it, and find enough information about the history of this house to make a project out of it. You know, like a timeline of the house's existence and the people who lived here."

Dad's eyebrows shot up. "We have an attic?"

I nodded. "There's a door in my closet. I found it yesterday and went up there this morning when the light was better."

"Wow." Dad grinned, his eyes bright. "I want to see that as soon as I'm done with breakfast. You might be onto something. This place has seen a lot of history."

I glanced over at Mom. When I first sat down, she had been talking away, eating her eggs and chugging coffee. But when I mentioned the attic, she'd gone oddly silent, her brow furrowed. "I... I'm not so sure going through that attic is a good idea," she said, staring at her cup.

"Why not?" I leaned forward. "Mom, this would be a perfect project." She avoided my gaze.

I sat back and crossed my arms across my chest, irritated by her lack of enthusiasm. "Besides, it's not like there's a lot of stuff for me to do here. Maya plans on dredging up the lake or something. Dad has his book, and you have your psychic hotline loonies to talk to."

Mom flushed. I knew she hated it when I mocked her so-called profession, but right then, I didn't care.

"Lina," frowned Dad as he put down his fork and turned to Mom. "I can't see that there's any harm in it. Sophia's right. There isn't much for her to do here. You don't want her sitting on her computer all summer, do you? I, personally, would love to learn more about the history of this house." Mom remained silent. I could tell she was ticked. She always shuts down if she feels like we're ganging up on her.

Dad sighed and rubbed his eyes. He just wanted to keep the peace. "Listen, I'll go up there with her, and if I think it even looks remotely dangerous, we'll call it off, okay?"

Mom didn't look any happier, but what could she say? "I don't believe it's a good idea. It feels... wrong."

She stood up. "I think I'd better consult my charts." With that, she disappeared up the stairs.

Dad and I exchanged knowing glances. Checking her charts should keep her busy for at least the next few hours. Dad rose from the table. "All right, show me the attic."

"Dad," called Maya as she gathered up her dishes. She was always conscientious like that. "Don't forget, you promised to take me over to the hardware store so I can get some stuff for my project. I want to get out on the lake once the weather clears up."

Dad assured her he hadn't forgotten, then followed me up the stairs into my bedroom. I opened the closet and showed him the door in the back wall. He studied it for a moment and nodded. "Guess this is why I never noticed it. I didn't check all the closets when I looked at this place." He pulled open the attic door and switched on his flashlight. I imagined him dressed like Indiana Jones ready to embark on another exciting adventure. Dad had that effect sometimes.

I followed him up the stairs, still shuddering every time a cobweb brushed against me. I'd have to remember to bring up a broom. As we reached the top, the dust stirred up by our passage tickled my nose. My sneeze sounded unnaturally loud.

Dad flashed his light around the attic as I rearranged boxes to find what might be hidden further back.

"Ouch!" I grimaced at the sharp pain in my shin. Cursing softly under my breath, I looked down and discovered an old wooden trunk. Curious, I shone my beam along its length. It was large, with a painted decoration on its flat lid. I carefully studied the ornate design and realized that flowing curlicues formed the letters "MMP". Someone's initials? That would be cool. Maybe the chest belonged to the MMP person. I heard Dad rummaging around behind me muttering to himself.

"Look at this!" He lifted a large, oval object. It looked like the portrait of a young woman from a hundred years ago. "Mercy May Parsons", he read looking at the back of the painting. "1855."

I moved closer. "Do you think she's related to Mom?" Mom's last name was Parsons before she got married, and according to Dad, her family was originally from around here.

Dad shrugged. "It's possible, I suppose. Your mother's ancestors departed shortly before the Civil War, but pretty much everyone in a small town like this was related by blood or marriage." Dad was our genealogist. "I don't remember anyone named Mercy May being connected to your mom, but she might have been a cousin or something. That's another thing you can find out." He set the portrait back onto the pile of junk.

I nodded, glancing at the chest. Did that belong to Mercy May? I smiled to myself, energized with excitement. Right now, there wasn't anything I wanted to do more than learn about the mysterious Mercy May.

"So, what do you think, Dad?" I asked, trying not to sound too eager. "Would it be possible to rig some kind of light up here?" I hesitated. "You *are* going to let me explore the attic, aren't you?"

Dad rubbed his jaw for a moment like he always does when he's weighing all the possibilities. He studied the attic. Then he shrugged. "I honestly don't see any reason why not. None of these piles looks big enough to cave in on you, and there aren't rabid bats roosting in the rafters. So, I say go for it!"

I grinned back at him. If I'd been alone, I would have even done a little dance, but I'm getting a bit old for that. "And the lights?"

"I believe there are work lights in the shed out back. They'll probably give you enough light up here."

As we started down the stairs, I turned to him. "What about Mom? What are you going to tell her if she starts saying something like the house of Jupiter doesn't want Mars inside, so that means the attic is off limits?"

Dad laughed. "Leave her to me. I'm willing to go so far with her obsession, but in this case, there's no reason why you can't go through the stuff in the attic. No matter what Jupiter and Mars say about it."

A weight lifted off my shoulders. My plan was now to head out to the shed, find the lights, and if I was lucky, meet Miss Mercy May Parsons up close and personal.

CHAPTER FIVE

It wasn't long before I had the lights set up and ready to go. Mom hadn't come out of her room since breakfast, but that didn't necessarily mean anything. When she communed with the stars, she might be incommunicado for hours. I was fine with that. Gave me more time to check things out. Dad and Maya headed out to the hardware store to get whatever she needed to collect frogs or weeds or the Loch Ness Monster. You never knew with my sister.

It took me several minutes to move the junk surrounding the chest. When I'd cleared enough space to allow me access without killing myself, I carefully studied the enigmatic trunk. I was reluctant to open it. It was like at Christmas when a big pile of presents waited under the tree. Until you actually opened them, the boxes might contain anything: jewelry, a TV, whatever. But the point is, the anticipation was almost the best part. Once they were all opened, that was it. No more dreams. You either got the new video game, or you got underwear. That's how I felt about the chest. Until I opened it, I could imagine it being chock full of Mercy May's most intimate secrets. Maybe I'd discover she'd hidden a treasure trove of gold and jewels inside, or passionate love letters revealing that she had fallen for a married man and ran off with him. The possibilities were endless.

The chest possessed a flat lid and was maybe four feet long and a couple of feet high with small square feet. I noticed two narrow drawers beneath the main body of the chest. I ran my fingers over the lid. It was as smooth as velvet. The chest was painted a pale blue and adorned with ornate flowers and birds along the front. It was really pretty. I gently traced the letters MMP on the top. "Mercy May Parsons," I whispered rolling the words around in my mouth. They were fun to say. I wondered if this was her hope chest. A long time ago, girls used to collect items to use when they started their married lives. Things like bed linens and dishes and they'd store them in chests like this.

Again, I experienced a strange reluctance to lift the lid. My shoulders were so tight they almost hurt. I drew a deep breath trying to release the tension. "Sophia," I muttered to myself. "This is stupid. Just open the damn box." I always felt a bit rebellious when I threw in the occasional curse word.

I took another breath then gently raised the top. A swirl of dust rose in my face, starting a sneezing fit. Dust and I don't usually do well together. When I finally got control of my nose, I cautiously peered into the chest, ready to jump back if something alive was in there. Rats and mice like to nest in odd places. I was lucky this time. No creepy critters.

A pale cloth, yellowed with age, protected the contents, its surface brittle and rough. It looked like what my mother called muslin. Would it fall apart if I picked it up? I considered this a moment. I didn't want to ruin anything, but my eagerness to discover the secrets in the trunk grew stronger. I pressed my lips tightly together and carefully lifted one edge of the material, slowly peeling it away, revealing the chest's mysterious contents.

More fabric made up the second layer. This time, a pale blue cotton with small delicate flowers. I removed the delicate material and allowed it to unfurl. A long dress met my surprised gaze. The fabric had browned in several places and disintegrated in others. The full skirt had three tiers of matching fabric that reached the floor, and there were long sleeves that tightened at the shoulders and belled at the wrist. Dainty pearl-like buttons ran down the front of the bodice. I held it up to myself and laughed. Even as petite as I am, there was no way I'd fit in that dress with its impossibly tiny waist. Then I remembered women back then wore corsets that would cinch you in to achieve that distinctive hourglass figure. I shook my head in disbelief. It was a pretty gown and finding it stuffed into a chest and forgotten for so many years depressed me.

I gently set the gown off to the side. My eyebrows rose in surprise at what lay beneath. A veil of yellowed lace lay sad and forlorn. With a shock, I realized this dress may have been Mercy's wedding gown. Tightness formed in my throat. Why the wedding gown of a girl gone for over a hundred years should make me so sad, I had no idea, but it did. I reached in and gently touched the delicate lace, afraid the frail fabric would tear in my hands. Holding my breath, I lifted it from the chest and laid it alongside the dress.

I carried the portrait over to the chest thinking I might as well keep all of her stuff together. I continued to search through the box but found mainly household goods. A set of blue and white china lay neatly stacked on the bottom. The images painted on the surfaces were all scenes of Japan. They called it willow ware. My grandma had some. Various tablecloths, napkins, towels, pillowcases, quilts, and so forth filled the rest of the chest. All things a young girl would want to start her new life as a married woman. I suspected that Mercy May Parsons may never have reached that goal.

Sneezing again, I glanced at my watch. It was already mid-afternoon. No wonder my stomach was grumbling. I sighed looking at the pile of stuff scattered across the attic floor. As I rubbed my itchy nose, I replaced the contents as I had found them, being careful not to damage anything. When I reached the blue dress, the tightness in my throat returned. What *had* happened to Mercy?

After I covered the gown with the muslin and shut the lid, I rose stiffly trying to get the feeling back in my feet. This was going to take longer than expected. But what else did I have to do? I stretched, working the kinks out of my back and turned off the work lights. Time to take a break I decided.

When I reached the kitchen, no one answered my call. No surprise there. I doubted Dad and Maya had returned, and Mom was probably on the phone busy predicting the futures of poor saps who had nothing better to do with their money. I could tell their futures… they would be receiving big credit card bills very soon.

As I made myself a turkey sandwich, I glanced outside. The rain had at last passed, and the sun was trying to make a break for it. Sandwich in hand, I stepped outside and took a deep breath of the cool, rain-washed air. After hours spent in that musty attic, the breeze smelled wonderful and fresh. I wandered down to the dock and stared out at the choppy water, a result of the recent storm.

"Hey, Sophia!" A distant voice broke my reverie, and I turned to see someone heading towards me. With a swoop in my stomach, I spotted Liam. He grinned and waved as he approached. He carried a large covered basket over his arm.

I moved to meet him. "Hey," I replied trying to act nonchalant. He had that unsettling effect on me. "What are you doing here?"

He held up his burden. "My mom sent some stuff for you guys. You know, fresh baked bread and cookies. A welcoming basket." He sighed dramatically. "I, of course, was *forced* to deliver this to you. I planned to spend my precious time cleaning the lodge bathrooms but no, I had to come all the way out here just to bring you some zucchini muffins."

Okay, I'll admit. I laughed. His melodramatic whining cracked me up. Yeah, it was stupid, but my mood lightened. "Well, I hate that we were the cause of so much distress," I replied solemnly. "I'll just relieve you of your burden, and you can get back to your plunger."

"Oh, no, no, no." Liam shook his head, pulling the basket away from me. "I was charged, upon pain of death, to deliver this directly to your house. *To... your... house*," he repeated for emphasis. "Not to your dock. And I am a man of my word."

I laughed again trying not to sound like some stupid, giggly girl. But he was funny, and I was losing my nervousness around him. "Okay, then. I guess you'd better follow me."

Together we walked up the hill to the house. I opened the door to the kitchen and followed him in. Dad leaned against the counter pouring himself some coffee. My brow rose in surprise. I hadn't heard the car drive up. He winked at me with a knowing grin. "Hello. You must be Liam."

Liam smiled his electric smile, and my knees went a little weak. "Yes, sir. From the Pine Forest Lodge. My mom sent this gift to welcome you to Little Loon Lake."

Dad looked pleased. I couldn't tell if it was because Liam had called him sir, or because he'd brought a basket of goodies. Kind of like a male Red Riding Hood. "Thank her for us. None of this will go to waste, I can assure you." Dad opened the lid and pulled out a veritable smorgasbord of baked goods: jars of preserves, cheeses, and smoked meat. My mouth immediately watered.

As Dad unwrapped some chocolate chip cookies, he eyed Liam. "Sophia tells me you're interested in history and dinosaurs."

Liam nodded, taking the cookie Dad offered him. "I love history. I'm really thinking I would like to become an archeologist or maybe a paleontologist." He paused. "Sophia told me you're writing a book about dinosaurs?"

Inwardly, I rolled my eyes. I could pretty much forget spending time with Liam. With that simple question, he'd opened Pandora's Box. Dad would never let him go until he'd shown poor Liam every model, cast, and fossil in the house. Dad couldn't bear to be without at least a crateful of artifacts no matter where we went. My eyes glazed over as my thoughts returned to the attic and Mercy May's chest. Maybe Liam would know something about her. I looked at my watch. Had twenty minutes passed since we came in? I sighed, resigning myself to losing Liam to Dad when the gods intervened. The phone rang.

The old rotary telephone, hung near the dining room, door jangled loudly, and Dad excused himself. I touched Liam's arm and nodded towards the back door. Liam looked at my Dad who gave him a little wave goodbye. I could tell it would be awhile before Dad got off the phone. From the conversation, he was talking to one of his dinosaur buddies. Those guys could talk for hours.

We wandered outside and strolled toward the path through the woods that led to Liam's lodge. "Liam," I began, still feeling a little odd being so chummy with this amazingly cute guy. "Sorry about that. Once Dad gets going, it's pretty hard to shut him up."

Liam just laughed. "Don't worry about it. Your dad really knows his stuff. I'd love to go on a dig someday. That would be really cool."

I tried to look enthused but just managed a lopsided grin. I glanced at him again. "Um, I realize you've lived here a long time, so I was wondering if you know much about the history of the area?"

Liam studied me with interest. "Sure. We've been here for generations. Since before the Revolution."

I licked my lips. "Do you know anything about the Parsons family? My mother's maiden name is Parsons, and since her family originally came from around here, I hoped to learn more about them." Why hadn't I asked him about Mercy? That is what I had intended to ask.

Liam frowned thoughtfully then grabbed my hand. "Come on. There's something you might find really interesting."

My mind blanked for a moment. *He was holding my hand!* I couldn't think of anything more interesting than *that*.

Fighting through my stupid foggy brain, I let him lead me through the forest to a second trail that wound further up the hill. He let go of my hand and the brain fog cleared. I now noticed the remains of stone walls visible here and there. Liam nodded when I pointed them out. "Most of this area used to be farmland.

You'll find these old stone walls all over the state. Come on, we're close."

We came to the top of a rise where it flattened out. I looked around, puzzled. Liam touched my arm and nodded to one side. "There!"

It took me a moment before I made out several lopsided gravestones peeking up through the brush. The remains of a decrepit iron fence circled the graves, but most of it had collapsed. A few tall trees, their limbs gnarled and twisted, stood sentinel.

Mesmerized by the forlorn tableau before me, I took one slow step, followed by another. My heart pounded in my ears, not scared exactly, but definitely anxious. We neared the first headstone. The weathered granite bore a thick coat of furry moss. I stared at the inscription trying to make out the words.

"Looks like William Parsons, 1789-1852." Liam traced the carved letters with his finger trying to scrape off some of obscuring moss. "This is the Parsons family cemetery."

My mouth went dry. I tore my eyes away from the old stone and looked around at the others. Maybe I would find Mercy's fate here.

CHAPTER SIX

The woods were chilly and wet from the recent rain. Water from the dripping brush soaked the bottoms of my jeans. I rubbed my arms as I looked around, trying to find more headstones in the murky shadows. There were more than I had first realized.

Together, Liam and I progressed through the graveyard reading the eroded tombstones. I found it odd that a lot of them dated from the 1850s. Sure, there was a fair number dated earlier, all the way back to the 1700s in fact, but there were a whole bunch from the mid to late 1850s. Had there been some kind of accident or plague? My feelings of foreboding concerning Mercy May continue to grow.

At last, I found her nestled near the roots of a massive oak. A small tombstone with an angel engraved in its pitted surface marked the grave. I knelt down and stared at the faded inscription: *Mercy May Parsons 1838-1855. The greatest attribute of Heaven is Mercy.*

My head swam and tears prickled the backs of my eyes. I was right. She had died young, just seventeen. Only three years older than me. I reached out and gently caressed the letters of her name. Her image filled my mind. I barely noticed Liam as he knelt beside me. He looked at me with a raised brow.

"Do you know who she was?"

"In a way," I replied softly. I blinked, trying to pull myself together. I still couldn't understand why this

44

dead girl had such a strong effect on me. "I discovered her portrait and hope chest in the attic of our house."

"Really?" Liam returned his attention to the tombstone. "Seventeen. They died so young back then."

"There was also a dress in the chest. I think it was her wedding dress, but I feel like she didn't make it to her wedding."

Liam said nothing. The fact that he took this seriously made him rise even higher in my estimation. Most guys I knew would have thought I was being an idiot getting so worked up over a girl dead for over 160 years. Liam was different. It was if he understood.

"We might be able to find out if she got married," said Liam at last. "There could be something in the county records or one of the local churches."

I turned to him, eyes wide. "Do you really think so?"

He shrugged. "It can't hurt to try. Genealogy is extremely popular these days so all kinds of records are available now. My mom is really into family history. I don't know when New Hampshire started recording marriages so we might not have any luck there, but churches usually kept records. We could get lucky."

I nodded. I glanced at the gravestone beside Mercy's. Carved into the granite was Elijah Parsons, 1835-1852. Next to him was Lemuel Parsons, 1837-1854. And beyond that, a third, Grace Elizabeth Parsons, 1840-1857. Were these Mercy's siblings? They had all succumbed within a few years of one another and even weirder, they were all seventeen when they died. It occurred to me that Maya would turn seventeen next week. I shivered again.

As the shadows lengthened, I figured it was time to go home. I had no desire to get stuck in some creepy, overgrown graveyard after sunset. It was eerie enough in the daytime. However, it had given me a lot to think about. I would have to ask Dad to give me some pointers on looking up family history stuff. I still wondered if these people were relatives.

All too soon, we had reached the house. I stood there awkwardly for a few minutes, not sure what I should say. I cleared my throat. "Thanks, Liam. At least I know where Mercy ended up. Now, if only I can find out how she got there. And if those others were her siblings."

Liam brushed his shaggy blonde hair out of his eyes. "Let me know what you find out. I knew the graveyard was there, but I hadn't thought too much about it. I mean, there are lots of those old abandoned family plots around here. My favorite is one with the victims of a massacre that occurred during King Philip's War back in the 1600s."

I looked at him again, amazed that this almost-too-good-to-be-true guy would turn out to be so interesting. We actually had something in common. Anyway, I assured him I would and watched with what I am sure was a moony look on my face, as he disappeared back into the woods. I would definitely have to find more ways to meet up with him.

With a happy sigh, I went inside slamming the screen door behind me. My stomach growled. I looked at my watch and realized it was past dinnertime. Funny. I didn't smell anything cooking. The house was dark. A prickle ran down the back of my neck.

"Mom?" There was no answer. I reached out for the light switch. Flicking it on, I gave a gasp of surprise. My mother huddled silently in the rocking chair in the corner of the living room, gazing at the door, her face blank and her breathing heavy.

"Mom?" I tried again. My voice quivered as if I might start crying. Truth is, I wanted to. I moved in closer and glanced around making sure there was no one else in the room. Where was Dad? Mom gave no indication that she even knew I was there. She just kept staring ahead, oblivious to her surroundings. I stood there for a minute unsure of what to do. Should I go find Dad? I didn't want to leave Mom here by herself. Finally, I reached out and gently touched her arm. "Mom, can you hear me?"

She made no response. I swallowed, fighting back those tears. I shook her arm harder. "Mom! Wake up! It's me, Sophia. Can you hear me?"

This time I noticed her hands tighten on the arms of the chair, her knuckles going white. Suddenly, her body began to shake, eyes rolling up into her head. I frantically scrambled backward, tripping over the small footstool behind me. I fell with a crash.

"Sophia?" Dad's voice floated down from the second floor. "Is that you?"

For a moment, my throat was so tight I couldn't get any words out. "Dad!" I finally croaked. "Come quick! It's Mom!"

By now, Mom had gone still, slumped in the chair, her face was a ghostly gray. At first, I thought she was dead until she coughed. It was a deep, painful cough that made me wince at the sound of it. I scrambled back to my feet and hurried back to her side. I took her hand. It was like ice. Dad's heavy footsteps sounded on the old wood floor behind me.

"Lina?" He now stood beside me looking at Mom with concern. "Lina! Are you all right?" Mom's eyes slowly opened. She blinked a few times then peered up at us in confusion. I was relieved to see some color returning to her cheeks.

"Roger? What's wrong?"

Dad now looked to me. I stared at my mother, trying to figure out what had happened. "You were just staring like some kind of zombie when I came in," I said slowly. "You didn't even notice me. I called your name, but I don't think you could hear me. Then you had some kind of fit. Just like before." I glanced at my father. "That's when I called for Dad."

Mom was sitting up straighter now and frowning at me. Then she coughed again. I bit my lip. I didn't like that. It sounded... dangerous. "I'm really not certain what you're talking about, Sophia. I feel fine. I fell asleep. Are you sure you didn't imagine all of this?"

Uh, right. I imagined my mother sitting there in some kind of creepy trance having fits. Not likely. Still, if she wouldn't believe me, what could I do? I began to suspect this house wasn't good for her. She'd been acting weird ever since we moved in. I mean, this was the second time I'd found her like this. It made me very uneasy.

"I just know what I saw," I muttered. I glanced at Dad who continued to study Mom. At least he hadn't simply dismissed what I'd seen.

Mom glanced at her watch and quickly rose. "Where has the time gone? I haven't even started dinner."

Dad put a hand on her shoulder. "I tell you what, why don't we go over to the lodge for dinner? It's a little late to cook, and what with the move and all, it would be a nice break."

Mom looked uncertain for a moment then shrugged. "Okay. If that's what you want. Let me find my purse." She disappeared up the stairs.

"Dad," I began, grabbing his arm. "I know what I saw. It was like she was in some trance, just like before. Then she had a fit or something. Her whole body began to shake. It was really freaky."

"I believe you, Sophia," he replied running his hand through his wavy hair. "When I looked in on her earlier, she was sitting there in front of her computer staring at the screen. She didn't even notice me when I came in. It wasn't until I shook her that she was aware of my presence. I told her she should quit working and go downstairs for a while. Obviously, that didn't help."

I wrapped my arms around myself. I didn't want this to be happening.

Dad sighed. "Well, let's go eat dinner. Maybe it's simply low blood sugar. I don't know if she's eaten anything since breakfast."

It took us about fifteen minutes to drive around the lake to the Pine Forest Lodge. It was a big old log building with the classic look of a rustic forest lodge surrounded by a huge wraparound porch with rocking chairs lined up near the railing. It was everything I imagined a New England lodge should be. There were several small cabins behind the main building, arcing away into the woods. Granted, I preferred my hotels more along the lines of a Hilton, but I could still appreciate its woodsy charm.

The lodge had a large dining room available to its guests and summer people staying in the area. It was about half full when we got there. A girl stood near the doorway, her bright blue eyes and long blonde hair identified her as Liam's sister. As we approached, she eyed me curiously making me wonder if Liam had mentioned me to his family. We were seated in a booth overlooking the lake as the distant call of a loon echoed across the still water; its lonely sound touched my heart.

I glanced at the menu and chose your basic hamburger and French fries. My tastes are simple. While Mom and Dad talked quietly together, I let my eyes wander around the dining room. I noticed one of the teenage waiters staring at Maya with obvious interest. And so it begins. I sighed. Most of the diners appeared to be tourists with that carefree look of people on vacation. But there was one man who caught my attention.

The man sat by himself in a corner of the dining room, out of view of most of the other patrons. He was tall, with long dark hair curling around the collar of his shirt, reminding me of an actor from some Jane Austen story with an aristocratic look, high cheekbones and aquiline nose. He must have felt my eyes upon him, because he slowly turned and stared directly at me. I went cold as my stomach dropped. A slow, knowing smile spread across his narrow face. His glance flicked towards Maya for just an instant. He glanced at me a final time with his dark, penetrating eyes, then returned his inscrutable gaze to the window.

"Hey, Sophia!" Startled, I turned to see Liam approaching us, a tray in his hands. "I see you decided to take me up on my offer." He smiled and set glasses of water on the table as he greeted my parents. I turned back to the man and frowned. He was gone. I glanced around the dining room, but he was nowhere to be found. Where did he go? I mean, I'd only looked away for a second. That was weird.

Liam followed my gaze. "Looking for something?"

"I... uh... no." Either I'd imagined the guy, or he somehow slipped out without me seeing him. Maybe there was another door. To be honest, I was glad he was gone. Something about him didn't seem right.

I introduced Liam to Maya, who eyed him with appreciation. How could you not be impressed by Liam? Liam was polite to her, but it gratified me to see he didn't go all gaga over her. A few moments later, Liam's parents joined us and started talking with Mom and Dad. Liam moved closer to me. "Any more thoughts about the Parsons family?"

I frowned. Since the event with my mother, I had forgotten all about Mercy May and the graveyard. I shook my head. "No, I haven't had a chance to think about them." I wanted to tell Liam what had happened to my mother, but now was neither the time nor the place.

Liam nodded. "I asked Mom about databases for early marriages, and she pointed me in the right direction. Anyway, I couldn't find any information on a bride named Mercy May Parsons in either civil or local church records." He shrugged. "I don't know how complete those online records are though. It might be better to actually go to the local churches and see if they have any there. Not all of those would be online."

I took a sip of water digesting this. I doubted it would matter how many churches we checked out; we wouldn't find any marriage certificate for poor Mercy May. A death record maybe, but certainly not one for a marriage. A deep sadness filled me. Our dinner arrived about fifteen minutes later. The food was fantastic. Certainly better than anything I could have scrounged together at home. Of course, having such a good-looking waiter didn't hurt.

The evening slipped by all too quickly, and before I knew it, we were on our way home. Mom and Dad commented on how nice Liam's parents were, and how they'd been invited back to the lodge to play bridge one night. Who knew my parents even knew how to play bridge? I always pegged my dad for more of the poker-type, and I don't think I've ever seen Mom handle anything but Tarot cards. Live and learn. Apparently, Maya had made a date with the cute waiter I'd noticed earlier. I somehow missed that. I guess it happened when I was talking to Liam, but it was definitely par for the course as far as Maya was concerned.

When we got home, Mom announced she was working a night shift on the psychic hotline and headed upstairs to the study. Maya disappeared saying she wanted to get organized for her expedition the next day. I watched Mom for a few moments hoping she'd be okay. I turned to Dad, eager to share what I'd discovered upstairs.

"So, you found a hope chest, eh? And an old wedding dress?" Dad sipped a glass of wine as he listened to me.

"Yeah," I replied curling up on the sofa. "Then this afternoon, Liam showed me an old Parsons family graveyard. I found Mercy May's headstone along with three others I think may have been her brothers and sister. They all died within a few years of each other. And," I paused for effect. "They all died at seventeen."

Dad's eyebrows shot up. "I've got to say, that is really strange. Why would they all die at seventeen? I mean, it's not uncommon for a number of children to die as disease runs through a family, but why did they all die at seventeen? And all in different years?" He shook his head in wonder.

I leaned back against the sofa. The fact that Mercy and the others all died at the same age creeped me out. What had killed them? What did they think as they watched one kid after another succumb to this unknown killer? It just didn't make any sense. Was it genetic? Some disease? Or did someone murder them? Why was seventeen the magical number? If we were related to these people, would I be affected as well? I thought of Maya again and her upcoming seventeenth birthday. The image of a gravestone with her name appeared in my mind as an icy finger of fear trickled down my spine.

CHAPTER SEVEN

The next morning after breakfast, I headed back up to the attic. It occurred to me that I hadn't checked the little drawers in the hope chest. I didn't expect to find much, but I was eager to investigate.

It was a lot quieter up in the attic now that there was no rain pounding on the metal roof. That was a huge relief. I swear my ears rang for hours after I came down yesterday. I turned on the work lights, approached the wooden box, and again, gently traced the initials. So many hopes and dreams cut short. I sighed and settled myself on the dusty floor next to the chest.

The chest contained two shallow drawers, each about a foot wide with pale, purple flowers painted across the front and a wooden knob in the center. I pulled on the knob of the first drawer, and it came out easily enough. Inside, I found a silver comb and hairbrush, both blackened by tarnish. Ornate swirls embossed the back of the brush along with the initials "MMP". I flipped the brush and gave a little start. Several long, dark hairs were caught in the yellowed bristles. Could these be Mercy May's? I studied them for a moment, trying to picture the girl brushing her flowing tresses each night before bed. Mercy May was becoming more real to me every day.

I returned to the drawer and found a string of small, lustrous pearls. I glanced at Mercy's portrait leaning against a box and noticed that she wore those same pearls. I set them aside with the brush and comb. The final thing in the drawer was a pocket watch strung on a frayed black ribbon. I seemed to remember that ladies in the olden days used to pin little watches on their blouses before the invention of wristwatches. The black case was adorned with a purple flower, maybe a violet. I opened the lid and inhaled sharply.

The watch was still running.

I stared in shock as the second hand made its methodical way around the watch face. I don't know much about antique watches, but I do recognize that in order to run they have to be wound. If this timepiece had been placed in the chest at the time of Mercy May's death, then it had been running for well over a hundred years. Impossible, yet, there it was. Maybe when I picked it up that got it started somehow. I glanced at my own wristwatch, a memento of my grandmother, and froze. The old watch displayed the correct time. Okay, Mercy May was becoming just a little *too* real for my liking.

Mouth dry, I thrust the watch back into the drawer as if it might bite me. I just didn't understand how it could still be working. I returned the comb and brush and closed the drawer. I sat back on my heels and rubbed my itchy nose. Dust again. An unexpected breeze lifted my hair. I shifted uncomfortably as my eyes flew to the dark corners of the attic. No ghosts or boogie men.

I turned my gaze to the second drawer. What would I find in there? Mercy's beating heart? I was beginning to get a little crazy here. Okay, I told myself, I can do this. I reached over and pulled on the knob. Nothing. It didn't budge. I frowned in irritation. Here I sat, all ready to be freaked out by some unknown creepy thing hidden away in the drawer, and I couldn't even open it.

I tugged harder. Still nothing. Whether it was stuck or locked, it was impossible to tell. I bent down and peered closely at the front of the drawer. That's when I located the tiny keyhole hidden below the knob. Damn. Locked. This stuff didn't belong to us, so I didn't want to damage it, but I was determined to get that thing open. I opened the other drawer once more and felt all around the inside. I removed it and carefully examined its outside, as well as the nook where it had nestled inside the chest. Still nothing. I even pulled out the trusty Swiss Army knife that Dad gave me when I was ten and tried to gently pry the lock open, but to no avail. I eyed the box in frustration, trying to picture any other little shelves or drawers inside, but as far as I remembered, it was one big open box full of wedding clothes and household goods.

Perhaps the key lay hidden in a sugar bowl or was sewn inside a pillowcase. I wasn't thrilled about having to check each item one by one, but what else did I have to do? With a sigh, I lifted the lid, inhaling the rich aroma of cedar and began my search.

It took me close to two hours to search everything in the chest. Honestly, I didn't think there had been that much in there, but once I got started, I realized how many tiny items were crammed in that tight space. I examined every handkerchief, tablecloth, and pillowcase. I looked in the teapot, sugar bowl and creamer and checked every plate and bowl just in case they taped the key to the bottom. I'm not even sure they had tape back then, but I figured better safe than sorry. Despite all my careful inspection, I remained keyless.

Putting everything back seemed to take forever, like completing a three-dimensional puzzle box. When at last I tucked the old muslin around the wedding dress, I closed the lid with a thud. I sighed and glanced at my watch. Time to eat lunch. I considered taking the pocket watch to show Dad, but truthfully, I wasn't keen to pick it up again. If he wanted to see it, he could come up and look at it himself.

After lunch, I decided to return to the graveyard. I wanted to record the names and other information engraved on the Parsons family headstones. It might help me unravel the mystery of all these dead teenagers.

The afternoon was a lovely 70 degrees and although a bit humid from the previous day's rain, my spirits were lifted. I shifted my backpack to a more comfortable position, and following our footprints still visible in the damp earth, made my way towards the graveyard in the woods.

Cursing softly, I swatted at an annoying mosquito as I approached the desolate burial yard. One of the bad things about walking through the woods, I mused, were bugs; nasty, biting, blood-sucking bugs. As I examined the latest bite, I was startled by a movement in the trees across from where I stood. I went very still, scanning the cemetery and woods around me. Had I seen someone? Of course, it might have been a deer, but I had my doubts. I took another step forward.

"Hello?" My voice quavered as I strained to hear any unusual sounds or detect further movement. Several long minutes passed, and all I heard was the chirrup of insects and the occasional birdsong. Slowly, I relaxed. Normally, I am not this nervous. In fact, I always considered myself a reasonably brave and level-headed person. I don't freak out at every little noise in the middle of the night or scream at bugs. However, since we arrived here, I've been a lot more high-strung. Maybe because of Mom's odd behavior or the mystery of the dead girl, but suddenly I was Miss Über Antsy. Everything spooked me. I needed to get a grip. I took a deep breath. "Here I come!" I called loudly, just in case anyone skulked in the bushes.

Cautiously, I crept forward, stopping every few steps to look around until I reached the dilapidated fence. I paused once more, gripping my notebook so tightly, the metal spiral dug into my hand leaving a painful indentation. When still nothing happened, I took another deep breath and released it. Paranoia did not suit me. Time to get to work.

I dug a pen out of my backpack and entered the graveyard. I decided I would write down the names and any additional information engraved on each of the headstones. Many of the stones had fallen and were now carpeted in a thick layer of fuzzy moss. A few were broken, with shattered stones scattered across the ground. On others, the writing had eroded to the point where they were almost impossible to decipher. I would just do my best.

It was an even more tedious job than I'd expected. The mosquitoes used me as their personal smorgasbord. I regretted not thinking to bring bug spray. I'd pay for that later. Mosquitos love me. For every one bite Maya gets, I get twenty.

After I finished copying down the information for one Benjamin Thomas Parsons 1800-1845, it was time for a break. I stood and stretched. I'd recorded about ten gravestones so far. For some, it was necessary to clear away a ton of brush to read the inscriptions. That had taken more time than I'd liked. There were probably twenty more stones visible through the weeds and who knew how many more still hidden. I sighed as I pulled a bottle of water out of my pack. Cursing, I smacked another mosquito. I considered heading home. Otherwise, I might not have the strength to leave after all those evil little bloodsuckers had drained me dry.

A crack of a twig brought me to full alert, my heart in my throat. I leaped to my feet as a shadowy figure materialized at the edge of the woods. I backed up, nearly tripping over one of the fallen headstones. I couldn't speak, the pounding in my ears drowned out all other sounds. The mysterious figure hovered in the shadows of the forest edge before stepping out into the sunlight and morphing into a man. I instantly recognized him as the mysterious guy from the lodge. He halted outside the fence and stared at me as if he had just noticed my presence.

"Oh, hello there," he said in a deep melodious voice. His smile was warm, but hesitant, as if unsure of his welcome. "I apologize if I startled you. Rarely anyone frequents this cemetery."

"I…" I swallowed, trying to will my heart to slow down. "I was just… uh…" I gestured helplessly at the notebook clutched in my sweaty hand.

The man nodded as if he understood. "Recording headstones?" He took another step towards me. He was at least six feet tall, with that long, dark hair curling over the collar of his white shirt, again reminding me of that actor, Colin Firth, who played a wonderful Mr. Darcy in one of the film productions of *Pride and Prejudice*. This guy was remarkably handsome, yet something about his deep-set eyes made me nervous. His smile might be welcoming, but his eyes most definitely were not. They were flat and cold.

I nodded and licked my dry lips. "Yes, um, for a project. I'm homeschooled, and my dad wants me to do a project about the history of this area, and my friend showed me the graveyard yesterday, so I thought I'd come and write down the names, and see if I could find out who they were..." My mouth ran on fast forward. It took all my concentration to make myself shut up.

The man's dark eyes continued to drill into me, never looking away. I clenched my notebook tighter in a vain attempt to keep my hands from shaking.

"That's very interesting," he said, taking another step towards me. "There are many intriguing stories in old graveyards. I, myself, have been recording them for years." He reached into his pocket and pulled out a small notebook as if to prove his point. "I am a historian of sorts. Amateur, really. But, I find old forgotten cemeteries fascinating, as I'm guessing you do as well."

"Well, I don't really spend much time in graveyards," I mumbled scrambling to gather my stuff. "In fact, I was about to head home. My mom is expecting me, and I need to go. So, you know, graveyards are kind of cool but I don't really know much about them..." Again, I was babbling. This definitely wasn't a trait I was happy to discover. I'd have to put in some serious effort to stop that.

The man glanced around the graveyard. "So much history here. So much tragedy." He turned to me once more. "You feel it too, don't you?" He glanced towards the large oak where Mercy May's headstone stood. I shivered, clutching my backpack tightly to my chest.

"Um, yeah, I'm sure lots of sad things happened here," I edged towards the gate. "I mean, when people die, it's always sad, right? And back then, lots of people died young." Why did I say that? I felt like I'd revealed a subject that shouldn't be discussed out loud.

The man's eyes gleamed with interest. "Yes, they did. Many died as mere children. Sometimes whole families died for no reason. Or so they thought."

I slung my backpack over my shoulder but froze at his words. Did he know something about the deaths of Mercy May and her siblings? I knew I should just get out of there, but couldn't resist. "Do you know what killed those people? The ones where whole families died, I mean?"

Suddenly everything changed. It was as if the world had been dropped into a vacuum creating a silence so intense, my head wanted to explode. The breath was squeezed from my body leaving me paralyzed. I had experienced nothing like it before and hope to God I never do again. Then it ended. Wide-eyed, I gaped at the man, but he seemed unaffected by the event. He stood as precisely as before, not a hair out of place, but he studied me with narrowed eyes. "Consumption."

"What?" The word sounded alien to me. I shook my head to clear it. Didn't help.

"Consumption," repeated the man patiently, never taking his eyes from me. "Today they call it tuberculosis. Back in the nineteenth century, they called it consumption. People believed the disease consumed

63

the body from within, wasting it away to nothing. Many people in these parts expired from that dread malady."

"Oh," I replied in a small voice. That was a start at any rate. I would look up tuberculosis when I got home, but now it was time to get out of there. "Uh, well… thanks for the information. I've really got to go. I'll see you."

I turned, and all but ran down the trail leading back towards our house. As I hurried away, I heard the man call, "By the way, my name is Hiram Parsons. I expect I'll be seeing you again. Soon."

Not if I can help it, I thought as a cold sweat ran down my back. I scrambled along the path trying to put as much distance between me and Mr. Hiram Parsons as possible, glancing over my shoulder several times, praying he didn't follow.

Panting, I stumbled up the steps to the front porch of the house and collapsed into one of the deck chairs. My heart raced. I didn't understand why Hiram Parson terrified me so much, but he did. Relief at making it home safe and sound flooded over me.

After I had finally caught my breath, I pulled out my notebook and flipped through the pages. I found the page with Mercy May and her possible siblings:

Elijah Parsons 1835-1852
Lemuel Parsons 1837-1854
Mercy May Parsons 1838-1855
Grace Elizabeth Parsons 1840-1857

I studied the names. What had that guy said killed them? Consumption? Or rather, tuberculosis. I knew little about the disease. I seemed to recall something about people coughing up blood and then they died. At least that's what happened to Nicole Kidman in that old movie, *Moulin Rouge*. Not a pleasant thought. I tapped my pen against the arm of the chair. Best thing would be to go look up consumption and see what the internet had to say. Dad would probably have some ideas on how to go about researching the names on my list. I could buy them all dying of a single illness, assuming it was contagious, but for them all to die at the age of seventeen? Explaining that would be a *lot* harder.

CHAPTER EIGHT

Dad was busy in his study working on his dinosaur book. I stood in the doorway and observed him as he rummaged through his pile of notes muttering to himself. It comforted me somehow.

"Dad?"

He looked up at me, blinking like some confused owl. "What? Oh, Sophia, it's you. What have you been up to?"

I leaned against the door frame trying to decide what to tell him. "Well, I went through some more of the trunk, and there are these two drawers. One was locked but the other I opened okay. It had a comb and brush and a watch."

Dad nodded absently as he studied a sheaf of papers. "Huh, well that's pretty cool."

"But, Dad, here's the weird part. The watch was actually running. I mean, don't you have to wind those old watches to keep them going?"

Dad set down his papers and peered up at me. "It was running? It just didn't start up when you jostled it or something?"

I shook my head. "It even had the right time."

"Whoa." Dad's eyes widened as he considered this. "That is freaky. How could it still be running after all this time? Those old watches had to be wound every day." Finally, he shrugged. "Well, that's beyond me.

There's probably some watch expert who could explain it."

I kind of doubted any watchmaker could explain a 160-year-old watch that ran without winding and kept the correct time, no less. "I also returned to that graveyard today and wrote down some of the names. Do you know how I could find some records about them?"

Dad rubbed his chin as he studied my list. "Well, we could go online and look them up in the 1850 census to see if these people were all in the same family; maybe find the names of their parents and so on. The 1850 census was the first one that recorded every person. Before that, you just got the name of the head of the household and a tally of other residents."

I grinned. "That's exactly what I need. I just want to make sure these aren't like cousins or something."

Dad looked at the paper again. "Hmm. Since the people on your list all died before 1860, then the 1850 census is the only one that would help you. Otherwise, you might find some kind of information in the county courthouse or local churches. New Hampshire didn't start keeping statewide records until the 1900s. Each town recorded local births, deaths, and marriages. More and more vital records are showing up on the internet so you might get lucky."

Before long, I found myself in front of my computer at the kitchen table searching a website with the United States census information. Since we knew precisely where the Parsons lived, it narrowed the search to a manageable number of potential Parsons. In a matter of minutes, we had our information.

I squinted trying to read the digitized image of a census page filled out over 150 years ago. Dad enlarged the image and Voila. There they were. All the names I had been searching for, plus a few more. I was antsy with excitement waiting for Dad to finish printing out the information.

The parent's names were Samuel and Elizabeth May Parsons. In 1850, they were thirty-six and thirty-four years old and Samuel's occupation was listed as farmer. Under their names, were seven more names. Seven! I had only four on my list: Elijah, Lemuel, Mercy May, and Grace Elizabeth. The census listed three more: Hiram, born 1834, Josiah, 1844, and Hannah, 1846. Interesting. Had these three avoided the strange curse that seemed to plague the family and somehow survived past their seventeenth birthday?

Dad also noticed the discrepancy. "Looks like you might have missed some gravestones."

"Yeah, the mosquitoes finally got to me." I was reluctant to tell him about the weird guy in the cemetery. What did he say his name was again? A cold lump formed in my stomach. Hiram. Hiram Parsons. I looked back at the census paper. Just like the one listed in 1850.

I realized Dad was still talking. "We can check later censuses to see if any of these people survived past the 1850s. Although, if Hannah got married, we wouldn't know her married name." We quickly scanned the later censuses for other Parsons. I was strangely relieved to find Josiah and Hannah in the 1860 report along with their parents. No sign of Hiram though.

"You might find this missing brother, Hiram, in the family plot someplace," said Dad gathering the printouts together. "Although he might have left Parsons Corners and died somewhere else."

I nodded. "A lot of the stones were knocked over or covered up. I didn't get to all of them. I'll need some help." And a ton of mosquito repellant.

Mom came down a little while later, her face pale but at least she acted like her normal self. She still continued to cough though. I showed her all the information we'd gathered but didn't mention finding the things in the trunk. She carefully read through all the census information. She sat back and tapped her lips thoughtfully.

"I'm wondering if we might be related to Josiah. The name seems familiar to me."

Dad's eyes lit up. "You could be right. I'd have to go check my records, but I think one of your great-great whatever grandfather's name *was* Josiah." He hurried upstairs to his computer where he kept all the family tree information. Ten minutes later he came thundering down the stairs waving a piece a paper.

"It's been quite some time since I've worked on any of this, so the names didn't register, but look! Here are all those names." He beamed at me with that goofy grin he gets with a success. "Your great-great-great-grandfather was indeed this Josiah Parsons!"

Speechless, I scanned the genealogy report Dad handed me. I was actually related to Mercy May. Mercy May Parsons, who had died at the ripe old age of seventeen, along with several of her siblings. Now the stark image of a headstone bearing *my* name popped into my head. I shivered and pushed my hair behind my ears.

After dinner, I settled myself down in front of my computer and was immediately pinged by Jenna wanting to chat. I usually loved hearing from her, but I had to admit, with everything that had been going on, I hadn't missed her as much as I expected. As I figured, she was more than a little interested in what I had to say about Liam. Eventually, her mom forced her to get off, but we promised to connect tomorrow.

I typed "tuberculosis" into the search engine and found numerous websites describing the disease. Caused by a bacterium, it spread from person to person through the air, usually settling in the lungs. An infected person might experience weakness, weight loss, fever, coughing and night sweats. Untreated, the symptoms gradually worsened, and the victim just wasted away. People living in close proximity spread the bacteria from one person to the next. With a fifty percent death rate, it wasn't unusual for half a family to die off from the infection over time.

I sat back against my chair to think. Five members of the Parsons family died during this virtual epidemic, but four survived. That fit with the statistics, but it still didn't explain why the children all died at the exact same age. And what happened to the oldest son, Hiram? Was he also in the graveyard somewhere?

That, of course, made me think about the current version of Hiram Parsons. Had lots of Parsons been named Hiram over the years? And why did he make me so nervous? I mean, he was super good-looking and seemed nice enough. He hadn't tried to get too close or act threatening, but he scared me just the same. Then I recalled his eyes. They had been dark, intense and bore right through me. What did he want from me? I frowned. Why did I think he wanted anything? I rubbed my burning eyes. It was past midnight, and I was beat.

As I climbed into bed and drifted off, I heard Hiram's last words echo in my brain: *I expect I'll be seeing you again. Soon.*

CHAPTER NINE

*A*s I walked along the forest path, the night surrounded me in a cloak of velvety darkness, yet I had little trouble finding my way. I had been this way many times before. Faint whispers echoed all around me, but I ignored them, determined to keep going despite the frantic beating of my heart. I had a purpose. What that purpose was exactly, I didn't have a clue, but I had to carry out my mission.

Soon I found myself in the old graveyard, but it was not the sad, neglected site I knew. The iron fence gleamed, looking new and well-cared for. The pale headstones stood upright and clear of brush; the rows of stones lined up like little soldiers. As I approached, I spied a young woman standing near the oak tree. I couldn't make her out at first, but I soon recognized the face from the attic portrait. It was Mercy May Parsons.

She wore a long white dress, like a billowy nightgown. Her pale face glowed in the moonlight, her long hair matted around her head. She looked ill. Worry tugged at my heart. "Mercy, what are you doing out of bed?" I asked. It was at that point, I realized I wasn't myself. I was Mercy's sister, Grace Elizabeth.

"You must get away from him," Mercy hissed, gripping my arm with a surprising strength. "Don't let him go free. He will kill you all."

"Who, Mercy?" I asked desperately. "Who will kill us?"

"Our brother." Mercy cried in a hoarse voice, and I recoiled upon seeing the ravages the disease had wrought upon her. Her eyes and cheeks, normally bright and sparkling with life and humor, were now sunken and dull with fever; her lips cracked *and bleeding. A small trickle of blood trailed along the side of her chin. "Hiram. He is the dangerous one. He will kill us all, one by one. You must be the one to stop him. You know what you must do." She then looked directly into my eyes. "He will kill you, Sophia."*

With a gasp, I leaped up in bed, my body drenched in a cold sweat while my heart raced in my chest. I had to take several long breaths to calm myself down.

"It was just a dream, Sophia," I tried to reassure myself in a shaky voice. "Just a really creepy dream." Absently, I rubbed my aching arm. Puzzled, I clicked on my bedside light and inhaled sharply. The pale flesh of my arm was marked by dark bruises, exactly as if someone had grabbed me. My head spun. I jumped out of bed and staggered to the bathroom, turning on the bright light. I was sweating like I had run a marathon and my damp t-shirt clung to my trembling body.

What was wrong with me? I turned on the water and filled my glass with water. My hands shook so violently, I thought all the water would slosh out before I ever got the glass to my mouth. I gulped down the entire glass, then stared at my face in the mirror. It looked bone white, my eyes dark pits. For a moment, I would have sworn it was Mercy's reflection peering back at me. I blinked a few times and sighed in relief as my vision cleared.

I stumbled back to my bed and lowered myself onto the edge, still trying to get myself under control. What had I dreamed?

I was in a graveyard, and Mercy May was there. She had warned me about something. I rubbed my aching head trying to remember. It had seemed so clear when I first woke up. Wait, she hadn't warned me against some*thing*, but some*one*. I thought harder. Hiram. That was it. She'd mentioned her brother Hiram, and that he was going to kill them all. I shook my head. That didn't make sense. Was she telling me that her brother some kind of serial killer?

Or could she have been warning me about the Hiram I'd met in the cemetery? Okay, wait I minute, I scolded myself. A dead girl did *not* just come back from beyond the grave to warn me about some evil guy I met in a graveyard. I mean, come on. I was just dreaming about him because he'd freaked me out. Sure, I was all for avoiding Mr. Hiram Parsons at any cost, but not because Mercy May told me so in a dream. But that wasn't exactly right. She'd definitely said her *brother*, Hiram. That Hiram must have died well over a hundred years ago, so he couldn't possibly be a threat to me, right? My head throbbed violently now as my thoughts went around and around in a circle.

It was a stupid dream! It's not true. Just. Get. Over. It. I was getting seriously annoyed with myself. A shudder ran through me as I suddenly pictured Mercy May staring into my eyes and calling me by name. That's what had awakened me. My heart beat faster as the hair on the back of my neck prickled. There had been a bit more. Mercy said I knew what to do to stop Hiram from killing everyone. Maybe she knew, but I didn't have a clue.

The remainder of the night seemed endless. I left on all the lights, and every time I started to doze off, I'd see Mercy May's haggard face in front of me, begging me to stop Hiram. Why wouldn't she leave me alone? Honestly, what did she expect me to do? Was he like a vampire? Was I supposed to drive a stake of holly through his heart? Or maybe he turned into a werewolf, and I had to shoot him with a silver bullet. Too bad I had left my collection of holly stakes and silver bullets back home.

By dawn, I had given up trying to sleep. I dragged myself out of my rumpled bed and retreated to the shower, hoping the hot water would revive me. By the time I made my way down to the kitchen, I was at least semi-conscious.

Dad was drinking his coffee and reading the paper. His eyebrow shot up as he took in my pale face and dark circles. "Bad night?"

I sighed deeply as I collapsed into the chair beside him. "I had this awful nightmare, and then I couldn't go back to sleep."

Dad nodded sympathetically. "Just like your mom. She tossed and turned all night. I finally came down and slept on the couch."

I got up and poured myself a bowl of cereal. With a yawn, I settled myself back in my seat and absently ran my spoon around the bowl pushing the soggy cereal. "Dad, do you think it's something to do with this house? I mean, weird things have certainly been happening since we moved here."

There was a moment of silence. I wasn't sure if Dad was trying not to laugh, or if he was seriously considering my words. He always tried to be fair and diplomatic no matter how stupid the idea. "That's quite a leap," he began slowly. "I admit that there are some odd things about this place, but it *is* a very old house. You have to expect some unusual events. But is the house causing you to have nightmares? I rather doubt it."

Well, that was pretty much the response I expected. After all, Dad is a man of science and according to him, all weird and wonky things must have some logical explanation. However, the longer we remained here, the more I suspected staying all summer might not be the smartest move.

I was trying to figure out what I should do with my day when a knock at the back door caught our attention. Dad got up and opened the door to find Liam standing there with a smile on his face and a bag of fresh cinnamon rolls in his hand.

"Good morning, Mr. Whelan," said Liam offering Dad the bag. "My mom sent these. We always end up with some left after the breakfast rush, so she thought she'd send some over."

Dad laughed and glanced at me. "I suspect it's more than delivering sweet rolls that brought you over here." I cringed, giving thought to crawling under the table. Why did he always have to embarrass me like that?

Liam ducked his head. I think he might have been equally embarrassed. Dad laughed, took the bag and invited Liam in. "I'll just take one of these rolls up to your mom," Dad said with a wink. He put a roll on a plate, poured another cup of coffee and headed upstairs.

"Sorry about that," I mumbled uncomfortably.

Liam laughed. How I loved that sound! "Don't worry about it. My parents pull that stuff all the time." He sat down across from me and pulled a gooey roll out of the bag. He broke it in half and handed me a piece. "But, he is right. I did want to see you again."

I dropped my eyes to the roll he'd handed me. A slow flush crawled up my face. To distract myself, I took a bite of the roll and nearly swooned as the pastry all but melted in my mouth in an explosion of buttery goodness. "Oh my god, Liam!" I swallowed. "This is amazing! Did your mom make these?" I crammed another large bite into my mouth. "I'd gain about a hundred pounds if I ate her food all the time," I said through a mouthful of pastry. "Please, I beg of you, don't bring these over again any time soon!"

Looking pleased, Liam nodded as he took a bite out of his half. "Yeah. I gotta say, Mom is probably the best cook on the lake." He swallowed. "So, did you find out anything more about your mysterious Parsons people?"

For a moment I wasn't sure where to start. "Do you know a guy named Hiram Parsons? He was in the lodge dining room the night we ate there."

Liam thought for a moment then shook his head. "No, I can't say I've heard that name. Why?

I peeled off a sliver of icing from my roll. "I met him at that graveyard yesterday, and he kind of spooked me."

Liam stared at me intently, his roll forgotten in his hand. "Did he try to hurt you? If he did, we can call the cops. We don't put up with that kind of stuff up here."

I tried not to smile. Knowing that Liam was outraged on my behalf gave me goosebumps. "No, no, he didn't try to hurt me or anything. In fact, he seemed very nice. Maybe a little *too* nice if you know what I mean." I paused, pondering Hiram's words. "I asked him what had killed all the Parsons kids, and you know what he said? Consumption."

"Consumption?"

"Tuberculosis. I looked it up last night and it was really common in the 19th century. Since it's contagious, it sometimes killed whole families."

Liam rested his chin on his fist. "Okay, I can buy that. But why seventeen? I mean, a disease like that doesn't usually kill at a specific age."

I shrugged. "Beats me. He merely said people died young back then." I tapped my fingers on the table. "It was so weird. He said something about there being a lot of sadness and tragedy in the graveyard, and that I could feel it too. As I was leaving, he said he expected

78

he'd be seeing me soon. Why would he say that?" I glanced at Liam.

"I don't know," he replied slowly. "but I'd stay away from him."

I laughed. "Oh, believe me, I have every intention of avoiding Mr. Hiram Parsons, whoever he really is."

He cocked his head at me. "Did you? Feel the sadness I mean?"

I considered this for a moment, then slowly nodded. "Yeah, I did. But it was a graveyard. Isn't feeling sad normal?"

About that time, Maya shuffled into the room and froze like a deer in the headlights when she spotted Liam. She wore flannel pajamas which certainly covered her well enough, but Maya never liked being seen by outsiders looking less than perfect. I stifled a laugh as she whirled around and vanished back through the door.

"How old is your sister?" asked Liam as he watched her disappear.

Still chuckling, I got myself under control. "She'll be seventeen next week."

"Seventeen?"

I stopped laughing as a cold chill ran through my heart. "Seventeen."

CHAPTER TEN

"I have something maybe you can help me with," I said to Liam as we finished our rolls. "Remember, I told you about Mercy May's hope chest? Well, yesterday, I went back up to check out the little drawers and opened one of them. There was a brush and comb but more importantly, there was a watch. A watch that was still running."

Liam's eyes widened. "Really? You didn't wind it or anything?"

I shook my head emphatically. "No way. It was running when I opened the case and even had the right time."

"Wow." Liam stared at me for a moment. "And?"

"And the other drawer is locked and needs a tiny key. I thought if you weren't busy, you could help me search the attic for it. I don't want to force the lock since obviously, the chest isn't ours, but I really want to know what's in it."

Liam's face lit up with excitement. "Yeah! That would be cool. It's pretty quiet at the lodge today. I don't think Mom will miss me for a while."

I smiled in relief. Having an ally was reassuring. Liam was quickly becoming more than just an idealized crush. He was becoming a friend. "Great. Come on. I'll show you the way." I led him upstairs and into my room.

Liam examined everything with interest. Fortunately, I hadn't left anything embarrassing lying around. He gave a low whistle when I opened the closet door exposing the second door to the attic. "I can see how you might miss this," he said peering up the narrow stairway.

A few minutes later we stood before Mercy May's hope chest. Liam lay on the floor to inspect the paintwork and details of the box. "You know, chests like these can be really valuable," he mused lifting the lid to examine the contents. "Especially if it comes complete with all the original stuff. I saw an empty one, not nearly this nice, sell for like a thousand dollars."

"Wow." I looked at the chest with a new appreciation. "Too bad it's not ours." Then I pointed to the two side-by-side drawers. "The one on the left opens, but the other one is locked. You can see the little keyhole right beneath the pull."

Liam hunkered down even lower, carefully studying the small hole. "Well, the key would be small and easy to hide." He ran his hand through his blond hair. "You said you checked everything in the box?"

"Yeah. I took everything out and searched thoroughly. I didn't find anything."

Liam reached under the chest and ran his fingers along the bottom and down the chest's stubby little legs. Next, he ran them along the outside of the chest feeling for any secret drawers or buttons. Lastly, he opened the top to examine the lid and the lip of the chest before closing the top with a thud. He pursed his lips and shook his head. I tried not to sigh. He looked so cute doing that. Brow furrowed, he opened the first drawer pulling it all the way out. I watched in fascination as Liam carefully examined every joint and seam in the wood. Still nothing. The only things left were the brush, comb, and watch.

Liam picked up the little watch for a brief moment before quickly returning it to the drawer. He turned his attention to the brush, testing to see if it opened in some way. No luck. He bit his lip, eyeing the watch doubtfully.

"Something wrong?"

"I don't know," Liam replied with a frown. "Something about that watch feels... off."

I reached down and picked up the watch, my eyes widening in surprise. The metal case felt warm to the touch. I ran my finger along the edge and stopped suddenly, feeling a bump. It was a tiny button. Without thinking, I pushed it and the back popped open. Inside the little door was a miniature portrait. Funny I hadn't noticed this before. I turned toward the light to get a better look and almost dropped the watch. Staring out at me were the dark, penetrating eyes of Hiram Parsons. My breath caught in my throat as I stared at the tiny picture in shocked amazement.

"Sophia?"

It took a few moments to get the words out. My throat was so tight I could barely swallow. "It's him!" I finally croaked thrusting the watch towards Liam. "It's the guy I met in the graveyard! Hiram Parsons."

With obvious reluctance, Liam took the watch and stared hard at the face. I stood beside him, relieved the thing was out of my hands. The style of the hair and clothing led me to believe the portrait had been painted in the 1800s. I frowned realizing that although the picture definitely looked like Hiram, it was a much younger version of the man. A teenager perhaps. A warm smile graced his lips. Was this really the Hiram Parsons I'd met in the graveyard or was he Mercy May's brother? The resemblance was uncanny. My stomach did a little flip.

Liam turned the watch around. "There's an inscription here." He squinted trying to make out the fine etching. "It says *Fear not death for the sooner we die, the longer we shall be immortal.*" He shook his head. "That's a weird thing to write inside a watch." Goosebumps erupted down my arms. I suspected that the quote's meaning was far darker than it seemed on the surface. Liam handed me the watch once more but my nerveless fingers couldn't grab it quickly enough, and the watch fell to the floor with a loud clatter.

I winced and reached down to pick it up. "Look!" cried Liam bending down beside me. In his fingers, he held a small silver key no more than an inch in length. I stared in confusion. Where had it come from? I turned back to the watch and realized the portrait hid another space. It must have popped open when I dropped the watch, releasing the key.

Solemnly, Liam handed me the tiny bit of silver. "I think you're supposed to open it."

My teeth chattered so much, you'd think we were in a freezer, despite the warm, stuffy air in the attic. I swallowed, knelt in front of the chest, and with a shaking hand, inserted the key. Carefully, I turned it until I heard a soft click. After a brief moment of hesitation, I removed the key and put it back in the case. Taking a deep breath, I gently pulled on the drawer. After so many years of disuse, it took several firm tugs before the drawer grudgingly slid open with a soft groan. Liam and I exchanged nervous glances as together, we peered into the open drawer.

We found nothing but dust. My shoulders slumped. Why would the drawer be locked if there was nothing inside? I gritted my teeth, reached in and pushed my hand as far back as it would go, hoping there weren't any spiders. Eyes wide, I froze. There *was* something. It was small and cool to the touch. Carefully, I pulled it out to discover a small, black book bound in leather.

Liam and I studied the book with interest. The dry leather had cracked and flaked leaving a few fragments in my hand. The edges of the pages, browned with age, seemed to be in good shape. I fingered the rough cover, hesitant to open the book in the dim and dusty attic, yet I was dying of curiosity. I would just take a peek. I licked my lips and gently lifted the cover. Inside, written in a faded sepia ink were scrawled the words:

The Diary of Miss Mercy May Parsons

I stared at the words for a long moment, a curious tingle running through my body. In my hands, I held the words written by the mysterious Mercy May. Over the past couple of days, my curiosity about the girl had intensified. I wanted to know all about her: Who was she? What were her hopes and dreams? Did she know she was going to die? I shivered at the thought. What would it be like to watch your family die around you, one by one, knowing you could be next?

"What is it?" Liam's hushed voice broke through my rather morbid reverie. Dumbly, I handed him the small volume. He took the book as if he might break it and read the first page. "A diary!" he breathed with excitement. He looked up at me, his eyes shining. "An actual diary from the nineteenth century." He fanned through the pages with care. I could see that the diary was over half-way full. Now I was eager to sit down and learn more about Mercy May and her life's secrets.

"Maybe we should take it downstairs where the light's better," I suggested, taking the book back. Liam nodded, and replacing the watch in its drawer, we closed up the chest, turned out the lights and retreated downstairs to the inviting sunlit kitchen. I guessed some entries might be difficult to read, and the kitchen had the best light in the house.

Liam and I sat side by side, the diary between us. Under normal circumstances, I would have been horribly self-conscious sitting this close to a guy, but my attention was so totally focused on the small book that it never even occurred to me to be embarrassed. Liam had truly become a friend.

Holding my breath, I turned the cover to the yellowed first page. The date was December 26, 1851. I began to read.

I am beginning my first diary. Aunt Margaret gave me this small journal as a gift for Christmas. I shall attempt to record the interesting aspects of my short life. Today, the weather is cold with much new snow. I helped Mother make new candles. Hiram is worse today. I can hear him coughing even when I am outside helping Father with the milking. Dr. Wilson came. He does not believe Hiram will see the new year.

Dec. 27 More snow today. Father and Elijah had much difficulty reaching the barn. One day Father hopes to build a back house to connect the barn to the house. Then we will not have to worry about the snow. Hiram continues to fail. I am so frightened. Mother often sits with him, but I am afraid to see him. He no longer looks like my strong elder brother. I thought nothing could ever hurt Hiram but the dread disease will soon take him.

Dec. 29. Hiram died today. He was but seventeen. Mother cannot stop crying. Father looks as if he would like to. Grace, Hannah and I cry as well. I am very frightened. Other families have been struck down by Consumption. The Waites lost all four of their children, including my friend Caroline. Will this happen to us as well? I notice Elijah does not look well. I pray he will not fall ill as well. We cannot bury Hiram until the spring thaw. Father will keep him in the icehouse until then.

January 1, 1852. It is a new year but there is no joy in my heart. I miss Hiram. Many neighbors have come to offer their condolences and food. I am grateful. Mother cannot do anything but cry. Grace and I are left to do the cooking and household chores. Hannah tries to help, but she is very small. Father spends much of his time working in the barn. I think he cannot bear the silence in Hiram's room. The boys help him.

January 15. It has been two weeks since I last wrote. The weather is desperately cold. Father thinks a blizzard will soon be upon us and has been busy making things ready. Elijah, Lemuel and little Josiah are helping him make the barn as strong as possible. We must protect the animals. Mother is no better. She barely eats, preferring to retire to her room and sleep. Sometimes she will sit at the window staring out, but she rarely speaks to any of us. Father is greatly worried. Grace and I spend our evenings spinning. There is little else to do. This is a very sad home indeed.

January 22. Father was right about the blizzard. It lasted three days. I was so frightened we would be completely buried in the snow and never get out. The wind howled, and the snow piled clear up to the second floor. Father and Lemuel spent hours trying to clear a path to the barn each day in order to feed the animals and milk the cows. Elijah was not feeling well. Father thinks it is nothing more than the grippe. I fear Elijah will soon follow in Hiram's footsteps. He did not like being forced to rest, but it is for the best. Mother was a little better today. She ate some soup. I am hopeful she will soon come back to us. I continue to pray for our family's health.

I stopped reading and exchanged glances with Liam. At last we knew what had become of the eldest Parsons child. Seventeen-year-old Hiram had been the first to die after all, and sometime in the coming year, Elijah would join his brother in the family cemetery on the hill.

CHAPTER ELEVEN

L iam looked at his watch and groaned. "I've got to go. I'm surprised Mom hasn't sent a posse out after me. Believe me, my brothers would jump at the chance to come drag me home if it meant getting out of work. Embarrassing me would just be an added bonus."

I laughed. I hated to see him go. Having someone to share this mystery with made it a lot more fun. Maya wouldn't be that interested. She's not much into history or mysteries for that matter. She's more interested in what she can see and measure. Her idea of a good mystery is trying to figure out what kind of beetle killed the pine trees or the secrets of dark energy. Whimsey is not part of her vocabulary, that's for sure.

Together we walked to the path. "I'll be back tomorrow," he assured me. "I want to find out what happens. It's like having to stop in the middle of a good movie." With a wave and another one of his brilliant smiles, I watched him go with a sigh.

I returned to the kitchen with slow, plodding steps. I slumped into a chair and rested my head on my hand. I gently touched the cracked leather of the journal. "Poor Mercy," I whispered.

"Who's Mercy?" came a sharp voice behind me. I turned to see Maya in the doorway. She peered around to make sure Liam wasn't still lurking someplace.

"Mercy May Parsons," I replied patiently, placing my hand on top of the journal. "She used to live in this house. I found her hope chest and portrait up in the attic. She's buried in an old cemetery up in the woods. It's really sad. She died when she was only seventeen."

"Hmph," I heard Maya grunt. She had her head buried in the refrigerator. "Lots of people died young back then. It was a fact of life."

"Yeah," I persisted, slipping the journal into my lap. "But it looks like her sister and three of her brothers also died when they were seventeen. Doesn't that seem weird to you? I mean, why would four kids in the same family all die at the same age?"

Maya shrugged, obviously uninterested. "Probably some genetic thing." She poured milk over her cereal. "Do you know where Dad is? He was going to show me how to use the electric motor on that little boat tied to the dock."

Now I shrugged. "Upstairs writing I would guess."

She grunted again as she shoveled cereal into her mouth. Maya could be a real pig sometimes. "I want to start collecting samples of aquatic plants," she mumbled through a mouthful of cornflakes. "I'm making a survey of all the different life in the lake. It should be fascinating."

I tried not to roll my eyes. Algae didn't exactly thrill me. "Well, I'm sure you'll have a great time," I said getting to my feet and slipping the journal into my jeans pocket.

"Trust me," she smiled. "I will."

I shook my head and headed outside. It was another beautiful early summer day. A gentle breeze ruffled my dark hair. I took a deep breath and let it go. As much as I hadn't wanted to come here, it was beginning to grow on me. I reconsidered my conversation with Jenna last night and sort of wished she was up here with me. Then I thought of Liam. Hmm. Maybe I didn't want her up here after all. Guys usually swarmed around Jenna. Perhaps it was just as well she wasn't here.

A swing dangled from a sturdy branch of a large oak tree by the side of the house. I meandered over, just enjoying the day, and settled in the swing, listening to the birds chirping up in the trees. I wished I knew what they were. The cardinal was the only song I recognized. After a few moments, when I was sure Maya wasn't going to come barging out of the house looking for me, I slipped the journal from my pocket. I gripped it tightly for a bit, both eager to continue reading but dreading what was to come.

Finally, I flipped the book open to where we had stopped. I hoped Liam wouldn't mind if I continued reading without him, but I simply couldn't wait until he had time to come over again.

Feb 1. Today would have been Hiram's eighteenth birthday. There is no celebration. Mother retreated into her room and has not come out again. I can hear her crying. Father and the boys work in the barn. Grace, Hannah and I made supper, but it was a grim affair. We miss you, Hiram.

Feb.11. Today is Elijah's seventeenth birthday. He has been doing better in the past few weeks. I am hopeful that he will not succumb to the same malady that took Hiram from us. Mother has also been doing better. She even made a small cake to celebrate Elijah's birthday. Sally Hopkins and her brother, Michael stopped by. Sally presented Elijah with a pair of new mittens she knitted herself. I always knew she was sweet on him. I know Elijah likes her as well. Maybe there is a wedding in our future!

Feb. 20. Everyone is sick with the grippe except for Mother and little Hannah. This is the first time I have felt well enough to think of writing here. I do not believe I have ever been so miserable in my life. Mother has almost worn herself out caring for us all. Father is well enough today to tend the animals.

Mar 10. Time goes by so quickly! Despite my best intentions to record my daily life, many days and weeks go by without a word from me. We all have recovered from the grippe although I find I still tire easily. Elijah is still pale and continues to cough. I believe he looks thinner. I am worried. Michael Hopkins came over today with Sally. I will admit, I find myself quite taken with him. I look forward to his visits.

Mar 20. Elijah is much worse. He can barely breathe and coughs constantly. The doctor has been here several times. He says Elijah has galloping consumption, and that there is nothing to be done. Elijah's fever is very high, and he often does not even recognize us. Mother never leaves his side. Father hardly talks.

Just goes about his chores in silence. I fear that our whole family will succumb to this terrible disease.

April 5. Elijah has finally gone to be with the Lord. His suffering has come to an end at last. Father wrapped him securely and placed his body next to Hiram's in the icehouse. The ground will soon be thawed enough that we will be able to bury them. Even now I can hear the awful pounding of Father's hammer as he builds their coffins. I cry all the time. To lose two of my beloved brothers in the space of four months is almost more than I can bear. Poor Mother will not eat or sleep. Lemuel, Grace and I do as much as we can. Even little Josiah and Hannah help as they can. Josiah is getting quite skilled at milking. But the pain we feel at the loss of our brothers can scarce be described. Both dead at seventeen. I pray this is not the start of a pattern.

April 20. We were finally able to lay our beloved brothers to rest. I pray they now sit by the side of the Lord. Many of our neighbors came. Poor Sally Hopkins was heartbroken. Pastor Martin from the Congregational Church presided. His words were a comfort to Mother and Father but I feel nothing but anger. Why should the Lord take two young men before they have had a chance to enjoy life? It is not fair. I know my parents would be horrified if they knew my feelings in this.

I looked up from the book. Wow. Two brothers dead just months apart. I can see why poor Mercy was scared. She'd mentioned earlier that entire families were wiped out by consumption. I would be terrified. I also knew Lemuel would be the next to die. Hiram died in 1851 and Elijah in 1852. According to the gravestones,

Lemuel joined them in 1854 and Mercy the year after that. Grace would survive until 1857. Only the youngest two, Josiah and Hannah would live to adulthood. A heaviness settled over me.

As I pondered the fate of the Parsons family, I wondered what had happened to Hiram's grave. I mean, he was supposedly buried at the same time as Elijah so wouldn't they be next to each other? I couldn't imagine them being buried in the same grave although I guess that could have happened. Yet, why wouldn't Hiram's name be on the gravestone along with his brother's?

I instantly wanted to go back to the graveyard and look for Hiram's stone, but even as the idea occurred to me, I paused, picturing that other Hiram Parsons lurking in the shadows. I ground my teeth in frustration. Why did that creepy guy have to be hanging around there anyway? I sighed, tapping my fingers on the rough wooden seat of the swing, the small diary in my lap. I decided I would take a break. Reading the faded ink and small cramped handwriting was giving me a headache.

As I stood up, voices floated on the warm breeze, and I spied Maya and Dad headed towards the lake loaded down with an assortment of nets and other fishing equipment. I wandered after them for a lack of anything more pressing to do. I got there just as Dad was starting to instruct Maya on how to operate the small outboard motor.

"I'll go out with you this first time," he said as he handed Maya a lifejacket. "Just to make sure you've got it down."

Maya rolled her eyes impatiently as she donned the fluorescent orange vest, but I would swear I could see a flash of relief pass over her face. Maya never wanted to admit there was something she couldn't do. But Little Loon was a big lake and she could get into trouble out there if she didn't know what she was doing.

I watched idly from the dock as the two of them headed out onto the lake. I had considered asking to go, but the thought of listening to Maya jabber on about fish or algae or whatever, was more than I wanted to deal with. Out there on the water, I'd be a captive audience. After a while, I turned with a yawn and headed back up to the house. I hadn't seen Mom today, and figured I had better check on her.

She was sitting on the porch when I reached the house. She looked troubled, but at least she didn't appear to be in some kind of weird trance.

"Hey, Mom," I said as I took the seat next to her. She smiled briefly, but her eyes were still worried. "Something wrong?"

Mom sighed. "I don't know, Sophia. Something about this house bothers me. It concerns me that I've gone into trances I don't even remember."

I turned and looked directly at her. "Do you think maybe you're sick or something?" Of course, the first thing that popped into my mind was a brain tumor.

Didn't they cause people to black out and forget things? I needed to look that up.

Mom shook her head as a tight smile passed over her lips. "No, I'm fine, but there is something in this house that feels... wrong."

"Like something evil?" I was getting into a Stephen King frame of mind here.

"Well, I don't know about that," laughed Mom a bit nervously, pushing her dark hair from her face. "I feel as if something is trying to warn me or send me a message. I just can't seem to interpret it and that worries me." Now she looked at me with narrowed eyes. "What did you find in the attic?"

I hesitated. Mom didn't like the idea of me exploring up there, but at the same time, I didn't want to lie to her. "Well, I found the hope chest of a girl who died in 1855. She was only seventeen. It contained her wedding dress and stuff. Really pretty sad." I decided to leave out the watch that never stopped and the diary. Mom took great stock in the power of personal items, and she might think they were the source of this unknown 'wrongness' and tell me I had to stay out of the attic.

"That is sad." She sat silently for a while. "I feel there has been a lot of sadness in this house."

I started to tell her about Mercy's siblings who also died at seventeen, but again, I didn't want to upset her. I honestly don't know how much of Mom's so-called psychic ability is real as opposed to just good intuitive guesses, but she takes it all very seriously.

"I'm afraid," she said in a soft voice, "There will be more."

CHAPTER TWELVE

Liam showed up later that day. My heart flipped when I spotted his blonde hair glowing in the afternoon sun. He waved happily as he approached the porch where I was working on one of my latest stories. He flopped down beside me with a weary sigh.

"Hard day at the salt mines?" I asked. My father always likes to say that.

He laughed, wiping the sweat off his brow. "We had a busload of tourists from Florida arrive at the lodge this morning. They'll be here for a few days. I should be over there now, but Mom took pity on me and told me I could have a couple of hours off. I've been telling her about this whole Mercy May story, and I think she wants to find out what happened as much as we do." He eyed me suspiciously. "You read more of the diary, didn't you?"

"Yeah, I'll admit it." I tried to look guilty, but frankly, I was simply too excited. I leaned forward. "I just read how Elijah died in April 1852. He got sick shortly after Hiram passed away and kept getting worse. But here's the weird part. They buried the two of them when the ground finally thawed in the spring. We know where Elijah's grave is, but where is Hiram's? Why isn't his right next to his brother's? I mean, since they were buried at the same time, it makes no sense that they'd be in different places."

Liam frowned. "That is weird. It must be there someplace. Maybe the stone was knocked down or stolen."

"We should go back and look. Do you have time?"

"I think so." He glanced at his watch and stood up. "Besides, if I get home late, I'll just tell Mom we were working on the mystery. That should appease her."

I grinned packing away my writing things. I then grabbed my backpack filled with bug spray, plant clippers, a trowel, flashlight and some bottles of water. I would be prepared this time.

Despite the bright summer sun, the air was chilly inside the dense woods. I rubbed my arms as I followed Liam up the path through the deep shadows. The intense silence was rather disconcerting and the hairs on the back of my neck prickled. Was someone watching us? Nervous, I glanced around, but there was nothing. After ten minutes or so, we reached the cemetery and stood quietly by the rusted gate that hung askew on its last hinge.

Licking my lips, I scanned the area, almost expecting to see that weird Hiram guy pop out from behind a tree. Liam looked at me, shrugged and pushed through the weeds into the graveyard. We made our way to the oak tree where Mercy May was buried. I figured that was the most logical place to begin our search for the missing grave.

We found Elijah's headstone with little trouble. "Okay, here's Elijah and Lemuel together," I said turning. "Hiram should be on the other side of Elijah." We pulled away the tangle of weeds and undergrowth just to the left of Elijah's tombstone.

Liam stopped for a moment and furrowed his brow. "This spot seems lower than where Elijah and the others are buried."

I stepped back, frowning in concentration. The ground was slightly sunken there. "You're right. Could they have moved him?" I peered through the thicket hoping to locate the errant tombstone.

Liam shrugged. "Well, the only way we'll know for sure is if we search the entire graveyard. I think you're right, though. It does look like a grave might have been there once. It could still be, and someone just took the stone."

"People do that?" I couldn't imagine why on earth anyone would want to steal a gravestone, but there were a lot of weirdos out there.

"It happens, especially if there's some kind of story associated with the person who died."

"Really?" I found this fascinating in a macabre sort of way.

Liam nodded. "There was a grave in another local cemetery they say belonged to a witch who was burned at the stake. There were lots of stories of her walking the graveyard at night, and people hearing eerie screams during the full moon. Anyway, her gravestone used to disappear all the time."

"Wow. Do people still take it?"

"Well, the city put up a new stone and anchored it so well, no one can move it. It's still there as far as I know."

I shook my head. Made no sense to me. "So, why would someone steal Hiram's? He wasn't a witch."

"That's the question, isn't it?" Liam sighed and slipped his hands into his pockets. He glanced across the small weed-infested graveyard. "Well, at least it's not a big graveyard. It shouldn't take too long to search."

I scowled at the brambles that had engulfed large sections the neglected cemetery. Images of ticks and snakes and other nasty things that might lurk in those tangled vines and tall grasses flit through my mind. I really didn't want Liam to think I was some timid little girly-girl, did I? Okay, part of me was perfectly fine with that idea, but mostly I needed to solve the mystery of the missing grave, and that wouldn't happen if I just stood there and watched.

I pulled out a couple of pairs of clippers and gardening gloves from my pack, handing a set to Liam as well as the can of bug repellant. My clothes already reeked of the bug spray I had soaked myself in before leaving the house. Starting at one end of the graveyard working our way across, and checking every stone and weed patch for the missing headstone, seemed like a logical way to progress.

"Okay," agreed Liam donning his gloves. "If you start at this end, I'll start at the other and we can meet in the middle."

"Yell if you find anything," I called as he headed to his corner.

It didn't seem all that hot when we first set out, but after an hour of pulling weeds, cutting through woody vines and crawling under pricker bushes, I was drenched in sweat, and scratches crisscrossed my arms. As I climbed out of a weed-choked hollow, I stared down at myself in disgust. Dirt and dead plant stuff covered my clothes and skin; my limp hair plastered to my grimy face. Exhausted, I wiped the stinging perspiration out of my eyes and groaned, stretching my aching shoulders. I spotted Liam coming towards me looking just as bedraggled as I felt. He looked discouraged.

"Find anything?" I asked with little hope.

He shook his head. "Nope. Nothing. I checked every stone and searched anyplace where there might have once been a grave, but no luck."

"Where can he be?" I winced at the annoying whine in my voice. "I mean his entire family is here, so where is *he*?"

"The only thing I can figure is they moved him to some other graveyard or," Liam hesitated for a moment glancing towards the fence. "they buried him outside."

"Outside?" I repeated, confused. "What do you mean? Like outside the fence?"

Liam nodded, his face troubled. "Sometimes, say if someone committed suicide, people didn't want them buried in the regular cemetery, so they buried them in unconsecrated ground."

I frowned, pulling my water bottle from my pack. "Yeah, I've heard of that, but we know Hiram died of tuberculosis, not suicide. Plus, I think that only applies to being buried in a churchyard. If he's outside this graveyard, it must be because they moved the fence."

Liam shrugged wiping the sweat from his face with the bottom of his filthy shirt. "Beats me. All I know is he doesn't seem to be here."

I plopped down on a large rock and closed my eyes. My shoulders slumped with fatigue. "If they buried Hiram elsewhere, I'm sure Mercy would have mentioned that in her diary. I mean, that's a pretty significant thing. Why would one brother be buried in the family graveyard but not the other?"

"Not a clue." Liam sounded beat. "Well, I hate to say this, Sophia, but I need to get home. It's getting late."

"Yeah, we better go." I looked at Liam and gently touched his arm. "Thanks, Liam. For taking me seriously. I couldn't do this alone."

Liam looked at my hand in surprise then grinned. My stomach swooped. "Trust me, I wouldn't miss this for the world. Nothing this exciting ever happens here." Suddenly he leaned over and quickly kissed me. Stepping back with a smile in his eyes, he said, "You have definitely made this a summer worth remembering. And it's just getting started!" He turned and headed over to replace his tools in my pack.

I stood there utterly shocked. That was absolutely the last thing I expected. My face burned while a chill ran through me. Had he just *kissed* me? No... really? He had! My brain whirled in confusion. I still felt the light touch of his lips on mine.

"Hey, Sophia! Are you coming?"

Flustered, I shook myself. "Uh, yeah, yeah, be right there." I gathered my things together, threw them in my backpack and hurried after Liam as he started down the path. I tried to focus on the mystery of the missing grave, but of course, my mind had other ideas. *He'd kissed me.* One of the cutest guys I'd ever laid eyes on actually kissed *me!* I stumbled over a rock as I continued to replay the kiss over and over like a big touchdown play in a football game. A random giggle threatened to erupt as I even replayed it in slo-mo. I simply didn't know what to do, what to think. Did he really *like* me? Or did I just happen to be the most convenient girl in the neighborhood?

Stop that, Sophia, I scolded myself. *You are not the total loser you always think you are.* Wasn't I? I was so confused.

As we walked, Liam continued to ponder aloud all the potential fates of our missing grave. He seemed oblivious to my inner turmoil. I made the appropriate sounds at the proper moments as he went on and on. I have not a clue what he said.

When we finally reached the house, we stood there awkwardly for a moment. Liam took my hand, squeezed it and gave me another one of those heart-fluttering smiles. "I'll see you tomorrow, Sophia." I nodded dumbly and watched him head down the trail to the lodge.

After he disappeared from sight, I wandered inside to my room and flopped down on my bed staring up at the ceiling. *He kissed me!*

CHAPTER THIRTEEN

That night I called Jenna to tell her everything. Other than chatting with her online, I hadn't gotten to talk to my best friend since we got up here. This, however, was much too important to discuss via chat. This required direct contact.

"He actually kissed you?" Jenna demanded.

I bristled at the obvious skepticism in her voice. "Yes, he *actually* kissed me. Why? Am I so hideously ugly you find it impossible to believe that a cute guy would want to kiss me?"

"I didn't mean it like that." Jenna tried to soothe me, but I knew she was a little irked that no sooner did I leave town, I turned into some femme fatale. Normally, guys flocked to her like a new video game, and she doesn't like competition. I mean, if suddenly the boys of Parsons Corners found me irresistible, what would happen when I got home?

"Listen," I tried not to snap at her. "It was one lousy kiss. Yes, maybe he is the cutest, nicest guy I have ever met, but it was just a kiss." I'm not sure my attempt at nonchalance fooled anyone.

"Come off it, Sophia. You know it was more than that. Otherwise, you would have just sent me an email!"

Yeah, she had me there. Jenn understood me all too well. "Okay, you're right. It was amazing!" I gushed nonstop. Everything running through my mind poured from my mouth in a rush. "But does he really like me?

I mean, it's not like there are a ton of girls his age up here. Maybe he only kissed me because I was there. You know what I mean?"

Jenna's long, put-upon sigh came over the receiver loud and clear. "Sophia, if he kissed you, then of course, he likes you! He's helping you figure out some kind of puzzle about a dead girl, right? Well, obviously you've dazzled him with your Scooby Doo mystery solving skills, and he's smitten."

I frowned hearing the sarcasm in her voice. Why did she need to bring me down? I always try to be supportive when she starts crushing on some cute guy, and believe me, with her, it's practically a new one every week. Yet here I was, at last finding my one true love, just like in the fairy tales, and she's Miss Negativity. I didn't appreciate it.

"Well, I think it's great you finally got a guy to kiss you," she purred. "You need to send me a picture of him. I'm dying to see what he looks like."

Again, with the subtle put-down. What was her problem anyway? I was tempted to make some smart remark but decided it just wasn't worth it. I didn't want us to fight and end up on a bad note. Time to turn the conversation back on her. Jenna was happiest when talking about herself.

When we hung up about twenty minutes later, I felt oddly dissatisfied. I had really looked forward to talking to Jenna about Liam, but it seemed her delicate ego couldn't handle that. Perhaps I needed to find a new best friend. Too bad there weren't many waiting in the queue. I sighed and trudged downstairs to get something to eat.

In the kitchen, Maya sat at the table eating a peanut butter and jelly sandwich. The food of the gods. She looked up when I entered, her face sunburned from being out in a boat all day. I opened my mouth to make some crack about her water weeds but decided I needed a friend more than a fight with my sister.

"So, how did your day on the lake go?" I asked reaching for the peanut butter.

Maya stopped chewing and stared at me suspiciously. "Why do you care?"

I shrugged. "Just curious. Did you find what you were looking for?"

Maya narrowed her eyes trying to decide if I was setting her up for something. "It went okay," she replied slowly, still watching me. "I found six different species of water plants including a couple of non-natives."

I finished making my sandwich and nodded as if this was all fascinating. "The non-natives, I assume they're bad?"

"Yeah," she nodded. "They're invasive and may eventually force out the native species." She stopped and frowned at me. "Sophia, I know perfectly well you couldn't care less about water plants. So, what gives?"

I shrugged again. "I just thought I'd ask. Is that a crime?"

Maya arched an eyebrow as she picked up her plate and headed for the sink. "No, but it's pretty weird. Something wrong?"

I opened my mouth then snapped it shut. Part of me wanted to pour my heart out to her. She's had a lot more experience with boys than me and could no doubt offer me some sage advice about Liam. On the other hand, it might just provide her with a whole new arsenal of weapons to use against me. I shook my head. "No, nothing wrong. I figured it might be nice to have an actual conversation for once without a fight."

For a long moment, no one said anything. Finally, Maya looked at me. "Thank you, Sophia. Maybe you're starting to grow up after all." She gave me an enigmatic smile and left.

I couldn't quite decide if that had been a compliment or an insult. I shrugged and swallowed a bite of my sandwich. A compliment, then. Life is short.

Later, as I sat in bed, I read some more of Mercy May's journal. I knew I could probably get through most of the diary in one sitting, but there was a certain amount of satisfaction in dragging it out. It was like reading a great story you didn't want to end. I wanted to keep it going in part because reading Mercy May's own words brought her to life. Once I finished, she would be gone. I know she's been dead a long time, but I had begun to think of her as a friend. That sounds weird, but let's face it, this whole thing was pretty strange.

I opened the diary to the next entry and settled in to read.

June 16. A glorious day. The rains have finally come to an end. The lake is very full. Much higher than I have ever seen before. Lemuel is eager to go fishing, but Father will not allow it until the water has gone down. Both Mother and Father have become very protective of all of us since the loss of Hiram and Elijah. Any little sniffle becomes cause for immediate alarm. So far, the rest of us seem healthy enough. I pray each night that the scourge has left our family.

June 30. We have received word that my cousin, Mary, has died. She was the daughter of Father's brother, Thomas and Aunt Symphronia. Mary was the same age as Elijah. Another one of the family gone at seventeen. Why? I am becoming more and more frightened. Lemuel will not be seventeen for another year and a half, so perhaps he is safe until then. I do not know. I wish we could move from this accursed place.

July 2. We have just now returned from Cousin Mary's funeral. Aunt Symphronia had to be carried away from the grave at the end. She refused to leave, so great was her grief. She has turned to Mother for support. Mother is all too familiar with the loss of a child. Uncle Thomas and Aunt Symphronia have two much younger children. I heard Uncle Thomas say he plans on leaving Parsons Corners. He fears for the lives of little Peter and Samuel. I wish we could go with them.

Sept 1. At last, I have my journal returned to me. I left it behind when Mother and I went to visit her sisters, Aunt Iris and Aunt Susan in Concord. Mother has been so very low since Mary's passing. She fears for her remaining children's lives more than ever. Now, we have heard that my cousin Jonathan has fallen ill. The doctor has diagnosed him with the same galloping consumption that took Hiram and Elijah. I begged Father to take us away from here. But he says this land has been in his family since before the Revolutionary War, and he will not abandon it. I fear in the end, he will have no one to leave it to.

Sept 17. A very strange thing has occurred this day. My Uncle John, Jonathan's father, has come to speak with Father along with Uncle Thomas and a third man I did not recognize. They claim he is a religious man from Europe. They have come to beg Father to allow them to dig up the bodies of Hiram and Elijah. When pressed for a reason, the man from Europe said he has done much study on families where consumption kills one person after another. He claims the reason for such destruction of life has to do with an evil entity that resides in the heart of one of the deceased. This entity thrives by drawing on the energies of the living, soon reducing them to almost nothing and eventually killing them. He said if they find fresh blood in either the heart or the liver of the deceased, they know they have found the culprit. They must then burn the offending organ, and if they feed the ashes to the ailing person, it will cure them. Father has refused. But could this be true? Could Hiram or Elijah be the cause of so much misery? I cannot believe this.

I sat back in shock. Were they talking about a *vampire*? A rising-from-the-grave, Bela Lugosi blood-sucking vampire? Come on. Really? I mean, surely these people didn't actually believe someone rose from the grave to suck the blood from the living? I hesitated. No, that's not exactly how Mercy May described it. She made it sound as if some, what did she call it? An *evil entity?* resided in the heart of the deceased, which then proceeded to suck the life out of someone else. The only blood she mentioned was that found in the heart or liver of the dead person. The victim didn't lose blood, only their health. Well, it didn't sound like Mercy May's father bought into the theory, but obviously, some members of the family were desperate enough to want to give it a shot. I guess Jonathan's father was ready to try anything to keep his son from going down the same fatal path as his cousins. I shook my head in wonder. I would have to do some more research on this.

That night my dreams were full of vampires and walking dead. Repeatedly, I jerked awake bathed in a cold sweat, my heart pounding. As the sun rose, I finally gave up. I decided if I could get Maya to take me, I should visit the library and search for information on this, for lack of a better word, vampire. I still found it hard to believe that rational people in 19th century New England believed in vampires. New Hampshire hadn't even been that big on witches, unlike say, Massachusetts where witches seemed to be as common as cows back in Colonial times. People in New

112

Hampshire didn't have time for the supernatural; they were too busy digging rocks out of their cornfields.

I found Maya later that morning making notes on her finds from the previous day. "Can you drive me to the library?" I asked.

She looked at me in surprise. "The library? Does this town even *have* a library?"

I nodded. "I looked it up. It's on Main Street. The Parsons Corners Free Public Library. I want to do some research on the town, and I'm hoping the library might have what I need."

Maya glanced at her watch. "I tell you what. It'll take me another hour or two to finish this, so I can take you after lunch. I wouldn't mind getting out of here for a little while."

I smiled and nodded. See? Not sniping at her yesterday about her water weeds paid off. Sometimes Maya can be okay.

CHAPTER FOURTEEN

The Parsons Corners Free Public Library was located in one of those big old Victorian houses you find all over New Hampshire. It was a pretty cool looking place with a tower and huge wraparound porch. Maya decided she would go look for some books on local flora and fauna while I began my own search.

I approached the librarian at the front desk. She reminded me of my grandmother with her silver hair and warm, friendly smile. "Can I help you?" she asked, peering at me over her wire-rimmed glasses.

I swallowed, a little unsure of how to begin. "Hi, I'm doing a research project, and, well, I wondered if there are any stories about vampires around here, say in the 1850s?"

The woman's eyebrows rose in surprise. "Well, that's not a question I often get, but, you're in luck. There have been places in New England where locals believed some vampire-like creature existed, killing entire families. Rhode Island had several such cases. In the 19th century, people would develop tuberculosis, a common disease at the time, and die. It's a rather contagious disease, and since large families lived in small spaces, it was easily spread. The theory was, one of the first to die continued to live by sucking out the life of other family members causing them to fall ill and ultimately succumb." She frowned and tapped her chin.

"I'm not sure there was a specific name for them back then, but today we refer to them as 'Yankee Vampires'. As for your Bram Stoker variety of blood-sucking vampire, I'm not aware of any documented stories."

"Do you know if there were any of the first kind around here?" I was excited that she understood what I was looking for but worried there wouldn't be any actual information.

"Well, many of the old newspapers are on microfilm if you would like to search. I can show you how to use the machine. Someday it would be nice to have it all online, but until then, we make do with the old technology." She gave me an apologetic smile. I was thrilled the papers were even available.

We entered a small room in the back of the library where a couple of ancient microfilm readers sat looking sad and forlorn. I wondered how often they got used these days.

"Can you narrow down the time period?" the librarian asked. "Otherwise, you'll be looking at a lot of newspapers."

I considered this. "Probably some time after September 1852." That would put it after Mercy May's uncles and the strange guy appeared wanting to dig up the bodies.

The librarian nodded and opened a large gray metal cabinet stocked with lots of small boxes of microfilm rolls. "The *Parsons Corners Gazette* only came out once a week on a Wednesday, so that will help you narrow the search," the librarian smiled. She pulled out five boxes. The first one was labeled *P. Gazette 1852*. "These will take you through 1856. If you want to look at other years, they're all in here in numerical order." I grimaced at the forbidding pile of microfilm. This was going to take forever.

The librarian loaded up the film and showed me how to use the machine. It was pretty straightforward, and I mastered it with little difficulty. I whirred through the images trying to reach September 1852. I had to avert my eyes as a wave of queasiness rolled over me. Who would have thought you could get motion sickness looking at old newspapers? Once I reached the September 1 issue, I stopped and carefully studied each page searching for anything that might indicate a vampire was running around.

I made it through the 1852 issues and most of 1853 before Maya finally appeared. "Are you done?" she asked coming up behind me to see what I was doing.

I yawned. There were still a lot more boxes to go through, but my eyes burned and my shoulders ached from sitting hunched over for so long. I grimaced at my empty notebook. So far, the newspapers had been less than helpful.

"Did you find anything interesting?" Maya asked, shifting the pile of books she carried in her arms.

I shook my head. "Nope. Not really. I'll need to come back again and go through some more of these."

Maya eyed the stack of boxes and shrugged. "Better you than me. Well, come on. I've already checked out these books. The librarian let me have a temporary library card, so I'm ready to go."

I followed Maya outside to the car and was about to slide into the passenger's side when the hairs on the back of my neck prickled. I had the distinct sensation of being watched. I scanned the area trying to appear natural but saw nothing out of the ordinary. Yet, the prickly feeling persisted. As I tossed my notebook into the car, I glanced upwards and froze. There, staring at me from an upper library window, loomed Hiram Parsons. My heart leaped into my throat as I stared back at him, unable to move.

"Come on, Sophia!" snapped Maya impatiently. "Let's go!" I wanted to say something but couldn't utter a peep. At the sound of my sister's voice, Hiram's gaze shifted towards her and abruptly grew more intense, almost hungry. His lips curled into an unsettling yet satisfied smile. He glanced at me one last time before dissolving into the darkness behind him.

Shaking, I slid into the seat. What was *he* doing here? Had he been watching me in the library? My stomach turned as I wrapped my arms around myself. I craned my neck to peer up at the window once more. It was empty.

"What are you looking at?" Maya scowled as she waited for me to close the door and put on my seat belt.

"I... I thought I saw someone up in that window."

"So?" Maya started the car.

"He looked like this creepy guy I met at the cemetery near our house," I explained still glancing upwards. "He was staring at us."

Maya gave me a strange look. "Why would he be staring at us? Did you talk to him in the cemetery?"

I nodded. "A little. He said his name was Hiram Parsons. He was the one who told me most of the people buried in the graveyard died of consumption."

"Tuberculosis?"

"Yeah. He seemed so odd, as if he knew who I was." I paused. "He was really good looking though. He had dark hair and looked a lot like that actor, Colin Firth. You know who I mean?"

"Mr. Darcy?" Maya loved all the Jane Austen novels, and Colin Firth was her very favorite Mr. Darcy. I knew she'd recognize who I meant.

"That's him. I just wish I knew what he wanted."

Maya frowned as she turned down the lane towards our house. "What on earth makes you think he wants anything?"

I shrugged. "It just seems really strange that every time I leave the house, there he is. I saw him the first time when we had dinner at the lodge. Later I saw him in the cemetery and now here at the library. Doesn't that seem weird to you?"

Maya grunted noncommittally as she pulled into the gravel drive leading to the house. "This isn't a huge town. You're going to run into people all the time. It's probably just a coincidence."

"Well, it seems weird to me," I persisted stubbornly. The fact that Maya dismissed this so easily made me even more determined to prove he was up to something, just to show her. The creepy look he'd given Maya resurfaced in my mind. I glanced at my sister and my chest tightened. I was suddenly terrified.

CHAPTER FIFTEEN

Dad decided to make me and Maya go camping with him for a few days, "To get the cobwebs out of our brains and experience the wonders of nature," is how he put it. I think he had just reached a sticky point in his book and camping was a way to avoid dealing with it.

Unfortunately, because I had to go commune with nature for a while, I wasn't able to do any more research on Mercy May and the fate of her family. But even out in the middle of the godforsaken woods, I feared I might run into that Hiram guy lurking behind every tree. It certainly made the trip a lot less relaxing.

Worst of all was not getting to see Liam for several days. I didn't realize how much I would miss him. I tried not to mope about it though. Maya was already giving me a hard enough time about him, calling him my "little boyfriend". It was so irritating. Personally, I think she was jealous.

We ended up being gone for five days. I worried about Mom being alone for so long. Dad had borrowed a satellite phone from the same guy who lent him the camper, so while we were out in the mountains where cell phone reception was spotty, he could check up on her every day. She assured us she was fine, but after her earlier bouts of strange behavior, it was hard not to worry.

I was so ready to get home and take a real shower and sleep in a real bed. I could deal with camping for a little while, but five days spent listening to Dad and Maya identify trees and discuss the effects of global warming on the environment should be considered cruel and unusual punishment. Guess I'll never make it as one of those survivalists.

We reached home early in the evening. My stomach growled and I hoped Mom had something for us to eat. I piled out of the car and trotted into the house where I promptly dumped my backpack by the front door. "Mom!" I called heading to the kitchen. "We're home!" I stopped and listened. An odd emptiness filled the house. I glanced into the kitchen. No one was there. "Mom?" I called again, peering up the stairs. "Are you up there?" Silence. My chest tightened as I hurried up the staircase still calling for her. I looked in all the rooms. They were empty. I thudded down the stairs in a near panic to tell Dad.

I found him and Maya methodically unpacking the car. "Dad!" I panted, "I can't find Mom."

Dad paused as he set down a cooler. "What do you mean you can't find Mom? Did you look upstairs? Maybe she's working."

"I did look upstairs. There's no one there." I glanced over and spotted Mom's car parked under the maple tree. She had to be here somewhere.

Dad hurried into the house calling Mom's name. I twisted my hands as I scanned the yard. I was terrified that I would find her under a bush unconscious or worse.

"She's fine," my sister assured me, but furrowed brow told me that she was just as worried as I was.

Dad returned a few minutes later. "You're right, Sophia, she's not here. But her car is, so she's got to be around someplace."

I chewed my lip, thinking. "Maybe she walked up to the graveyard."

"The graveyard?" Dad turned to stare at me.

"Yeah, the one up in the woods. The one Liam and I have been checking out."

Dad nodded slowly. "Show me."

It made sense, really. I mean, if Mom is actually psychic, wouldn't she be drawn to a graveyard, especially one like the Parsons'? I'm sure with all its sad stories, it would be a powerful magnet to someone with true psychic abilities.

We hurried up the pathway through the woods, swatting at the clouds of mosquitoes that swarmed around us. The trail seemed much longer than I remembered it. We finally got to the top of the hill and sighted the old fence. "It's up there," I pointed. Dad picked up his pace with me and Maya hurrying to keep up.

"Lina!" he called. I detected a note of fear in his voice. "Lina, are you up here?"

"Dad!" cried Maya staring into the distance. "Look! She's over there!" Dad and I both turned and spotted Mom near the oak by Mercy May's grave. Like a specter, Mom stood there unnaturally still and pale. Her eyes were closed, and she seemed to be speaking to herself, oblivious to our presence.

Now that we'd found her, no one wanted to interrupt her trance or whatever it was. We approached cautiously like we would a wild deer, then stood silently observing her for several long moments.

"Lina?" Dad moved closer and placed a gentle hand on Mom's arm. "It's me. Roger. Can you hear me?"

Mom's lips stopped moving and her body became impossibly still. I wrapped my arms around myself to keep from shaking. Fear gripped me. Of what, I'm not sure, but it felt wrong. Finally, Mom's eyes opened ever so slowly. She stared straight ahead for a few minutes before she registered Dad standing two feet in front of her.

"Roger?" Her brow furrowed in confusion. "Roger, what are you doing here? I thought you were camping with the girls." She turned to scan the area. Her frown deepened. "What is this place?"

"It's the Parsons family graveyard," I told her coming closer.

"Oh, yes," she said faintly but not really like she was listening. She acted vague and unsure.

Dad took her arm. "Perhaps we'd all better get home," he said. He glanced at me and Maya. "It's time for dinner, and we're starving."

As Dad led Mom down the path, I turned to examine the spot where Mom had been standing.

"Look," I said, pointing to something white buried in the weeds. Maya picked it up and stared at in surprise. It was a white rose. Someone had placed it on Mercy May's grave.

"A rose?" I asked, frowning. "Where'd that come from? Did Mom bring it?"

Maya shrugged, her eyes glued to the luminescent blossom. "I don't know," she whispered, rubbing her finger along one of the silky petals. Suddenly she cursed and dropped the flower, a small dot of crimson standing out against the pure white of the flower. Maya stuck her bleeding finger in her mouth.

"Are you okay?" I asked, staring at her in concern.

Maya nodded, examining her finger. "I'm fine. It was just a thorn." Her eyes darted nervously around the cemetery as she absently ran her hands up and down her arms. "I don't like this place," she said in a low voice, "I think we'd better get going. Dad will wonder what happened to us."

As Maya quickly retreated down the path, I took one last look around. I didn't blame Maya for feeling a little freaked out. It did feel unusually creepy here today. Again, there was the sensation of someone watching me, and it was growing stronger. With a final shiver, I picked up the rose, trying not to look at the spot of blood, and replaced it on the grave. A slight tingle ran up my arm as I released the flower. With a soft cry, I hurried after the others.

By the time we got home, Mom was her normal self and chatting to Dad about our camping trip. Maya, on the other hand, seemed to retreat into herself more and more as the evening progressed. She answered Mom's questions with one or two-word answers, then finally excused herself saying she wasn't feeling well. Mom's eyes followed her with concern.

Uneasy, I considered my sister as she disappeared upstairs. Maya would turn seventeen the day after tomorrow. I know there was no reason for me to worry, but I'd seen the way Hiram stared at her at the library. There had been a disturbing intensity in his gaze, and I didn't like it. I had no idea if he was one of those perverts you always read about or what, but I decided I needed to be on my guard more than ever.

Liam showed up a little after breakfast the next morning. I tried not to show my excitement and blushed when he handed me a bunch of colorful wildflowers.

"They aren't much," he said looking embarrassed, his blue eyes glancing down at the ground, "But they were pretty, and I thought you'd like them."

I sighed, feeling a bit moony-eyed. No guy has ever given me any kind of flowers, and I didn't care if he'd stolen them off the front desk of the lodge; they were gorgeous to me. "Thanks," I mumbled, shy at this display of affection. "I... I better put them in water." Thank goodness flowers always needed to go into water right away. Tracking down a vase gave a girl a minute to collect herself.

"How did your camping trip go?" Liam asked as he followed me into the kitchen. "Did you have fun?"

"It was okay, I guess." I rummaged under the sink for something to hold the bouquet. "It was beautiful and peaceful, but I missed my bed." I held out my arm, mottled with nasty red bumps and welts like some horrible skin condition. "Too bad the mosquitoes didn't seem to understand the purpose of bug repellant. I think it attracted them more than chased them away."

Liam winced in sympathy. "I guess you need a stronger brand."

I grunted in agreement as I finished arranging the flowers in the old mason jar I'd found. They looked quite pretty. I smiled. I glanced over at Liam and noticing that he followed my every move, I smiled at him, too. "Thanks again," I said. "I really love them. They're beautiful." He seemed to relax.

"Now that I'm home," I continued, moving the flowers to the table, "We can start working on the Parsons mystery again. Listen, I didn't get a chance to tell you about the whole vampire thing." Just as Liam was about to respond, Mom and Dad strolled into the kitchen.

"Oh, hello, Liam," Dad grinned, looking back and forth between the two of us. "I didn't know you were here."

"What lovely flowers!" Mom had noticed the vase on the table. "Did you bring these, Liam? They're beautiful." She glanced at me, and I could tell she was trying not to smile. It was time to go.

"Come on, Liam," I said my face burning again. "I've got something to show you." With a final word to my parents, Liam followed me out of the kitchen and up the stairs to my room. I pulled the diary out of the bottom drawer of my dresser. I opened it to the last section I'd read about Mercy May's uncles wanting to exhume Elijah and pushed the book into Liam's hands. "Here, check this out."

Liam scanned over the entries; his eyebrows rose in surprise. "That's weird. I've never heard about this before."

"I know they don't say *vampire*, but that's what it sounds like, doesn't it?"

Liam nodded slowly. "Sort of, but it doesn't sound like something that comes in the dark and sucks your blood like a traditional vampire. It sounds more like it just drains away your life." He shook his head. "But that's stupid. We know these people died of tuberculosis. Not by some evil spirit hanging out in a corpse. That's just some old superstition."

"I went to the library to see if I could find anything about vampires or people digging up bodies," I said taking the journal back. "But, so far no luck."

Liam sat down on my desk chair. "It's possible they never actually dug them up. Mercy May said her father wouldn't let them."

"True." I turned to the diary in my hands. No doubt the answer was in here. If they had exhumed the bodies, Mercy would have certainly recorded such an incident. Assuming it happened before she herself passed away.

I opened the journal once more and glancing at Liam, who gave me a nod of approval, began to read.

CHAPTER SIXTEEN

September 30. Cousin Jonathan continues to fail. Uncle John has come twice more begging Father to allow them to exhume Hiram and Elijah's bodies. He is desperate to save his son. Father still refuses. He says this is all wild superstition and cannot understand how his own brother can condone such nonsense. I have to agree with Father in principle, but what if exhuming the bodies really could do Jonathan some good? Mother came into the room the second time Uncle John came by. Father had not told her of the request to dig up the bodies. When she heard of this, she became quite hysterical and fainted dead away. The doctor was called to tend to her. Uncle John left, but it is unlikely he will give up the fight.

Oct 10. Today I turn sixteen. I can scarcely believe it! Mother allowed me to have a few friends over for tea and cakes. I invited Betsy, Louise, and Agnes. They are my best friends at school. It was a most delightful day. It was made even better when Michael came over with a special gift for me. It was a lovely silk handkerchief. I must confess, the best part came when he kissed me! Of course, it was improper but most exciting. I wouldn't mind being Mrs. Michael Hopkins someday.

Oct 12. Lemuel discovered Uncle John in the graveyard with that odd Dr. Kiev, starting to dig up Hiram's grave. He came home and told Father straight away. Father told him to ride for the constable while he himself went up to the cemetery. I wanted to follow, but Mother would not allow it. Father had taken his shotgun, and Mother feared there would be violence. Lemuel told me later that when he arrived at the graveyard with Constable Lowell, Father had both men tied together. According to Lemuel, Uncle John was nearly in tears begging Father to allow him to check Hiram and Elijah's bodies for fresh blood. He truly believes he might be able to save his son if he discovers this. The Constable took them both away. Father says he will not press charges, but he has warned Uncle John to stay away.

Dec 3. Jonathan has passed after a long and painful illness. I do not know if digging up my brothers' bodies would have saved him, but now we will never know. My friend, Louise told me some say it is my Father's fault since he would not allow his sons' bodies to be exhumed. I pray no more die from this awful malady.

Dec 26. Another Christmas has passed. It was a most somber affair without Hiram and Elijah to join us. Often, we go to some relative's home for Christmas dinner or they come to ours. However, this year it seems we are no longer in favor with the rest of the family. Ever since Father refused to allow them to dig up poor Hiram and Elijah, many of the family will no longer speak to us. Even some of our friends look down upon us, saying we let Jonathan die when we could have helped. Sometimes I wonder if they even listen to what they say. Do they truly believe that if we had allowed Uncle John to burn poor Elijah's heart and made Jonathan drink a concoction made of those same ashes Jonathan would be cured? That sounds like something akin to witchcraft, and no God-fearing person would condone such behavior. It is madness.

Jan 17, 1853. Today is Lemuel's seventeenth birthday. Given the family's past history, we all secretly fear for his life. I am happy to report that today, all seems well. Lemuel spent the morning chopping wood for Mother and seems his usual healthy, happy self. I continue to pray that the plague of consumption is done with us and has moved on. We killed a chicken especially for Lemuel's birthday dinner. It has been some time since we have had a chicken. The winter has been especially cold, and we have lost several of our hens, thus Mother has been sparing with them. The meal tasted delicious. Lemuel seemed to like the socks I knitted for him. I was glad.

Jan 30. Lemuel has been troubled these past few days. When I asked him why, he was at first reluctant to talk with me. Finally, he confided in me that he has been having disturbing dreams. Dreams of Hiram. He says Hiram comes to him at night and speaks with him. When I pressed Lemuel for more details, he claimed not to recall the exact conversations, but he had the impression that Hiram was apologizing for some wrong he would be committing. I expressed my confusion at the future tense of this event. Lemuel was likewise puzzled. However, he felt it was a bad omen and was fearful. I know he suspects he will be the next victim of the dreaded consumption. I assured him he was healthy and had nothing to fear. I am not sure I persuaded him.

Feb 1. Today is poor Hiram's birthday. He would have been nineteen. Is that possible? Sometimes, I wake in the night thinking I hear his voice calling to me. It is but a dream, but it seems so real. Would he be married now? Before he died, there was talk of him and Annie Powell marrying. She has since married Martin Bannon. I have also heard that Sally Hopkins will soon marry Samuel Stevens. I am saddened by what might have been. How happy Mother would be to be a grandmother now and I, an aunt. If only.

Feb 11. Today we remember Elijah. He would have been eighteen this day. The weather is terrible and ice covers everything. We lost one of our cows. She slipped on the ice and broke her leg. Father had to put her down. I noticed Lemuel looked pale and tired this evening at supper. I said nothing, for I fear I look for illness where there is none. Grace calls me a worrywart, and perhaps she is right, but I have seen her obvious concern for our brother.

Mar 2. Lemuel has confided in me again of his dreams concerning Hiram. He says the nights he dreams of our brother, he wakens in the morning tired and weak. I detect no sign of injury on him, and he claims there is no bodily harm, just weakness. I find this troubling.

Mar 10. I fear my journal has become nothing but a record on the health of our family. Yet, recording the weather or how I spent the day knitting or sewing seems trivial in comparison. Last night I woke from a terrible dream. Elijah came to me. His skeletal form hardly looked as I remembered him. He warned me that Lemuel faced great danger and must leave Parsons Corners for someplace safer. Someplace where he will stay well. I asked Elijah if Lemuel was ill. Elijah declared Lemuel would not see his eighteenth birthday. I awoke at this point in great distress.

Was this truly an omen or simply my own fears manifesting themselves in my dreams? I do not know.

I stopped reading here as I suddenly remembered my own seemingly prophetic dream.

Liam eyed me with curiosity. "Is something wrong?"

"No," I replied slowly. "I was just thinking about a dream I had."

"Really?" Liam sat forward, his eyes bright. "What was it? Did Elijah come talk to you too?"

I could tell he was kidding, but he was closer than he realized. "Not exactly. It was Mercy May. I dreamed I was in the graveyard and she was there. Suddenly I wasn't me. I was her sister, Grace. Mercy warned me that I must get away, or Hiram would kill me. Then she called me Sophia and said he'd kill me too. It was a really disturbing dream."

Liam sat back, his brows knitted. "Could she really have been warning you about the Hiram guy you keep seeing? Maybe he's some kind of serial killer or something."

There was a chilling thought. Could that really be what the dream meant? I remembered thinking that she'd been warning me about the present-day Hiram. Surely it was nothing more than what it seemed - a weird dream. "Did I tell you I saw that Hiram at the library?"

"No." Liam frowned. "He sure does seem to pop up wherever you go. I'm beginning to suspect that it's not a coincidence. Maybe he's following you. Did he say anything?"

I shook my head. "No, in fact, I spotted him in the upper window of the library just watching me." I paused and corrected myself. "*Us.* He was watching Maya, too. In fact, I think he was watching her more than me. He knew I saw him, but I could tell he didn't care. It was almost as if he wanted me to see him watching her. It was really creepy."

"Have you told your parents?"

Again, I shook my head. "Not about the library. I told Maya about him, but she acted like it was no big deal. She probably thinks I'm just imagining the whole thing. I mean, no one else has seen him except me."

Liam tapped his fingers on the nightstand. "I recognize most people around here," he mused. "At least by sight. Although, he could be a summer resident. There are tons of those around now."

I sighed. "Well, I'm probably just being paranoid. So many strange things keep happening here that I'm probably blowing it all out of proportion. Maya's right. In a town this small, I'm bound to run into the same people all the time."

Liam grunted. "But in the graveyard? Nobody ever goes to that graveyard. Now suddenly it's like Walmart at Christmas. Why is he so interested?"

"His name is Hiram Parsons," I replied thoughtfully. "He could be working on his family history and is related to the people buried in the cemetery."

"Hmm." Liam looked skeptical. "But that doesn't explain why you keep seeing him. I'll try and keep my eyes open and see if he shows up at the lodge for dinner. I don't remember him from that night you guys were there, but I wasn't working the tables either."

About that time, Dad called me down for dinner. Liam looked at his watch and groaned. "Damn! I'm going to be late. I told Mom I wouldn't stay long. I gotta run. She's going to kill me." I walked him down and out the front door. He gave me a warm smile, squeezed my hand, turned, and trotted down the path. I was a little disappointed that he didn't kiss me this time, but also a little relieved. As much as I loved being with Liam, I'll admit that the idea of some kind of romantic relationship scared me. He was so easy to be with and always listened to me. If we evolved into girlfriend/boyfriend would that change things? I felt very confused at the moment. I sighed and returned to the house.

Dad and I whipped up some hamburgers while Mom sat talking to Maya about her impending birthday. "So, what do you want for your birthday dinner?" Mom asked.

"I'd really like to go to the lodge," Maya replied squirting a mass of ketchup on her burger. It was disgusting, really.

"I think you just want to see that cute waiter again," I threw out.

"Ha! Like you should talk." Maya glared at me. "Seems like you spend an awful lot of time hanging out with Liam." She leaned forward with a smirk. "And those are some mighty pretty flowers he brought you."

My face burned. I was too new at the boy thing to feel comfortable talking about it at the dinner table.

Dad obviously caught on to my discomfort. He poked Maya in the shoulder. "Leave her alone, Maya. Sophia and Liam are just... friends. Right, Sophia?"

My face burned even hotter. I kept my eyes glued to my plate. "Yes, Dad, we're just *friends*." I felt like such an idiot.

"But that waiter is pretty cute... isn't he, Maya?" Dad laughed and dumped some potato chips on his plate. Now it was my sister's turn to blush.

Suddenly Mom turned to me, her face serious. "Sophia, I want you to be very careful, and definitely stay away from that graveyard. It's dangerous there."

That came out of the blue.

I tilted my head and frowned. "Dangerous? How? I doubt there are any snakes up there, and I certainly didn't see any big holes or cliffs. It's just an old graveyard, Mom."

She shook her head firmly. "It's more than that. Evil lurks in that place. I fear it means us harm. I don't think we need to invite it in."

I rolled my eyes even as I experienced a slight flutter in my stomach. I know most of what Mom says is a lot of hokum, but sometimes she actually gets it right. I was fully aware that something *was* wrong in that graveyard, but in my teenage superiority, I found difficult to agree, especially when it meant I'd have to stay out of the cemetery. "Mom, I don't imagine any zombies are wandering around Parsons Corners."

Mom didn't even crack a smile. "I'm dead serious, Sophia. There is something up in that graveyard. I don't know what it is, but I sensed something evil. It drew me there. Promise me you won't go up there anymore."

I sighed my deepest put-upon teenaged sigh. "Fine. I'll stay out of the graveyard."

Mom nodded, looking relieved. "Good. I'm sure there are plenty of other things you can find to do besides hanging around old cemeteries."

Sure, I wouldn't go inside the fence into the actual graveyard. However, Mom didn't say anything about staying out of the woods *around* the graveyard. You just got to love those loopholes.

CHAPTER SEVENTEEN

M aya's birthday turned out to be a chilly, dreary day. I woke up to gray skies and the musty dampness you only really get in old houses. I peered morosely at the torrent of rain falling outside my window. Ugh. Guess I'd be staying inside today.

I stumbled down the hallway to the bathroom and took a shower. That helped wash the cobwebs out of my brain. I'd been having weird dreams all night, but I couldn't quite remember them. When I woke up for good, I had that tense, uncomfortable feeling you get when you've got an unpleasant dentist appointment coming up. I didn't like it.

I pulled on a sweatshirt and jeans and clumped my way down the stairs to the kitchen. As I arrived, Mom slid a tall stack of pancakes into the oven to keep them warm. The tangy aroma of hickory smoked bacon made me swoon with hunger. "How long till breakfast?"

"Whenever Maya shows up." Mom tossed me a banana.

I sighed. Who knew how long that might be? I flopped down in a chair and peeled the banana, still gazing longingly at the crisp strips of bacon Mom piled on the platter. If Maya didn't get out of bed soon, I'd go wake her up, birthday or no birthday. I was starving.

Dad arrived soon after I did, and Maya wandered in about five minutes later looking disheveled but hungry. "Something sure smells good," she said.

Mom might not be the world's best cook, but she does make a mean breakfast. I'm not usually a big morning eater, but I definitely ate more than my fair share of pancakes and bacon. The eggs tasted pretty good too.

For her birthday, Mom had promised she'd take Maya to Berlin to do a little shopping. Berlin wasn't exactly New York, but it certainly had more than Parsons Corners. Parsons Corners only had a single general store, best suited for emergencies and miscellaneous groceries. Anyway, it would be a mother-daughter outing leaving me and Dad at home. When they returned, we'd all go out for dinner at the lodge.

After breakfast, I retrieved the gift I had gotten her. It was a journal with a beautifully hand-tooled leather cover decorated with an elaborate Celtic knot on the front. Just the kind of thing Maya loves. Abruptly, I was reminded of another journal and glanced at the small black volume laying on my nightstand. I hoped Maya's story would have a happier ending than Mercy May's.

Presenting her with the gift as she and Mom prepared to leave, Maya ripped off the paper and her eyes widened. "Oh, Sophia! It's beautiful!" I saw she really liked it which made me happy. Sure, we might fight and not see eye to eye on a lot of things, but for a sister, she could be okay.

After they left, Dad disappeared into his study to work on his book. I flopped down in the ratty old easy chair near the fireplace in the living room to think about my project.

I tapped my finger on the arm of the chair as I considered everything that had happened in the past, along with the odd things still happening today. Finding Mercy May's diary was quite the eye-opener, but it was more than that. There were Mom's weird spells. Her telling me not to let *him* in, and then later finding her in the graveyard. And who could forget the mysterious Mr. Hiram Parsons who kept popping up? I frowned. Really, who was that guy? How did he fit into all of this?

I sighed deeply. So, where did I go from here? I still wanted to go back to the library to search for more information on this "vampire" story. I also wanted to locate Hiram's grave. Since Liam and I had been unable to find it in the graveyard, it stood to reason Hiram's father had relocated the grave elsewhere. I glanced out the window at the steadily falling rain. No illicit trips to the graveyard for me today. Well, I thought as I heaved myself to my feet, there's always the attic. I'd only looked in Mercy May's trunk. Maybe there was something else up there of interest.

Five minutes later I stood at the top of the attic stairs, and I winced at the ear-splitting sound of the rain reverberating on that stupid metal roof. I'd forgotten how noisy it could be up here. I glanced at Mercy May's trunk, and a wave of sadness wash over me as I picked up her portrait and sighed. "I'm really sorry you died so young, Mercy," I whispered, wiping dust from the picture. "Do you know what happened to Hiram's grave?" I waited in silence for a moment as if I thought she might actually answer. With a sigh, I replaced the portrait on top of the hope chest and surveyed the rest of the junk piled in the attic.

I hesitated and turned back to the chest once more. I knelt down and opened one of the drawers. Carefully lifting the pocket watch, I clicked open the case. Goosebumps erupted up and down my arms as the second hand made its relentless journey around the face of the small timepiece. It had a mesmerizing effect traveling around and around, over and over again. How many times had it done that? How many times had those hands made their circle around the face? Must be millions. I shook my head in wonder. Why did it never wind down? What would happen if it did? An unexpected shiver crawled down my back, and I froze. Was someone up here? Straining my ears, I heard nothing besides the roaring of the rain. My eyes darted around the attic, but of course, I was alone. This house really had me spooked.

I put the timepiece back into the drawer and closed it again. *Pull yourself together*, I chided myself and climbed to my feet. With a deep breath, I surveyed the attic, trying to decide where to go next. It didn't really matter, so I pushed my way further back into the pile of junk, past the heaps of old lamp shades, boxes of dishes and racks of moth-eaten clothes. It was unlikely anyone had ever thrown away a single thing in the history of this house. We could probably open a museum. However, as interesting as some of it might be, I was only keen on stuff that came from the mid-nineteenth century; when Mercy May and her family lived here.

As I shoved some boxes to one side, a second chest, resembling Mercy May's, caught my eye. After stirring up a massive cloud of dust and cobwebs, I managed to excavate it from the surrounding boxes and bags. It looked identical to Mercy May's but painted on the top, I read the initials GEP. My mouth went dry. *Grace Elizabeth Parsons.* Mercy May's sister.

I chewed on my lip as I stared at the forlorn trunk for several minutes, the sound of my pounding heart drowning out the rain. I inhaled slowly as I carefully lifted the lid. Hardly able to breathe, I leaned forward to peer inside, not knowing what I might find, but what I didn't expect was an almost empty trunk. I released my breath with an audible whoosh. *Oh, come on!* I thought furiously staring at the few random items lying at the bottom of the trunk. There was supposed to be a wealth of information stored in this trunk like family secrets, illicit love letters, or revealing photographs. But no, at the bottom of the trunk lay a pitiful bundle of tattered papers tied together with twine. That was it. Not even some cool period dress from the 1800s. Grace was as much of a mystery as before.

I growled, sitting back on my heels as I contemplated the pile of paper. It might very well have some interesting information about the Parsons family, yet I hesitated. There was just something about that paper that unnerved me. Yes, I know that sounds weird. How can a pile of paper seem scary? But it did. I didn't want to touch it.

I shook myself. What was wrong with me? Was everything in this attic going to creep me out? Mom's foreboding words didn't help to ease my litany of chills, racing heartbeat and clenched gut, but what exactly did I expect an old pile of paper to do? Shred me with paper cuts? With an impatient grunt, I forced myself to reach in and grab the packet and pull it out.

Yellowed and brittle, the paper felt dry to my touch. It disturbed me to see how much my hands were shaking. The ringing of the raindrops on the roof had abated some as the morning progressed, but my head was throbbing just the same. I wanted to drop the papers back in the trunk and get away from it as quickly as possible, yet my curiosity burned to discover what it contained. I glanced around the attic. Mercy May stared down at me with that odd flat stare so common to portraits in the early 19th century. I swallowed. Okay, I told myself, I should just take the stack downstairs and look through them there. If nothing else, it would be quieter.

I turned off the work lights and scurried back to my room. With a sigh of relief, I dropped onto my bed, my body heavy like lead. I didn't want to move. In fact, I could barely keep my eyes open. I frowned. Where had this sudden fatigue come from? I hadn't exactly been doing anything strenuous. The unexpected weight of my eyelids forced them closed, but my mind whirled on.

First a diary and an unstoppable watch in Mercy May's trunk, and now this weird pile of papers in Grace Elizabeth's. Was it a journal of some kind as well? It took some effort, but I opened my eyes and turned to stare at the packet sitting on the table beside me. I gently chewed on my lip. I needed to stop doing that. With a grunt, I pushed myself up to a sitting position and grabbed the papers. It was stupid to drag this out. Maybe this pile of paper would solve the entire mystery.

CHAPTER EIGHTEEN

I dug in my pocket and pulled out my faithful Swiss army knife. Gingerly, I cut the twine and pulled it away from the stack of paper. The top sheet was blank; nothing to explain what this pile represented. Nothing that said, "Secrets Revealed Here". I ran my finger along the rough texture of the sheet. It didn't feel like writing paper, but more like the type used for drawing. I tilted my head and carefully lifted the cover sheet from the pile. With a small gasp, my eyes widened to find the image of Mercy May looking up at me. The picture was similar enough to the painted portrait in the attic, but this one was livelier. Mercy May was smiling; her eyes showing a vitality missing from the portrait. I noticed there was something written at the bottom: "Mercy May, 16 yrs. By her sister, Grace Elizabeth 1854." It appeared Grace was quite a gifted artist.

I lifted the drawing of Mercy and gently set it on the table, careful not to damage the brittle edges. The next picture was that of an older couple. The man's weathered face spoke of a lifetime spent outdoors. The woman was smiling, but a deep sadness filled her eyes. The caption on this one read, "Samuel and Elizabeth Parsons, 1854 by their daughter, Grace Elizabeth Parsons". This must have been drawn after Hiram and Elijah died. I really was impressed by the girl's talent. She totally captured her parents' heartbreaking grief.

From the dates on her gravestone, she would have been about fourteen when she drew these.

Below the pictures of her parents, I found a portrait of a young boy about twelve followed by one of a little girl two or three years younger. These must be the two youngest Parsons children, Josiah and Hannah. I knew Josiah escaped the dread disease, he was my great-great-whatever grandfather, but what of little Hannah? I wondered if I would ever learn her fate.

Below Hannah's drawing, I found a portrait of a young man. His face was thin and drawn, but his narrow lips curved in a warm smile. Yet, when I studied his eyes, I saw stark fear there. This was Lemuel, with the date, 1856, at the bottom. The year he died. No wonder he looked terrified. He'd just watched his brothers and two cousins die, and it was apparent he was not well himself. He understood what was coming. I shivered and quickly put the picture aside.

The next drawing showed another teenaged boy, skeletally thin and sickly. His cheeks were sunken and dark bruise-like circles underlined his eyes. Unlike his brother, there was a twinkle in his expression, not fear. He might have at least one foot in the grave, but his eyes smiled as if amused by some inside joke. I dropped my gaze to the caption: *Elijah, 1855.* No doubt drawn shortly before his death. My own eyes abruptly filled with tears. This was stupid. I was mourning for a kid I'd never met. Yet, the story was such a tragic one and seeing this sketch made it seem all too real.

I lifted away Elijah's drawing and found myself faced with one more young man, gaunt and haggard but with features so similar to Elijah's they had to be brothers. With a jolt of alarm, I recognized this face. It was Hiram. I shuddered. Unlike his brothers, Hiram's eyes did not reflect fear or amusement but pure anger. The drawing was very different from the small portrait concealed the watch. That had been of a healthy, smiling Hiram. In my head, I pictured those same eyes peering at me over the fence of the graveyard and from the window in the library. They were identical to those of the Hiram Parsons of today.

I frowned. Well, it was obvious they couldn't be the same person. This Hiram had died 160 years ago, but no doubt the two were related. It was kind of cool thinking a person could so closely resemble a long-dead ancestor. Or maybe it was just creepy. I couldn't decide.

I quickly moved Hiram's picture to see the final drawing. It was of a young teenaged girl and labeled *Self-portrait, 1856 by Grace Elizabeth Parsons*. I smiled. The girl's solemn expression seemed to indicate that the act of staring at herself in a mirror and drawing her own image had been serious work. Studying her face, I experienced a certain sense of familiarity, then I gasped as it hit me. She looked like me! Well, not exactly, but there was definitely a similarity in the eyes and mouth. Fascinated, I stared at the picture for a long time before a gentle knock at the door startled me back to reality.

"Sophia?"

My heart leaped at the sound of the voice. "Come on in, Liam!" I called. "I've got something really cool to show you."

Liam opened the door and looked in with some hesitation. "Your dad said it was okay to come up. I hope I'm not interrupting anything."

"No, really, it's cool. Look!" I held up one of the pictures. "I found these in Grace Elizabeth's trunk up in the attic. She drew everyone in the family. She was amazing."

Liam pulled a chair closer to the bed to get a better view of the sketches. His eyes widened as he picked up Grace's self-portrait. He looked back and forth between me and the drawing. "I might be crazy, but this looks a lot like you."

I sighed in relief. I wasn't nuts. "You see it, too? I was afraid I just imagined it."

Liam shook his head firmly. "No, it's weird, but you could be sisters." He carefully examined the drawings of the other family members. He spent a long time looking at Mercy May and her two dead brothers. Then he paused at Lemuel's portrait. He glanced over at me. "He knew what was coming."

I nodded slowly. "Just look at his eyes. He was terrified. Grace did an incredible job capturing the emotions in her drawings, didn't she? She might have become a famous artist if she hadn't died when she was seventeen. She was very talented."

I reached over and picked up Hiram's portrait and held it up. "Here is another image of Mercy's brother,

Hiram. Age him about twenty years and you'll get an idea of what the Hiram I keep seeing looks like. He must be related to Mercy's family, and that's why he was hanging around the graveyard."

Liam studied the picture, then shook his head. "If he ate in the lodge that night, I sure don't remember him." He paused. "This guy looks really ticked off."

I nodded. "Maybe he was mad about being sick? Who knows?" I gathered up all the portraits. "Seeing these makes Mercy and her family seem even more real. First, she wrote about what happened to all of them, and then I find these drawings by Grace Elizabeth. I feel as if I know these people. Like they're still here and didn't die over a 160 years ago."

"I know what you mean," agreed Liam watching me put the pictures away. I pushed the drawer firmly shut.

"Every time I come over here and find you've discovered some new piece of the puzzle, I get more excited," he continued. "I want to learn everything there is to know about this family. Usually, my summers are incredibly dull, but this is like some TV mystery show. And believe me, none of the girls around here are nearly as interesting as you."

I laughed. "Well, I can honestly say, this is my first experience with a real live mystery. Just call me Nancy Drew. It is exciting, isn't it?" Suddenly I blushed. "I'm really glad you're here to help."

He leaned closer and my heart raced. I actually started to tremble when my father's voice bellowed from downstairs, "Sophia, lunch is ready!"

Liam and I leaped apart as if Dad had walked right into the bedroom. My face burned in embarrassment, and Liam stifled a laugh. "Just like in some bad sitcom," he said with a shake of his head.

Now I had to laugh. He was too right. We both stood to leave. However, I hadn't even taken a single step when Liam turned, stepped towards me and firmly pressed his lips against mine. My first startled response was to pull back, but the warmth of his lips drew me forward. My heartbeat pounded in my ears. I was only aware of Liam and the warmth of his body. His arm circled my waist and pulled me slightly closer. I melted into him and threw my arms around his neck. This wasn't bad at all.

"Sophia!" Again, we leaped apart, my eyes wildly spinning towards the door at the sound of my father's voice. "C'mon! Lunch is ready!" My knees weak, I stumbled backward. I glanced over at Liam who grinned at me as he ran his hand through his blonde hair. I smiled back in relief.

"Coming, Dad!" I opened the door, and we slipped downstairs. Dad had a pile of golden grilled cheese sandwiches waiting on the table. I guess he figured Liam would eat enough for five or six people.

Dad eyed us suspiciously. "Awful quiet up there."

I tried not to look guilty. "I found some drawings of the Parsons family," I quickly replied, sitting down and grabbing a sandwich. "Grace Elizabeth was an incredible artist, and she drew pictures of all her brothers and sisters as well as her parents. We were looking at them."

"Yeah, and the picture of Grace looks a lot like Sophia," added Liam through a mouthful of bread and cheese.

Dad lifted an eyebrow as he settled into his own seat. "Really? You'll have to show me after lunch. Where did you find them?"

"In Grace Elizabeth's trunk up in the attic. In fact, they were the only things in there." I paused a moment. "I wonder what happened to all the stuff that would have been in her hope chest."

"Maybe her younger sister took it," suggested Liam.

I shrugged. "That would seem kind of morbid. I'm not sure I'd want to start my new life as a married woman with my dead sister's sheets and towels."

"Maybe not." Dad grabbed another sandwich from the pile. "But if your family didn't have much money, it would have made sense. It would have been a real waste to leave such valuable items in a chest forever."

"They did with Mercy May's," I replied.

A moment of silence hung over us as we all pondered this point. All I could figure was perhaps after packing away one daughter's dowry, they couldn't afford to do it a second time.

By the time lunch was over, the rain had stopped and the sun struggled to break through the dense barrier of clouds. I walked Liam to the path where he gave me another quick kiss. I watched him disappear down the trail toward the lodge, my heart going with him.

Tingling with excitement, I returned to my room. With a happy sigh, I flopped down on my bed picturing Liam's golden smile. I touched my lips remembering the warmth of his on mine, and a slight thrill ran through me. I turned over onto my side, and my gaze fell upon Mercy May's diary. I wanted to drag it out and savor every entry, yet I was desperate to know what really happened to her. With a deep sigh, I sat up and reached for the book.

CHAPTER NINETEEN

*M*arch 20. Mother has been ill for several days with the grippe. The doctor came and said we must keep her warm and make her drink as many fluids as possible. She is burning with fever and coughs badly. Sometimes she doesn't recognize me. We are all so frightened that we will lose her. Please Lord, please do not take another of our family.

March 30. Thank you, dear Lord, at last Mother has begun to recover from her illness. Today she took some broth. Lemuel has also taken ill but less severely so. I pray that he too will recover quickly. I have sent Josiah and Hannah to Grandmother Parsons until the sickness has passed. Grace and I must stay to support father and tend the sick. Grace looks unusually fatigued, and I fear she may also become ill soon.

April 17. It was not Grace who next fell ill, but myself. I awoke one morning feeling very tired and achy as if I had not rested at all. My head throbbed horribly. I went down to make breakfast, but my stomach recoiled mightily at the thought of food. Grace took one look at me and banished me back to my room. I will admit that although I protested, I was glad to return to the comfort of my own bed. I remember little of the days that followed. I do recall having terrible dreams and that Hiram and Elijah were often there. But as to what the dreams were about, I have no further memory. Today, I was able to sit up and Grace brought me some broth and toast. I am beginning to feel better at last.

April 22. I am bored. I am still weak, but my mind is active. I have been doing a lot of knitting while I rest in bed, but I long to get up and do something. We all yearn for periods of inactivity until we are forced into them. Now I would like nothing more than to be allowed to go out and milk the cows. Lemuel has visited me several times. He remains pale and seems slow in regaining his strength. Mother is almost completely back to normal. I am so very relieved. Lemuel tells me they feared I would die. I told him I feared the same would happen to him. We all live with that secret fear in our hearts. Lemuel has just come in with a game of checkers. Bless him.

May 1. A beautiful spring morning and I am finally myself again. I continue to tire easily, but am able to do more and more each day. I am happy to say that Grace was spared the illness and Josiah and Hannah have returned home. We are all so glad to be together once again. Mother prepared an entire chicken just to celebrate the gathering. Even Grandmother Parsons came. I am beginning to feel hopeful that the worst is behind us now.

When I reached the end of this section, I realized several pages had been so damaged by water they were illegible. Blast. Well, I hoped there was nothing of consequence in there. I forged ahead.

Sept 16. Lemuel is worse. He tries not to complain, but his bloody cough betrays him. Most mornings I must change his bedding as they have been soaked through by his frequent night sweats. I am devastated. We all understand what this means.

Hiram and Elijah both walked this same path. Lemuel has some good days, but they are fewer and fewer as time goes on. He assured me today that he was feeling much better, but I knew he was lying. There is a terrible fear in his eyes. Grace was in this morning sketching him. She has made it her goal to draw a portrait of each of us. 'So we will not forget', is what she said. My heart breaks to hear this.

Nov. 22. I have had little heart to write in my journal. Sadness permeates everything in my life and writing it down only makes it seem more real. I believe Lemuel will soon join our brothers with the Lord. He coughs up so much blood, I wonder that he has any left in his feeble body. He never leaves his bed now and is fully dependent upon us to tend to his needs. How can I watch another beloved brother die? I want to die myself and end this pain. I wonder if that strange doctor was right. Could there be something evil in Hiram or Elijah's graves that is sucking the life from poor Lemuel? Father is obstinate that the graves remain undisturbed.

Nov 25. I have spoken to Mother about exhuming Hiram and Elijah. She was horrified and claimed I would go to Hell for even suggesting such a blasphemous deed. But is it really? Might it not be the one thing that would save Lemuel? He continues to fight, telling me he refuses to follow Hiram and Elijah into the grave. But, how long can he continue? To gaze upon him is to see a dead man.

Dec. 2. Uncle John has come to Father again to demand we dig up the boys. His son, Jacob is now sick. I overheard him and

155

Father fighting, and Uncle John accused Father of all but murder. He claimed that by not allowing them to open the graves, he was condemning their children to death.

Dec 10. Father caught Uncle John and Uncle Thomas digging up Elijah's grave. They had just opened his coffin when Father came upon them. He was furious and threatened to kill them both. I saw him run out of the woods and return there a short time later with his shotgun in hand. I wondered what he had seen. Later I learned that when he had returned with the gun, Uncle John and Uncle Thomas agreed to leave. I suspect they did not find any fresh blood in what was left of Elijah's body. Father chose to rebury Elijah by himself.

Dec. 12. Father has decided to move Hiram's grave to prevent anyone from secretly digging him up. Mother will go and help, but he does not want Grace nor myself to learn the location of the new burial site. He believes it to be safer if fewer people know. I asked him if he will check to make sure there is no fresh blood in Hiram's heart before they rebury him. For the first time in my life, I feared Father would strike me. He finds the whole idea of some evil entity residing in his son's body so repellant that he refuses to even consider such a thing. After Mother and Father left, I sat with Lemuel to read to him. I have been reading him one of Mr. Dickens' novels. It is called David Copperfield. *Lemuel claims that hearing of David Copperfield's travails makes his own seem minor in comparison. How I will miss my dear brother.*

Jan.10, 1854. Another beloved brother is lost to us. Lemuel passed from this kingdom into the next early this morning. How much more of this can we take? I fear Mother will not recover from this blow even though she was aware it was coming. She has now lost her first three children, her three precious sons. How can any mother bear such pain? Father continues to be stoic, but he looks so much older these days as the pain of loss bears him down. I fear what will happen to Grace, Josiah, and Hannah if they should fall ill as well. Please Lord, let this be the end of it. Let my family live together for a long time. Or will it be my turn next?

I slowly put the diary down. Wow. This had to be the most tragic thing I'd ever read. Mercy May has now seen three of her brothers and two cousins die within the space of a couple of years. How could she not fear for her own life? Hot tears prickled the backs of my eyes. I just felt so sorry for her. Well, for her whole family. Could I survive watching my siblings die one after the other? I thought of Maya and a cold chill ran down my back. I only had one sister and didn't even want to think about how I'd feel if she died.

I quickly closed the book and shoved it into my purse. I didn't like this premonition of impending doom that had settled over me. Reading the diary was making me very depressed. I hoped when we went to dinner, I might have a chance to show it to Liam. In the meantime, I needed to find something else to occupy my mind.

I rolled off the bed and headed to my desk to boot up my computer. Checking my email, I was delighted to see a message from Jenna. It was such a relief to do something normal like answering email. I had been a little peeved with Jenna about Liam, but at the same time, I couldn't bear losing my best friend. Fortunately, she felt the same way and sent me a long chatty email and expressed interest in learning more about this 'Liam guy' as she put it. I smiled. Jenna could be a real pain, but it was nice to have her to talk to, even if it was just through email.

Shortly after I got off the computer, Mom and Maya returned from their day of shopping. I heard Maya laughing as she told Dad how Mom had managed to get them lost in the booming metropolis of Berlin, population approximately ten thousand. I walked down the stairs and peered through the kitchen door where all three stood around the table. My heart rose in my throat at the thought of losing any one of them. Mercy May's words echoed in my head, *Please Lord, let my family live together for a long time.*

CHAPTER TWENTY

That night, we headed to the lodge for dinner. Again, Hayden, Liam's sister, took us to our table, but a different girl served us. I kept looking around for Liam, but saw no sign of him. Well, I figured, he must be working in the kitchen or someplace. However, Adam, the waiter Maya had gone out with that one time, kept coming over to talk to her. I thought it was pretty funny and gave her a hard time about it.

"So, have you picked out your bridesmaid's dresses yet?" I inquired buttering a roll. "I hear orange is all the rage this year."

"Shut up, Sophia," muttered Maya giving me a shove. "I only went out with him once."

"Hm hmm." I stuffed the roll into my mouth and narrowed my eyes. "He's awfully cute."

"Yeah, that's the problem." Maya frowned as her eyes followed Adam across the dining room talking to a couple of girls. "He attracts the attention of every girl that walks by. Pretty soon I felt invisible."

I came very close to choking to death on my roll. How on earth anyone could ignore my sister was beyond me. Not only was she drop-dead gorgeous, but she had that amazing knack of knowing how to talk to people so they always felt like the most important person in the room. I really envied her that. It was like

159

some kind of superpower. If anyone tended to blend into the background and be ignored, it was me.

Our steaks arrived a short time later, and I was delighted to find Liam carrying the plates of food. As he place mine before me, he whispered, "Can you meet me by the kitchen before you leave? I need to tell you something."

I stared at him for a second then nodded. He looked excited as he passed out the rest of the plates and gave me a brief smile before he quickly retreated back to the kitchen. I couldn't imagine what he might want to tell me. Did he want to reveal to me his passionate and undying love? I almost laughed out loud at that one. Not likely. Sure, I knew he liked me, but I can't say we were quite to the stage of declaring our passionate and undying love. Still, it was intriguing.

I hurried through my meal, anxious to meet him. It was kind of a waste to gulp down such excellent food so quickly, but my curiosity definitely got the better of me. While Maya and my parents continued eating at a more leisurely pace, I excused myself and headed over to the kitchen. Liam slipped through the door a moment later and led me outside to the back porch.

"What is it?" I asked, unable to contain myself a minute longer. "What's so important?"

Liam leaned close to me. "I spotted that Hiram Parsons guy today. It's amazing how much he looks like the kid in the drawing. Just a lot older."

My heartbeat sped up. "What was he doing?"

"Well, he came in for a late lunch. Hayden served him, and when I asked her about him, she just said he seemed really nice. Anyway, he stayed for about an hour, sat out on the porch for the longest time then got into his car. I figured he was going to take off, but he continued to sit in the parking lot. It wasn't until you guys drove up that he finally left."

I frowned. "That's weird. Do you think he was watching for us? I mean, how would he know we were even coming?"

Liam shrugged, glancing back towards the busy dining room. "Maybe he was waiting for you so he could rob your house when he knew you wouldn't be there."

A chill ran down my back. Rob our house? What could there be in our house that would interest Hiram Parsons? The pictures that Grace drew? What about the diary? At least I had that with me. But what should I do? I'd sound nuts if I told my parents I thought someone was robbing the house, and by the way, did I mention he looks exactly like the Hiram Parsons who died back in 1851? No, I'd need another plan.

"Listen," I grabbed Liam's arm. "I only have a second, then I'd better get back and figure out a way to convince my parents to go home. I read in Mercy May's diary that her father moved Hiram's grave after he found her uncles digging up Elijah. That's why he isn't with the others."

"Really? Where did he move it to?"

I sighed. "I don't know. Apparently, he didn't want anyone else in the family to know except for him and Mercy's mother. It can't be too far from the cemetery. I mean, he'd want Hiram safe, but I can't see him lugging a coffin that's been in the ground for a couple of years all over the countryside. Be a little obvious, don't you think?"

Liam nodded. "Yeah. I imagine it would have to be a spot reasonably close to the cemetery." He frowned. "But if his father didn't mark the grave, how on earth will we find it?"

"I don't know, but I want to go back out there as soon as possible to look. If it's not raining, would you have time tomorrow?"

Liam brushed his straight blonde hair out of his eyes, thinking. I bit back a little sigh. "I should have some time in the afternoon," he finally replied. "I have to take a group out fishing in the morning, but we should return around lunchtime, so maybe I can sneak away after that."

"Great." I grinned at him, wanting to say more, but then I remembered Hiram. "I'd better go and try to convince my parents to leave." Liam nodded, squeezed my hand and disappeared into the kitchen. I hurried back to the table.

I was happy to discover that Maya and my parents had actually finished eating. Guess I was absent a little longer than I'd realized.

"Are you okay?" asked Mom with a concerned frown. "You were gone a long time."

"I…" I hesitated. "My stomach isn't feeling that great. Do you think we could go home?"

Mom stared hard at me. I tried to look ill, but honestly, I'm not very good at faking things like that. However, since they had all finished, everyone decided to humor me. Dad called for the check, and we soon headed out. I caught sight of Liam and gave him a grim wave.

As we drove home, I kept fretting about what we might find when we got there. Probably nothing. I was most likely blowing this all out of proportion. Hiram Parsons had no reason to break into our house. How would he even know about the pictures or the diary? It made no sense. Still, I found myself chewing on my fingernails all the same.

As we drove up to the house, I stared hard through the headlights trying to detect any motion or the beam of a flashlight in the windows. Except for the light Mom had left on in the living room, they were dark. When we went inside, nothing obvious was out of place. I heard the others chattering away as my eyes scanned the interior looking for anything unusual.

I stood at the bottom of the stairs and listened hard. All I could hear was the pounding of my heart. Step by step I made my way upstairs, still focusing all my attention for any little sound. Slowly, I approached my bedroom. The door hung slightly ajar. I pressed my lips together. Had I left it that way? I couldn't remember. The stupid doors in this house are always swinging shut. Drives me nuts. Still, it's possible I'd left it like this. My mouth was as dry as dust now. Holding my breath, I pushed the door, watching it swing open, as the rest of me prepared to turn tail and run screaming.

The room was utterly dark. I reached in as far as possible without actually entering the room and flicked on the light switch. I immediately jumped back, my nerves like a tightly wound spring. Nothing happened. This time I cautiously stepped to the doorway and peeked in, still not setting one foot beyond the threshold. It appeared exactly as I had left it. Almost. I frowned. The drawer in the bedside table stood open just a bit. I clearly remembered putting the portraits inside and firmly shutting it all the way. Slowly, I took a few hesitant steps into the room, continuing to stare at the table. I came to a halt, and taking a deep breath, pulled the drawer completely open.

The sketches lay all stacked nice and neat. With care, I lifted them out one at a time. They were all there. All but one. Hiram's picture was gone. My hands shaking, I thrust the papers back into the drawer and slammed it shut. I whirled about expecting Hiram to leap out from my closet or from under the bed. My entire body tingled as I backed out of the room, not daring to turn around.

Suddenly, I was brought up short up against a warm body. With a shriek, I spun around, prepared to fight or run. Whatever seemed most logical.

"Sophia!"

I gasped in relief, my hand resting on my pounding chest. "Dad, you scared me!"

He stared at me, one eyebrow cocked. "Are you all right? You look like you've seen a ghost."

Gulping air, it took me a moment to calm myself to speak. "Dad, someone's been here. Someone has been in my room."

"What?" Dad immediately went on high alert. He quickly peered under the bed and flung open the doors to the closet and the attic. Nothing. Finally, he turned to me, running a hand through his hair. "What makes you think someone has been here?"

I reached over and opened the drawer again, pulling out the drawings. "There were eight pictures in this pile. One of them is missing." I paused, realizing I had never told Dad about Hiram Parsons lurking in the graveyard. How could I explain why this guy would break into our house just to steal a sketch of his namesake?

"Maybe you misplaced it?" asked Dad, studying the drawings. "Did you ask Maya or your mother? They seem like more likely candidates than some stranger breaking in just to take an old drawing. How would someone even know you had it?"

I opened my mouth, then closed it again. Dad shook his head and started for the door. "Wait!" I said reaching towards him. He turned back looking at me expectantly. Time to spill. "There was this guy, at the graveyard, the day I went by myself. He told me *his* name was Hiram Parsons. He seemed really interested in what I was doing. Then I saw him again at the library. He was watching me and Maya. I don't know how he'd know about this picture, but Liam told me he saw Parsons hanging around the lodge this evening. He left as soon as we arrived. Doesn't that seem pretty suspicious to you?"

Dad listened to me with a sober expression. "Do you think this Parsons guy has been stalking you?"

I wasn't sure what to say. "No," I replied slowly. "But I think he's curious about what I'm doing. He might have just broken in looking for something to steal and found the sketch."

Dad glanced around the room again. "Is there anything else missing?"

I shrugged. "I haven't had a chance to check, but I bet he took the picture because it looks just like him."

"So why would he want to take it? It's not like you don't know what he looks like, right?"

"I don't know, Dad!" My frustration was building. I had no idea why he took it, just that he had. The fact that creep had been in my room made me feel, I don't know, violated. Like it wasn't safe here anymore. I crossed my arms tightly across my chest.

"All right," he soothed. "Let's go on downstairs. The door was locked when we came in, but I'll look around and see if there are any signs of a break-in. If not, I'm not really sure there's anything we can do. I mean, I could call the police, but I doubt they'd be terribly concerned if the only thing stolen was an old drawing." He put his hand on my shoulder. "Come on,

166

kid. Mom and Maya are waiting to do birthday cake. They'll be wondering what happened to us.

With a deep sigh, I got up and followed him out of the room. I took a final backward glance and shuddered. Was Hiram still hiding someplace in the house? I promised myself, I would make Dad search the place from top to bottom tonight. There was no way I was going to sleep until I was certain that guy was gone.

CHAPTER TWENTY-ONE

As agreed, Liam showed up the next afternoon shortly after lunch. Mom was working the psychic hotline, and Dad was doing some writing. Oddly enough, Maya was taking a nap. Maya wasn't known for sleeping during the day. Anyway, Liam and I headed out to the ·cemetery without having to go through a lot of explanations and half-truths. I mean, I had promised Mom I wouldn't go *into* the graveyard again, but since we thought Hiram had been buried outside the fence, I figured I was good.

Armed with my trusty can of bug spray and water bottles, Liam and I headed up into the woods. I swore under my breath as a deerfly took a bite out of me. I doused myself with another quart of repellant. The warm, muggy air was like walking through a sauna. It wasn't long before I was dripping wet.

We came to a halt about ten yards outside the cemetery gate. The hairs prickled on the back of my neck as I craned my head around. I didn't see anyone, but Hiram Parsons really had me spooked. Other than the occasional bird song and bug noise, it was quiet. Liam wiped the sweat from his face. "I think we should keep walking up the path. My guess is Hiram's father would pick someplace away from the graveyard, but close enough to walk to."

I nodded thoughtfully. Just how far would Hiram's father go? With only his wife to help, they wouldn't be able to carry the heavy coffin far. Maybe the used a wagon? I turned and began to hike further into the woods, looking carefully for any likely spot. I wiped my brow again in disgust. There were probably a million such places where they could have buried him. It couldn't be too obvious or others would have found it.

We searched for at least a couple of hours. My hair clung to my face in sodden tendrils. I hate that. Even Liam looked wilted. There were simply too many places to look. With a groan, I collapsed onto a large boulder, pulled out a bottle from my pack and took several long gulps of the tepid water. Didn't help much. Liam had gone on a bit further to check the top of a knoll. I was beat. The path was barely visible any longer. Could Mr. Parsons have even gotten a wagon this far? I sighed deeply and rested my head on my hands.

"Are you lost?" My head snapped up with a sharp gasp. Hiram Parsons stood about ten feet away, leaning nonchalantly against a tree. I just stared at him, mouth open, unable to move. How had he gotten there? I hadn't heard a thing.

"N… no," I finally managed. I glanced up the hill praying Liam would appear. *Where was he?* "I… I'm fine. Just resting."

The man nodded. He smiled his warm, friendly smile, but his dark eyes remained cold and penetrating. Mr. Darcy's evil twin. "I simply wondered. This area is a bit off the beaten path as it were." His smile broadened as he took a few steps towards me. My heart pounded. I wanted to stand up, run, get away, but I couldn't move. I was like a mouse being mesmerized by a snake.

"You know, Sophia," he continued conversationally in his deep, hypnotic voice. "Family history is all well and good, but there are stones that should be left unturned."

I stared at him, unsure if he was expecting a response or just giving me some sort of vague warning. I tried to swallow. "I'm not sure I know what you mean." There. I got that out. Go me.

Hiram's handsome face hardened. "Don't you? I think you know exactly what I mean. You've been digging around in things that do not concern you. It would be best if you found a new project. Unpleasant things… could happen if you don't."

This was beginning to sound like some abysmally bad horror movie. I'm not really brave, but now I was getting annoyed. I wanted to ask this guy who wrote his lines because he definitely needed a new screenwriter. Okay, maybe I didn't say that, but I was finally able to move and leaped to my feet.

"What do you mean *things?*" I snapped. "And what exactly do you know about the Parsons family? You told me before that they all died of tuberculosis over 160 years ago. What could be such a big secret now?"

Hiram never took his eyes off me. My breath froze in my lungs as I clutched my backpack protectively to my chest. I stepped back but was blocked by the boulder.

"I told you, Sophia," he hissed. "There are things best left alone. I am warning you. Do not persist in this. People will suffer if you continue."

The soft crack of a twig behind me caused him to start, his eyes darting up the hill. It must be Liam returning. Suddenly Hiram appeared beside me, and I cried out in pain and shock. His cold hand gripped my wrist in a band of iron as his hard gaze burned into my soul. "Remember. I warned you." He flung my arm aside and strode away into the woods, disappearing into the curtain of underbrush.

I collapsed back onto the boulder, my head spinning as I gasped for air. Had I actually been holding my breath? It certainly felt like it. I rubbed my arm. It burned where he'd gripped it. His words kept echoing through my mind. What had he meant by *people will suffer*? My body trembled as I listened to Liam making his way down the slope.

"Hey, Sophia!" he called. "Where are you?"

My first attempt at a response erupted as a feeble croak. I tried again. "Here!" A few moments later, Liam came into sight. Filthy and soaked in sweat, he limped towards me. I frowned. "Are you okay?" I handed him a bottle of water as he collapsed on the ground beside me.

"Yeah," he mumbled between gulps. "I fell down the hill."

"You fell?" My eyes scanned his body looking for any sign of injury. He seemed all right.

Liam nodded as he finished off the bottle. With a grimace, he wiped his mouth on his sleeve. "Yeah, I was standing on a rock trying to see the bottom of a ravine when the stone suddenly gave way. Next thing I know, I'm rolling down the hill. I'm lucky I didn't break my neck."

"Wow." Was this a warning from Hiram? I took a deep breath. "Hiram Parsons was here."

Liam's head whipped around to stare at me. "Just now? Did he hurt you? What did he say?"

Unconsciously, I rubbed my aching wrist again. "He didn't hurt me. Scared me pretty bad though. He told me I should leave things alone or... or people could suffer."

Liam frowned. "What people? You? Me? Was he talking about this whole Parsons family thing?"

"He just kept saying that there were things that were best left alone. My guess is he doesn't want me looking into Mercy May's death, even though he didn't come right out and say that. But why would he care? She's been dead for well over a hundred years."

"I don't know." Liam pushed himself to his feet, wincing. "But I think we should keep digging. This sounds awfully suspicious. Is there like a buried treasure or something valuable he's afraid we'll discover before him? Makes no sense." He reached down and gave me a hand up. I stumbled, my legs still shaky after my encounter with Hiram.

We decided it was time to call it quits. Liam needed to get back to work the dinner shift at the lodge. I wanted to get home and think about all of this. How far was I willing to go, and what would happen if I didn't back off?

Liam gave me a quick kiss and a big grin when we parted ways; him to return to the lodge and me back to my house. No one responded to my call when I entered, so I decided to take a quick shower to remove the half a ton of dirt and sweat. Ugh.

Later I made my way down to the kitchen, drying my wet hair with a towel. Maya sat there with her head resting on the table. I stopped and stared at her in surprise. "Maya? You okay?"

Slowly, she lifted her head and considered me with red-rimmed eyes. "Yeah. I think maybe I'm coming down with something. I'm so tired. Everything aches."

I froze, a frisson of fear running down my back. My mind instantly went to Mercy May's diary and the descriptions of her brothers' illnesses and ultimate deaths. *Don't be an idiot, Sophia*, I scolded myself. *Those people lived in a time when tuberculosis was everywhere. No one catches that here. She probably caught a cold or the flu.* Still, a blanket of unease settled over me.

"Did you tell Mom?" I asked sitting down beside her. I touched her arm. It felt warm.

"Nah." Maya shook her head. "She's been up there all day on the chat line, talking to those looney tunes. Do those people really believe she can read their future over the phone? And Dad is in his study." She paused and rubbed her eyes. "I'm sure it's nothing more than some bug." She grimaced. "Great way to celebrate turning seventeen."

Again, my stomach clenched. *Seventeen*. That was the magic number, wasn't it? Hiram, Elijah, Lemuel, Mercy, Grace, and at least their cousin Mary, all died at seventeen. I wasn't sure about cousin Jonathan, but my money was on him being the same age. I examined my sister. The deep circles under her eyes were like dark bruises against her pallid complexion. What were the symptoms of consumption? I thought hard. Night sweats. That was one. Also coughing. Coughing with blood. Weight loss, which is why they used to call it consumption; it was as if the person wasted away. Fever, chills and loss of appetite. Those were the only ones I could recall. So far, I didn't see any of these in Maya. Well, maybe she had a fever, but lots of things caused fevers. In fact, lots of things caused most of those symptoms. I sighed. I'd just have to keep an eye on her. Although how Maya would have contracted TB was beyond me. It isn't common in the United States. Most people infected come here from other countries. Regardless, I didn't like her coming down sick, especially after she'd just turned seventeen. It seemed like a bad omen.

I stood up. "Are you hungry? I was going to make myself a sandwich."

Slowly Maya shook her head and pushed herself to her feet. "No thanks. I'm not hungry. I think I'm just going to go back to bed. I'm so tired." I chewed on my lip as she shuffled from the room. No. I didn't like this one bit.

CHAPTER TWENTY-TWO

When Mom appeared sometime later, I told her that Maya was sick. She immediately went to check. I waited anxiously to hear what she had to say. Mom came down about ten minutes later.

"Well?"

Mom smiled. "She's probably coming down with the flu. She's running a fever of 101° and has a slight cough. But I think she'll live."

A cough? I tried to mask my dismay. A cough was one of the primary symptoms. My fear level ratcheted up as my common sense tried to convince me I was being stupid. *TB doesn't show up overnight! It can take weeks and weeks. She does not have tuberculosis. Get. A. Grip.* "Maybe we should take her to the doctor?" I tried not to sound desperate.

Mom stared at me in surprise. "I think it's a little early for that. She just got sick." She patted my head. "Don't worry, Sophia. I'm sure it's just some virus. She'll be fine. I suggest you stay away from her though, in case it's contagious." She turned away to pour herself a cup of coffee.

My mind whirled. Mercy May's siblings and cousins all fell ill after they turned seventeen. Now Maya was sick, and technically we were part of the same family if Dad's genealogy was correct. Restless, I got up, heading to my room. I needed to read more of Mercy May's diary. Maybe there was some clue. As I picked up the journal, a cold chill ran through me. Hiram. What had that guy said? If I didn't quit digging someone might suffer? In the next room, I heard Maya cough. Damn.

I stared at the diary for a few moments. When had Mercy May died exactly? I dug out my notebook. October 5, 1855. I opened the diary to last entry I'd read, January 10, 1854, the date of Lemuel's death. I flipped ahead and noticed there weren't a lot of entries for 1854. The few I skimmed were perfunctory and described little more than daily activities like milking the cows or doing laundry. It was as if all the life went out of Mercy after Lemuel's death. In August, another cousin died.

August 3, 1854. Cousin Catherine has now passed. She was one month short of eighteen. Uncle Thomas has sold his farm and will be moving West to Ohio. He says he can no longer live in this blighted place. Uncle John says he has also put his farm up for sale and has plans to follow.

I didn't blame Uncle Thomas and Uncle John for skipping town. I'd be worried too if my kids were dying one after another. I knew that since Mercy May's brother Josiah was my great-whatever grandfather that the family eventually left New Hampshire for Ohio to join the others. I guess for the same reasons. Mercy May's father was hoping to save his last two children.

I found nothing else of interest until I got into March of 1855 and Mercy May's seventeenth birthday. I decided this was the best place to begin.

March 8. Today I turned seventeen. Normally such a day would be a cause for celebration but unlike last year when I turned sixteen, I feel nothing but dread. I find my parents watching me for any signs of illness. I can already detect the despair in their eyes. They do not believe I will reach my eighteenth birthday. I fear they are right.

March 15. Michael has at long last asked my father for my hand in marriage! I am so excited. Mother and I have worked on my trousseau since I was eleven. I have sewn most of my linens and we collected dishes a little at a time. Now we will plan my wedding dress. Mother said she wants to make me a special dress for my nuptials. We plan for an October wedding. The trees are so beautiful then. Michael wishes to build us a house and it will take some time. Perhaps, at last, we are having some good luck for a change!

March 23. I awoke from a nightmare. I found myself soaked in perspiration. In my dream, I met my brother, Hiram. He looked alive and well. It was so wonderful to see him. I dreamt that we walked through the meadows together. It was a beautiful day. The sun was shining and flowers were everywhere. He handed me a beautiful white rose. I was so happy. But, as we progressed, he took my hand, and a weariness settled upon me. I noticed the flowers were wilting and the skies turning a dismal gray. Soon everything around us was withered and dead. There were spots of red marring the purity of my rose. I dropped it in horror seeing blood upon my fingers. I looked down and spied the bodies of my lost brothers and cousins in a pile off the path; their clouded eyes staring into mine. Then Lemuel's hand reached out to me, it was rotten and putrid. I heard a whispery voice in my head. It said Do not let him in. *I wanted to scream and it was then that Hiram forcibly gripped my arm and pulled me away. I turned to him to protest but instead of my brother's face, I found myself peering into a horrifying death's head, its empty sockets burning into me. I could feel myself starting to fall. Then I awoke. I know it was some kind of omen. I am very frightened and wish I could go be with Uncle Thomas and his family in Ohio.*

With a jolt of fear, I looked up from the journal A white rose? Like the one we'd found on Mercy's grave? In my mind's eye, I pictured that rose with a drop of Maya's blood lying on the ground in front of Mercy's gravestone. I swallowed. Not a good omen. I returned to my reading.

April 5. It has been three years since my beloved brother, Elijah, was taken from us. I awoke this morning from another horrifying dream although I cannot recollect the details. I am very tired and achy today.

April 17. Today I developed a cough that will not go away. Just a tickle in my throat, but I fear it is a harbinger of worse to come. I am still tired and feel as if I may be coming down with the grippe. I hope it is nothing more than that. I say nothing to

179

Mother or Father, but I fear Grace has already seen through my subterfuge.

April 29. Michael came over today to take me to church. I put on my prettiest dress, but I was dismayed at how pale I looked. I pinched my cheeks hard to bring a little color to them. I have consumed as much tea and honey as I can tolerate to relieve my cough. It is not so bad but does annoy. I did not want him to think I am ill.

May 9. I am feeling somewhat better today. I have been a bit poorly the past few days with a fever. I dread the terror I see in Mother's eyes. Michael is confident that it is but a minor illness, and I will soon be as good as new. I do not think he wants to believe that perhaps it could be something more serious. He comes to see me as often as he can. It always cheers me to see him.

May 16. Mother showed me the fabric she ordered for my wedding dress. It is pale blue with small sprigs of white flowers. It will be lovely and later provide me with a new dress for church on Sundays. We have been looking at fashions in Godey's Lady's Book. I am very excited. It has been so long since I have had a new dress. This one will be beautiful.

May 29. Michael and I went for a long ride in his buggy this afternoon. It was such a beautiful day. He took me to the site of our new home. He has cleared the land with the help of his father and brothers. His father has given him fifty acres as a wedding present. The house will be simple but it will be ours. He *showed me how the house will lie and the arrangement of the rooms. I cannot wait to see it rise from the wilderness. Unfortunately, I tired quickly, and we were forced to return home sooner than either of us would have liked. I took to my bed for a nap when I got home. I pray that I will regain my energies soon.*

June 15. I am feeling much better these days and am beginning to think perhaps I will not succumb as did my brothers and cousins. Their maladies progressed very rapidly, yet it has been weeks since I first felt out of sorts and am still able to do most things as before. Maybe it is my love for my beloved Michael that sustains me. He is so strong and seems to lend me his strength when the weakness comes upon me. I am truly blessed.

July 4. It is Independence Day. The town had a picnic to celebrate. At first, I was not sure I wanted to attend. I did not sleep well last night being much alarmed by nightmares once more. However, Michael wished to go, and I did not want to disappoint him. It was quite warm today and sunny, yet I still felt chilled. The unsettled feeling from my dreams did not leave me for a long time.

July 10. Michael continues to work on our house. Mother has finished my beautiful dress but had to take it in once again. I will admit, I have not had much of an appetite of late. I believe it is the hot and humid weather that saps all my energy.

July 27. A rainy day. I am feeling poorly today. Grace brought me some tea. She asked me if I was going to die. I did not know what to say. I do not believe I will die, especially not before I am wed, but only the good Lord knows what our future will bring. I try to keep up my spirits and act as if nothing is wrong, but we have been through too much for my family to be fooled.

Aug 9. My cough is worse and I was horrified to find my handkerchief stained with pink. Mother has been working on my dress having to take it in yet again. Neither of us speaks of my health. Perhaps if we say nothing, it will go away. If it is consumption, we both know there is nothing to be done. I have heard of some sending the afflicted away to drier climes, but I have never heard that it actually helped.

Aug 17. I am weaker today and so scared. As I rested in my room, I looked out the window and could see my brother, Hiram, standing outside watching me. I gave a little scream which brought Grace to my side. I told her what I had seen, yet when she looked, no one was there. Perhaps it was another dream, yet it seemed so real. Every time I dream of my eldest brother, I seem to fail further. Could my uncles have been right? Could Hiram somehow be draining me of life? What would I find if I could dig up his grave?

Aug 31. Michael took me once more to see the new house. The outside is finished. Now he and his father and brothers are working hard to finish the inside before our wedding on October 15. He is sure it will be completed in plenty of time. I wish I could feel as excited as he. It is beautiful and normally I would be so happy, but I fear I will not live long enough to ever reside there. I have begun to cough up more blood and have lost so much weight Mother has given up taking in my dress until closer to the wedding. If I should live that long.

Sept 10. The doctor has at long last confirmed it. I have consumption. Michael is devastated. Mother and Father look so defeated. I cannot bear thinking I am the cause of so much unhappiness. Grace stays with me as much as she is able. Josiah and Hannah have again been sent to Grandmother Parsons. I heard Father say he wants to sell this accursed place and move to Ohio to join Uncle Thomas and Uncle John. I know I will never leave New Hampshire but will soon join my brothers.

Sept. 17. I am quickly weakening. I dream of Hiram almost every night now. I know he takes a piece of me every time he comes. Perhaps that is the fever speaking, but I believe it is true. I know now that I will never marry my dear Michael. He comes to see me each day, but his eyes are full of grief. He knows it for the truth as well. Grace tells me he no longer works on the house. This saddens me. I grieve for a future I will never have.

Sept 20. I do not leave my bed now. I am coughing up much blood and unable to eat. Mother cries whenever she sees me so it is mainly up to my dearest sister, Grace, to care for me. She has a look of resignation, believing that she sees her own future. I fear this is true. Father comes and sits with me sometimes, reading passages from the Bible. Like Mother, I think he cannot bear to see yet another of his children waste away to nothing. I no longer have the energy to weep.

Oct 1. I do not think I will be able to write again. I am dying now and do not believe I will see more than one or two more sunrises. Dear Lord, please spare the rest of my family. Please protect them from Hiram. He must be stopped before he takes any more lives.

Oct 5, 1855. My dear, dear sister, Mercy May Parsons passed away this morning at 9 o'clock in the morning. She was seventeen years of age and ten days short of her wedding day. May she rest in peace. Grace Elizabeth Parsons

That was it. The final entry. I sat staring at those words for a very long time. I was glad Grace had taken the time to add the little note, yet it pulled at my heart. Poor Mercy May tragically died just ten days before her wedding. Poor Michael. So much pain in this family, and Grace would be next. How did those people survive that? Tears pooled in my eyes. I unconsciously wiped them away.

With a lump in my throat, I skimmed over some of the entries again, then frowned. Mercy May had mentioned Hiram several times. She seemed to imply that he was somehow the source of her illness. Just like her uncles had claimed. Could that be true or were those just the ravings of a dying girl? If she was right, how could I find out? Maya's face suddenly came to me, and a cold fist clenched my heart. I needed to figure this out before Hiram took another life.

CHAPTER TWENTY-THREE

A fog of depression settled over me after finishing Mercy May's diary. Somehow, Mercy's death seemed so immediate, like it had just happened. I know that was stupid. She'd died in 1855, long before even my great-grandparents were born. Yet, I had started to experience a connection with her. Poor Grace was all alone now. She and her older sister were obviously very close. I wondered if their parents brought Josiah and Hannah home or decided they were safer at their grandparents'.

I heard Maya coughing in the next room; a deep rattling cough. It scared me. How would I feel if I lost my only sister? Locating and opening Hiram's grave became more important than ever, but the thought both terrified and repulsed me. The notion of digging up a 160-year-old body was hardly appealing, but I had to know. Was Hiram the source of all this death and misery? If I did find a heart full of blood, and the very idea of that was enough to make me want to puke, would I have the guts to pull it out and burn it? Is that even legal? Probably not. I guess they could arrest me for something like defacing a corpse or graverobbing. I needed to talk to Liam. I bet he would help me.

The next day, Maya was worse. I stood in her doorway and hesitated before entering. She lay against the pillows; her face pale with sunken eyes, dull with fever. She gave me a wan smile when I sat down next to her bed.

"No, you can't have my stuff," she rasped, her voice as pale as her face. "I'm not dead yet."

I laughed even though my heart wasn't in it. "How are you feeling?"

"Like crap. Everything aches. My head is killing me. I have this awful cough, and I can hardly breathe."

I chewed my lip, hesitating. "Did... did you have any weird dreams?"

She frowned. "No, not that I can remember."

I almost sagged with relief. At least Hiram hadn't come visiting. Yet.

After leaving her room, I looked at my watch. It was still early. I decided to give Liam a call to see if he could come over. It took a few minutes for his sister to track him down, but in the end, it didn't matter.

"I'm really sorry," Liam sighed when I asked him. "A big group arrived last night and another is coming in this afternoon, so I won't be able to get away. I hope it wasn't anything too important."

What could I say: *No, no, just that I wanted to go find old Hiram's grave and dig him up before his evil spirit sucks all the life out of my sister?* But, wait, Liam had been with me since the start. If anyone would understand, it would be him. I took a deep breath, "Liam, my sister is sick. She's got a fever and a bad cough." My voice caught. "I'm really scared. Maybe she's only got the flu, but I'm worried it's something more." I paused. "I've *got* to locate that grave."

There was a long silence at the other end of the phone. Did Liam think I had finally lost it completely? "I wish I could, but I really can't make it over there tonight," he said slowly. There was another moment of hesitation. "But Sophia, promise me you won't go up there alone. That nutjob might be hanging out in the forest again."

I didn't want to agree. I wanted to go to the woods right this minute and search for that grave. "Liam, I can't promise that. If something happens and you can't come, I'll have to go look for it myself. The way Maya is going, I don't think it's going to take months for Hiram to kill her. I promise I won't go without you unless Maya starts getting worse. That's the best I can do."

I hung up the phone feeling a tad desperate. How long could I afford to wait to find that grave? Mercy May and the others took weeks or even months before the disease finally killed them. Maybe Hiram had come up with some new and more efficient technique for consuming a person's soul which could mean Maya had only days. How had he survived so many years? Had he'd been sucking the lives out of other relatives elsewhere, or just hanging around here hoping some random Parsons would come along?

I wandered outside to sit on the dock and wrapped my arms around myself, chilled despite the muggy air. I kept trying to convince myself that Maya had nothing worse than the flu. She certainly hadn't been exposed to anyone with TB, and from what I had learned, it wasn't that easy to become infected, so how could Maya have caught it?

I picked up some stones and absently tossed them into the lake. I ran my thumb over the smooth surface of a particularly flat one and smiled, remembering when I'd first met Liam. Taking careful aim, I skipped the stone across the tranquil water. Five skips. Liam would have been proud of that one.

I stared at the dark surface of the water. It reflected my mood. A couple of ducks quacked at me hopefully, but I had nothing to give them. I rubbed my eyes. Earlier, I had gone online and done a little more research on these so-called "Yankee Vampires". Apparently, they were all the rage in Rhode Island in the 1800s, and even New Hampshire had a few of its own. However, there didn't seem to be any real evidence that destroying organs of the recently deceased helped the ailing family member. Still, I couldn't help wonder if in this case, it just might.

My growling stomach motivated me to move inside and prepare myself a sandwich. Dad came in as I was clearing away my dishes. He looked tired.

"How is Maya?" I asked staring hard. I wanted to make sure he wasn't trying to gloss things over.

"I don't know," he sighed flopping into a chair. "She's got some kind of nasty virus, that's for sure. I figure if she's not better in another day or two, we'll take her to the doctor." He ran his hand distractedly through his shaggy hair. "I just hope the rest of us don't catch it. I have deadlines to meet and can't afford to get sick."

"Maybe you shouldn't wait. What if it's something serious, like pneumonia?" I would feel better if a doctor checked her out.

Dad shrugged. "I'm sure she'll be fine. You kids have always been extraordinarily healthy. But don't worry, we'll be keeping an eye on her."

I nodded doubtfully. There was no way I could explain to Dad my fears about Hiram Parsons without sounding like a lunatic. While Dad searched for something to eat, I headed upstairs to talk to Mom. I figured with her psychic background she might be more open to my concerns.

I found her making notes in the journal she's required to keep for the psychic hotline people. She looked up as I entered and smiled. I noted that like Dad, she also looked tired with dark shadows under her eyes. "Hi, honey."

"Hey, Mom." I settled into a chair next to her desk. I watched her for a minute. "Mom, I'm worried about Maya."

Mom turned to fully face me. "Honey, she just has a virus. I'm sure she'll be fine in a few days. If not, we'll take her to the doctor." She and Dad must have talked.

I leaned forward. "Mom, I'm almost certain it's something more serious than that. Weird things are happening in this house. You've experienced some of them yourself." I hesitated and took a deep breath. "I think Maya's life is in danger."

Mom frowned. "In danger? From whom?"

"Hiram Parsons."

"Hiram Parsons?" Mom's frown deepened. "Who is Hiram Parsons?"

I fidgeted with a pen from her desk. How to explain this without sounding completely nuts. "I'm pretty sure he's what people used to call a 'Yankee Vampire'. Hiram Parsons died in 1851, and since then some evil entity has resided in his grave. That thing, whatever it is, basically sucks the life out of any local Parsons relation when they turn seventeen." Okay, I hate to say it, but that sounded totally ludicrous. I certainly wouldn't believe me.

Mom stared at me for a long time. "There *is* something very odd here," she began slowly. "I've felt it, even though I've tried to deny it." She shook her head. "But a vampire? I'm not sure even I buy that."

"Mom, this isn't a Count Dracula blood sucking type vampire. It's some ancient evil that resides in the heart of the first to die and continues to survive by draining the life energies of someone else in the family. Everyone assumed the kids died from consumption, I mean tuberculosis, but a few feared it was something more sinister. Hiram Parsons died in 1851, and then one after another, his relatives died—his two brothers, his sisters and some cousins. All when they were seventeen." I paused to swallow and gripped my mother's arm. "*Maya* is seventeen."

I saw a tiny glimmer of fear in my mother's eyes as she shook her head again. "Sophia, we know several tragic deaths occurred here in the past, so I can certainly acknowledge the existence of spirits in this house. I've even sensed some residual energy both here and in the graveyard. There is a lot of pain. A slow death by tuberculosis is not a pleasant way to go. However, I still can't accept that this Hiram Parsons caused the deaths of his relations. At least not in the way you suggest."

"Mom," my voice grew louder as I tightened my grip on her arm. "I *need* to find Hiram's grave. His father moved it when people wanted to dig Hiram up and look for evidence of this evil being. I need to see for myself."

Mom rolled her eyes. I was losing her. "See what for yourself, Sophia? A box full of moldering bones? You said Hiram died in 1851. That's over *one hundred and sixty years ago*. Surely you don't believe that someone who died back then is still killing people today? Tuberculosis was a common illness in the nineteenth century and killed thousands while today it can be effectively treated with antibiotics. Plus, it's simply not prevalent in this country anymore. Maya would need to have been in close contact over a period of time with someone with an active infection. As far as I know, that hasn't happened."

Mom was right, of course, but still, I knew, absolutely *knew*, that Hiram was killing my sister. I sighed deeply. I wasn't going to get any help here. If I had told her Hiram's ghost was wandering around the house, that she would have accepted, but make him

191

into some sort of oddball vampire, forget it. "You're right, Mom. It does sound crazy. I guess I just got so caught up with Mercy May's diary, that I started to forget what was real and what wasn't." I stood up. "Regardless, you ought to take Maya to a doctor sooner than later. She could still have something serious."

Mom reached out and grabbed my hand, squeezing it tightly. "Honey, I didn't mean to make fun of your concerns. I mean, look at me! Working a psychic hotline. But, I'm beginning to worry that there may be dark energy in this house that's having a negative impact on you."

I tried very hard not to roll my eyes. I loved my mother, but I hated when she talked like that. Even if I suspected there was some truth in what she said. No doubt it was that dark energy that had affected her so strongly when we first got here. Or maybe Mercy had been trying to use Mom's abilities to warn us about Hiram. Regardless, Mom didn't want to listen to what I had to say. I gave her a wan smile and returned to my room. All right, the time had come. I was going to have to go out to the graveyard myself.

CHAPTER TWENTY-FOUR

That was my plan, anyway. As I gathered my backpack the next morning, a deep rumble vibrated through the house. I froze and cursed. Darting to the window, I stared at the solid bank of black clouds churning towards me. Intermittent flashes of lightning cut a jagged path through the dark sky, followed by another deafening clap of thunder. The tall pines surrounding the house bent under the force of the buffeting winds. I growled. There was no way I could go wandering out in the woods in a storm like this unless I wanted to get fried by lightning or crushed by a giant tree. Frustrated, I slammed my hand down on the windowsill, then quickly pulled the window shut as the first drops of rain spattered violently against the glass.

I turned away and flopped down on my bed. Now what was I supposed to do? I felt so helpless. I was desperate to search for Hiram's grave. I knew, deep down, that was the key to this whole thing. I was certain that the Hiram of today was the same Hiram of over a hundred years ago. Sure, that sounded totally insane, like a bad horror story, but I was convinced. After reading Mercy May's diary of death, I had no doubt in mind that Maya was next up on Hiram's hit list, and I couldn't let that happen.

I was certain the weather would improve by the following day, but despite my predictions, it continued to rain all week. I roamed around the house like a lost soul. I pretended to work on my research project to keep Dad off my back, but really, I spent my time watching Maya. It was a huge relief when by the weekend, she started to show signs of improvement.

"See?" said Mom one morning at breakfast. "Her fever is down and she's feeling better. I told you; it was a virus. Now, don't you feel silly worrying about some evil, life-sucking vampire?"

My face went hot. Who was she to accuse me of having silly notions? I mean, she's had more in a single hour than I've had in my entire life, but I decided if I couldn't say anything nice, I'd better just keep my mouth shut. It didn't change a thing. I was sure Hiram wasn't done with us yet.

After breakfast and another grim observation of the never-ending deluge outside, I dragged myself back to my room. Jenna and I talked a couple of times during the week but with everything on my mind, I found her mindless chatter grated on my nerves. To be honest, right now, I couldn't care less if Ashley liked Michael, or that Kendra got the worst haircut in the history of haircuts. I was too worried about Hiram sucking the life out of my sister, but how could I explain that to Jenna? She'd probably figure I'd been out in the woods too long.

So, spending time with Jenna was hardly a distraction. I hadn't seen much of Liam either. He'd been sick with what his sister claimed was just a summer cold. Thank goodness he wasn't related to the Parsons family, or I would have been a wreck.

It finally stopped raining a couple of days later and with the sun, came Liam and his shining smile. I'd missed him.

"Sorry I haven't been in touch," he said as we sat outside on the porch swing. The air smelled freshly washed. "I was pretty sick most of the week and at the end, Dad had me help entertain bored tourists with bingo. I'm pretty good at calling those numbers now. Just like a pro."

I laughed. "You are obviously a man of many talents."

He nodded, his face serious. "You have no idea." He grinned and put his arm around my shoulders. A thrill ran through me. "So, how is Maya?" he asked his voice still a bit hoarse. "When I last talked to you, you were really worried she had come down with the same thing that had killed all those Parsons kids way back when."

I made a face. "Yeah, well, she seems to be better. She came down this morning, ate a big breakfast and griped that I had used up all the good syrup. So, she's definitely going to live. Pity. I really wanted her stuff." I paused as an unexpected chill ran down my back. "But, I don't think everything is okay," I continued in a low voice "I still feel that Hiram has it in for her. We have to find his grave and you know, make sure."

Liam frowned. "Do you honestly think opening his grave is a good idea? I mean, I don't know about you, but I'm not too keen on this whole digging up the dead thing. Seeing them do it on TV is one thing, but I doubt it's going to be all that easy in real life."

I understood exactly what he meant. I was working very hard at *not* thinking about what opening an old grave would entail. If I did, there is no way I could go through with it. If a dead bird creeps me out, how would I deal with the moldering remains of some guy who died back in the 1850s? Would I really be able to pull out his heart and check for blood? My stomach did a flip. The image horrified me, but I would do what was necessary to save my sister.

"Well, we have to find the burial site first," I reminded him. "Maybe I've blown this whole thing with Maya out of proportion, but it wouldn't hurt to at least know where the grave is. Just in case."

Liam sighed and nodded. "Yeah, you're right. Nothing says we have to actually dig up the grave, especially if your sister recovers. I'd be happier if that Hiram guy disappeared. I saw him eating at the lodge a couple of times this past week." He hesitated. "I got the feeling he was watching me."

I tensed. Did Hiram have Liam in his sights now? I shook my head. That was stupid. Liam wasn't a Parsons… was he? I turned to him, my heart beating quickly. "You… you aren't related to the Parsons, are you?"

He laughed that deep throaty laugh that made my heart spin. "No way. I even double checked with my mom just to be sure. Our family has its own oddballs, but fortunately, vampires aren't on the list."

"I wouldn't call Hiram a vampire, exactly," I said snuggling closer. I could really get used to this. "Sure, he seems immortal, and apparently sucks the life out of unsuspecting teenagers, but he's nothing like the vampires in books or movies. Some of those are downright sexy. This guy is anything but."

Liam laughed again. "I thought you didn't think vampires were sexy."

I shrugged. "I don't, but my friend, Jenna, loves all that crap. She can quote every *Twilight* book by heart. She has posters of sexy vampires all over her room. I think it's stupid, but then who am I to talk? To me, the Phantom of the Opera is hot, and he's only got like half a face."

"So, would you like me better if I started wearing a mask?"

I turned and studied him critically. "It might help."

He punched me lightly on the arm then kissed me on the lips. I leaned into him, wanting time to stop. I think it was official. I was now one of those girls who went gaga over guys. What a shame. I smiled.

I would have been happy to sit there all day, but Dad chose that moment to come out onto the porch. He eyed the two of us with a knowing grin. I moved away from Liam, a little embarrassed. I mean, we weren't doing anything wrong, but having your father seeing you all snuggled up next to a guy was kind of awkward.

"I didn't mean to interrupt," said Dad, still smiling, "But I just got some new images from a tyrannosaur dig in Montana my friend is conducting. I thought Liam might be interested."

Liam's eyes lit up, then he turned to me, obviously torn. I laughed. "Oh, go on. Who am I to stand in the way of a geek and his dinosaurs?"

A look of surprise on his face, Liam stood. "Thanks, Sophia. I'll be right back." He gave me a warm smile and hurried inside.

I shook my head. I was not going to become one of those girls who kept an iron grip on a guy and demanded his complete attention. Liam was interested in the pictures and hey, if it got him in good with my father, then so much the better. If Dad couldn't trust a fellow dinosaur aficionado with his daughter, then who could he trust?

I sat on the swing, fully aware of the empty space beside me. Shifting my thoughts, I considered the mystery of Hiram's final resting place. How were we ever going to locate it? Maybe if we could borrow a cadaver dog, we'd have a chance, but there were a lot of woods out there, and Hiram had been buried so long ago, we'd be lucky to find any evidence of the grave. Somehow, I doubted his father put a headstone up. That was like erecting a 'dig here' sign. Well, as long as Maya's health improved, there was no to rush to find it. Or so I kept trying to tell myself. Panic constantly flittered around in the edges of my mind warning me I was running out of time.

Liam returned about twenty minutes later. He looked excited. "That was so cool! Your dad said that he might be able to arrange for me to work on a dig next summer. I've wanted to do something like that my whole life."

I almost rolled my eyes. If he enjoyed sitting in the blazing sun, sifting through half a ton of dirt and rocks hunting for petrified hunks of dino poop, then I'm sure he'd have a blast. Although, if he did go on a dig, it would make digging up dino poop a lot more interesting as far as I was concerned.

"Listen," I began, trying to get off the topic of dinosaurs, "If you're not doing anything, maybe we could spend a couple of hours looking for the grave. If we started making a map of all the places we've checked, it would be really helpful."

Liam shrugged. "Okay. Mom said I didn't have to be back until three." We quickly gathered our stuff together and headed for the woods.

Three hours later found us trudging back towards the house, hot, sweaty and covered with bug bites. Even worse, we hadn't found the least little clue as to the location of that stupid grave. The entire search was looking pointless. For all we knew, when the Parsons left New Hampshire, they took Hiram's body with them. That seemed a tad unlikely, but you never know what weird things people will do.

When we reached the main path, Liam and I went our separate ways. He had to return to the lodge to help with dinner, and I was headed for the showers. A twinge of abandonment coursed through me as Liam disappeared around the curve. I'm not sure what would happen when the summer ended, and we went home to Manchester. I pushed that thought back into the darkest recess of my mind. I hitched up my backpack and turned toward home.

I had only taken a few steps when a wave of dizziness washed over me. I stumbled and collapsed onto an old tree stump as my legs gave way beneath me. I fought down a bout of nausea as a my body went hot them cold. Must be the heat. Or the humidity. Or both. I fumbled in my pack for my bottle of water. As I unscrewed the top, I looked up and froze. Hiram Parsons stood ten feet away, his dark eyes burning into me with such intensity, a cold, hard knot of fear filled my gut.

"I warned you before, Sophia," he said in a low, throaty voice that under other circumstances, might have been sexy. "I told you to stay out of things that do not concern you." He took a few steps closer. "I have needs, and I will not allow you and your little boyfriend to stand in my way." His eyes never left mine. Like before, I was paralyzed and my beating heart caught in my throat. Hiram advanced. My mind screamed at me to get up and run, throw something, yell, anything, but my body seemed to be on a different wavelength. I couldn't move a muscle.

Hiram's tall figure loomed over me. Seizing my chin, he forced my head back making it impossible for me to look away. He stared deeply into my eyes, into my very soul. Spasms of terror shook my body and the bottle of water slipped from my nerveless grasp.

"I don't want to hurt you, but you need to understand that you are dealing with things beyond you. This will be your last warning." His silky voice sent a ripple of fear down my spine. Hiram gave me a small, thin-lipped smile and ever so gently, placed his other hand over my heart. A jolt of electricity slammed into my body. I whimpered softly as the color faded from the world.

CHAPTER TWENTY-FIVE

A painful throbbing in my chest gradually brought me back from the darkness. I moaned softly and stirred.

"Sophia? *Sophia!* Are you okay?"

A voice echoed through my brain, and I had trouble focusing on it. Why were they calling me, anyway? It couldn't be time to get up.

"C'mon, Sophia, wake up!" The voice now sounded a little panicky. Slowly, I pried open one eye and then the other. Liam stared down at me, his face pale beneath his tan, his brow furrowed. When he realized my eyes were open, he blew out a relieved breath and ran his hand through his hair. "Sophia? Can you hear me? Are you okay?"

Why did he keep asking me that? I gradually became aware of my surroundings. I seemed to be lying on the ground, the trees towering above me. I frowned, trying to figure out how I ended up there. I started to push myself up, then gasped in pain. My entire body ached, kind of like I'd been run over by a tank. Or at least how I imagined it would feel after being run over by a tank. I groaned and grimaced as I struggled to sit up.

"Not too fast," said Liam, propping me against the tree stump. "Take it easy. That's it." He was surprisingly gentle as he assisted me. I settled against the stump and rubbed my aching chest.

"Sophia," said Liam looking into my eyes, "Do you remember what happened to you? I realized you still had my compass, so I came back and found you lying on the ground." He paused and swallowed. "You looked like you were... dead." There was an unmistakable note of fear in his voice. I found it strangely endearing. Still, what *had* happened to me?

"I... I'm not sure," I mumbled. All my muscles were stiff and numb like when your leg goes to sleep. I struggled to remember. I had just parted from Liam, was headed home and... And what? My stomach clenched. What was wrong with me? Why couldn't I remember? I started to shake and looked at Liam again, my distress reflected in his eyes. He turned to his pack and pulled out one of those emergency solar blankets. The silver ones that look like something astronauts would use. He wrapped it carefully around me. Despite the heat of the day, it felt good. He was just like a Boy Scout—always prepared. I gave him a wan smile.

"We'd better get you home," he said looking around. "I don't want to leave you here by yourself. Do you think you can walk?"

I was about to answer him when a flash of memory nearly blinded me. I saw Hiram looming over me, his hand reaching towards my chest, then a really sharp pain and after that, nothing. "Hiram" I gasped, my eyes wide.

"Hiram?" Liam moved closer, holding my hand. "What about Hiram?"

"It was him." My voice sounded faint as if the mere effort of speaking sapped all my energy. "He warned me. Told me we needed to stay out of his business. He... he did something to me." I shuddered as the memory of that jolt through my body resurfaced. I absently rubbed my aching chest.

Liam's face darkened. "Okay, enough is enough," he said, his voice hard. "It was one thing when we just *thought* he might be doing stuff, but now that he's actually hurt you, we can get his sorry butt thrown into jail for assault at least."

I slowly shook my head, still dazed. "No, I don't think so." Why had I said that? I was all for throwing Hiram's sorry butt into jail. I'm not sure exactly what he did, but I did know it would be hard to prove that he had even touched me. I pulled open the neck of my t-shirt and studied my chest. Not a mark on me.

"What do you mean?" demanded Liam. "Look at you! Who knows what might have happened if I hadn't come back?"

I sighed, exhaustion enveloping me like a cocoon. "Liam, no one else saw him here. The only proof something happened was you found me unconscious on the ground. It's hot and humid, and we've been tromping through the woods. The cops would just say I fainted from the heat or dehydration and dreamed the whole Hiram thing. My parents already think I'm a little obsessed with him."

Liam dropped down beside me. He was silent for several moments. "Okay, maybe you're right. But this is serious, Sophia. Can you tell me exactly what happened?"

I tugged the crackly blanket closer around me. I should be broiling, but I still felt chilled. "I remember you had just left, and I was starting home. Suddenly, I started feeling sick and had to sit down." I glanced at the stump I was using as a backrest. "Then, there he was. Hiram, I mean. He looked mad." I frowned, trying to remember exactly what he'd said. "He told me he'd warned me before about getting in his way, and that if you and I didn't quit, we'd be in big trouble. Or at least that was the gist of it. He said this would be my last warning." I decided not to add the boyfriend part. "Then he touched my chest." Unconsciously, my hand massaged the very spot. "I felt this sharp pain and that was it. Next thing I remember is you calling my name."

I was suddenly parched and reached for my opened water bottle on the ground nearby. Most of the water had drained onto the ground, but there were still a couple of good swallows left, soothing my burning throat. As I considered what had happened, my anger surged.

"He must have really wanted to make his point," said Liam wiping sweat from his brow.

I yanked the blanket off my shoulders and began to roll it up. "Yeah, but it doesn't matter. I am not giving up. This just proves he has plans for Maya. I'm not going to sit around and wait for her to get sick again and waste away to nothing." I looked into Liam's troubled blue eyes and experienced a rush of warmth.

"Liam, you're the only one I can trust. No one, including my mother who supposedly buys into all this paranormal crap, believes me." I grabbed his hand again. "I can't do this alone."

Liam smiled crookedly and gently touched my face. "You won't have to Sophia. There is no way I'm letting you do this by yourself. Remember, every superhero needs a sidekick."

I laughed and snuggled up closer to him. He wrapped his arm around my shoulders. I felt much safer.

"Well, we still need to get you home," said Liam. He studied me doubtfully. "You look awfully pale."

"Just give me a hand up. I'll be fine." Or at least that's what I told myself as Liam grasped my hands and hoisted me to my feet. With a gasp, I clutched his arms as the world spun around me. My stomach dropped and for a moment, I thought I was going to barf. That would have been romantic. I closed my eyes and heard Liam's steadying voice tell me to take some deep breaths. It took a few minutes, but I felt a little steadier. I eyed Liam.

"Where did you learn this great bedside manner?"

He laughed. "Remember, I deal with needy tourists all day long. I've taken all kinds of first aid and CPR classes. You'd be surprised how many people hurt themselves on a simple nature hike."

I nodded. Then took another deep breath. "Okay, let's see if I can walk." It took a few awkward attempts but eventually, I could put one foot in front of the other without falling flat on my face.

"I think you're a natural when it comes to this walking stuff," commented Liam with obvious approval.

I glanced at him, then grinned. "Just like skipping stones. I am practically a prodigy."

Liam laughed but stayed nearby in case I stumbled. By the time we reached the house, I was marching ahead on my own and feeling pretty much back to normal. Still, I couldn't help but be unnerved by the experience. Hiram was proving to be even more dangerous than I'd originally suspected.

Liam left me at the front door with a kiss and a warning to be careful. I turned and watched him until he disappeared down the path. A chill ran down my back as I experienced a sense of déjà vu. Shaking it off, I opened the door and slipped inside. It was dead quiet. I went upstairs where Mom was asleep on her bed. She had worked the late shift on the psycho hotline. Dad and Maya were nowhere to be seen. I glanced out my bedroom window and noted the little motorboat was gone. Maya must have been feeling well enough to take a spin on the lake and no doubt Dad went with her.

With a long, weary sigh, I flopped down on my bed and closed my eyes, letting my body relax. Every single muscle throbbed with exhaustion, but my thoughts whirled, trying to figure out what to do next. I wasn't going to let Hiram scare me off. Not if it meant sacrificing my sister. Maya might be a royal pain in the butt, but she was the only sister I had. It all boiled down to finding his grave. I turned over on my side and plumped up my pillow. If only there was someone I could ask. If only. I immediately fell into a deep sleep.

❖ ❖ ❖

I was in the graveyard again. I had been searching all day for Hiram's burial spot, but no matter where I headed, I ended up by Mercy's grave. I was frustrated and decided it was time to go home. As I turned to leave. I found myself face to face with Mercy May, her face lined with worry.

"You cannot allow Hiram to take another life. You must stop him. Only you can do this. But, you must take care, as he can hurt you as well."

"But I'm not seventeen," I protested, trying to ignore her warning. "He can't suck the life out of me."

She stared at me with grave eyes. "That is not all he can do. This very day you tasted his power. He could have greatly injured or even killed you if he had so desired." Then she looked away. "It is not Hiram who does these monstrous things, but the evil that has overtaken his soul. You must find his burial place. You must destroy it before another innocent life is ripped away."

I frowned and sighed in frustration. "But I've looked and looked, and I get nowhere. These woods go on for miles. He could be buried anywhere." I paused, eyeing her hopefully. "Maybe you can tell me where he's buried?"

She shook her head, her pale face sadder than ever. "Alas, I cannot. But," now she looked directly at me. "Perhaps you are looking in the wrong place."

I rolled my eyes, ready to explode. "Duh! Of course, I'm looking in the wrong place. If I'd been looking in the right *place, I would have found the grave by now."*

She regarded me as if I had the brains of a gnat. Anger rose within me. Who was she to judge? It was obvious she wasn't going to be very helpful. Dire warnings were all well and good, but unless she could come up with the goods and provide me with a map or directions of some sort, she had no room to complain. Then I paused. A map. Could there be a map someplace? Would Hiram's father have been willing to take that risk and actually record where his son was buried?

I turned back to Mercy May. She nodded and faded away into the darkness. "You know where to look." Her faint words echoed in my head. "You know where to look."

I sat up abruptly, the words still ringing in my mind. *You know where to look.* Did I? The woods were so vast that trying to find Hiram's grave without some kind of clue or map was pretty hopeless. Map. There was that word again. I needed a map. But, where would I find one? Then it hit me. Where had I found all the important information so far? In the attic. Of course! How could I have been so stupid? If there was any map to be found, the attic was the most logical place.

Even though my aching body screamed for rest, I couldn't just lie in bed all day. I had to *do* something. I turned my head and eyed the door to the attic. With a grunt, I rolled off the bed and hobbled stiffly to the closet. As I reached for the attic door, I felt a brief surge of fear. I sure hoped Hiram wasn't lurking around up there just waiting for me. Squaring my shoulders, I took a deep breath, yanked open the door and marched up the stairs into the dusty gloom above. Happily, no one waited to ambush me.

Once in the attic, I surveyed the relics of so many past lives. I felt a familiar twinge of sadness when I spied the hope chests of Mercy May and Grace. Was there was anything here that belonged to their brothers or parents or had all that been taken west? I carefully picked my way through the maze of boxes and piles of dusty junk. I sneezed several times. It made my head hurt.

The work lights were on, but they didn't even make a dent in the shadows filling the back corners. I switched on my flashlight and tried to make out what hid in the darkness. There just had to be something. I felt it in my bones. In one of the farthest corners, my light swept across a piece of furniture piled high with dusty boxes. It took my mind a moment to register what it was. I moved the light back to get a better look. It was a desk. My stomach gave an excited swoop. Desks could be treasure troves of information. They often held important papers, and my gut was telling me this could be just one of those desks.

I climbed over enough junk to furnish a couple of houses in my quest to reach the desk. Jeeze, did these people ever throw anything away? It took me about ten minutes, and as many sneezes, to finally reach my destination. I studied the cartons piled on top. Some of them looked pretty old, but I didn't think they used cardboard boxes in the 1800s, but what did I know? I hefted the first box, staggered a few feet and dropped it with a loud thump, hoping it wouldn't bring up my mother. I paused for a few moments but nothing happened. I knew if she showed up, she'd probably chase me out of the attic. She still didn't like me messing around up here.

I rearranged the other boxes a bit more carefully and peeked into a few. They held books. That explained why they were so heavy. When I had removed the final carton, I found myself staring at an old-fashioned roll-top desk. My grandfather had a similar one. Only his wasn't covered with dust and disgusting cobwebs. I sneezed again and began to check out my find. The back half of the desk was made up of a series of small cubbies and drawers. Using the flashlight, I peered into the cubbies only to find a dense network of spiderwebs and an assortment of dead insects. My skin crawled. I don't like bugs. Did I mention that?

Next, I turned my attention to the drawers. Some opened easily, but others were good and stuck. It wasn't long before I was covered in both dust and sweat. One of my very favorite combinations. I managed to get all the drawers open but, surprise, surprise, nothing. They were totally empty. I sat back and frowned as I wiped the perspiration from my face with the bottom of my t-shirt. I was so certain this desk was important. I'd been drawn to the two chests, and they'd turned out to be veritable gold-mines, so what was the deal with the desk?

Then it occurred to me that sometimes these old desks had secret compartments. At least they did in movies, but hey, it was worth a shot. First, I examined all the drawers looking for false bottoms or sides. That seemed like the most likely scenario. Nothing. I looked inside where the drawers belonged but still didn't find any secret hidey-holes. I sat back and thought hard refusing to give up. I remembered a Chinese puzzle box I had where to open the box, you pulled out a little drawer part way to trigger the next step of the mechanism. Could this have something similar? Carefully I pushed all the drawers back into their slots and slowly pulled out the first drawer. I froze when I felt a small tug, like the drawer had caught on something. I turned to the second and tried the same thing. My heart sped up as I felt a second tug. Quickly, I repeated the process with each of the ten drawers in the desk. As the last drawer settled into place, I heard a distinctive click and a small decorative panel set along the front of the desk popped open.

I squealed, jumped to my feet and did a little victory dance. Was I a great detective or what? I was becoming a regular Nancy Drew. Once my heart had settled down, I studied the drawer a moment before cautiously pulling it open. Inside was a worn black notebook. I stared at it for a long time. Another diary? My breath caught in my throat as I reached in and picked it up. It was about six inches tall and four inches wide, bound in cracked leather. With a flutter in my stomach, I opened the notebook.

CHAPTER TWENTY-SIX

If I had been expecting an emotion-filled diary written by Hiram's father including detailed directions to Hiram's grave, I was seriously disappointed. If I had been hoping for a dry account of planting schedules, daily weather, and annual crop yields, I hit the jackpot. I glared at the book in my hand. All that buildup for *this*? This was like expecting a computer for Christmas and getting a vacuum cleaner. I was that disappointed.

I tossed the notebook back on the desk and growled. What a waste of time. Whoever cleaned out the desk must not have known about the secret compartment. Otherwise, why leave *that*? I'm sure it was very useful way back when, but hardly of any great historical importance today. I frowned, tapping my fingers on the desk. Why would a seemingly innocent farm record be hidden anyway? It's not like it contained top secret planting information. I tilted my head and stared hard at the book. Could there be more in that little journal than meets the eye?

I reached out and picked up the book again and this time, I carefully examined each and every page. I wasn't sure what I was looking for, but surely there had to be some reason someone had hidden the book. Frowning, I noticed that the paper on the inside back cover didn't look quite right. The marbled endpaper sat slightly askew. It wasn't something you'd catch unless you looked closely. Taking a deep breath, I tugged at a loose corner. It didn't take much for the old glue to let go, and I carefully peeled the paper away from the cover. My heart gave a little jump as I turned the paper over.

It was a map.

It appeared hastily sketched and didn't contain a lot of detail, but surely for anyone familiar with the area, it showed enough landmarks to make the location clear. A small x in the map's center drew my attention along with the single word written beside it: Hiram. Goosebumps erupted up and down my arms. This *had* to be the map of Hiram Parsons' final resting place.

Abruptly, a sharp pain stabbed my chest. With a cry, I slammed the book shut and whirled around. I swore I heard the echo of a deep laugh. Was someone else in the room? Frantically, I swept my light across the attic, but I saw no one. Didn't matter. I scrambled to my feet and dashed back downstairs to my room, the book clutched firmly to my less than ample bosom. Without this map, it would be impossible to find Hiram's grave.

The pain faded by the time I slammed the attic door shut. Panting, I massaged my chest. The stabbing sensation occurred in the exact spot where Hiram had zapped me. I didn't like that. Did he somehow know what I'd found? My jaw tightened as my eyes dropped to the book in my hands. I must never let the paper out of my sight. If Hiram learned that I had a map showing the location of his gravesite, it would disappear just like his portrait.

This whole thing had me spooked. Shakily, I lowered myself onto my bed and pulled the map from the book. I chewed my lower lip studying the drawing. None of the landmarks made any sense to me. If Mercy May's father had at least marked the location of the old graveyard, that would give me a place to start. But if he had, anyone could easily find Hiram's grave and that was the last thing Mr. Parsons wanted. In my opinion, he should have let the uncles dig up Hiram and be done with it. It would have saved everyone a lot of grief in the long run.

I flipped through the notebook one more time hoping for some other clue, but the map was it. Everything else pertained to the farm. I sighed and rubbed my fingers along the soft leather of the cover. First of all, I should make a copy of the map. I didn't want somebody sneaking in and making off with the only record of Hiram's burial.

As I got up to go make the copy in Dad's study, I heard the front door open, and Dad calling my name. Shoot. The copy would have to wait. I didn't want him asking me about the map.

"I'm here, Dad," I yelled. I stepped out of my room and looked down the stairs to where my father stood below, his face reddened by sunburn. Maya sagged on the bench beside the front door, her head resting in her hands.

"Where have you been?" I asked walking down the stairs to meet them. My eyes continued to study my sister.

"Oh, Maya wanted to go for a trip around the lake. Check some of her fish traps."

Maya lifted her head. Despite being in the sun all day, her face appeared oddly pale. "I didn't want to leave the fish trapped any longer than necessary. I want to record all the species I find in the lake." Her voice was rough with fatigue.

"Maybe you should have waited," I said. "You look beat."

Maya shrugged. "Maybe. But I didn't want the fish to die. I meant to check the traps at least every other day. It's been close to a week." She closed her eyes and leaned back.

"I think you should go up and take a nap, Maya," said Dad. I lifted my eyebrow. Dad's a great guy, but unless you were bleeding on one of his dinosaur bones, he probably wouldn't notice if you were injured. It surprised me he picked up on Maya's exhaustion.

Maya nodded. "Yeah, you're probably right. Being sick all week has really sapped my energy." She struggled to her feet and with a heavy sigh, trudged up the stairs.

I looked at Dad. "I still think you ought to take her to the doctor."

Dad shrugged. "I suggested that on our walk back from the lake. She says she's feeling better." He leaned over and kissed me on the head. "Don't worry.

Sometimes it can take a while to shake a virus. She'll be fine." With that, he followed Maya up the stairs.

I rubbed the back of my neck. Okay, it's possible she did have a virus, but there were simply too many weird coincidences. I made a decision and headed up to Maya's room. I found her lying on her bed with her eyes closed.

"Maya?"

She opened her eyes and squinted at me. "Yeah?" Her voice sounded raspy.

I stood silent for a moment, then forged ahead. "I need to ask you a question. It might sound kind of weird, but have you been having any strange dreams lately?"

Maya frowned and pushed herself up on one elbow. "Yeah, but how did you know?" She rubbed her eyes. "I keep dreaming about some guy. He looks like that actor, Colin Firth. I know it's not him but looks just like him. Anyway, he stood outside the window and told me to let him come in, that he could help me. I have no idea what that means. Bet Mom would know. When I woke up this morning, I felt worse." She lay back down with a soft moan and closed her eyes again.

I felt ill myself right then. *Hiram.* Just like with Mercy May and all those others. He was coming for my sister. I had to find his grave before she got any worse. Everyone thought the uncles were nuts claiming Hiram had sapped the life out of their kids, but it was beginning to look like they were the only ones that had had a clue.

I regarded Maya for a few moments more before returning to my own room. Things were moving way too fast. If Maya had started dreaming about Hiram, it was only a matter of time before her symptoms got worse. I suspected Hiram wasn't going to be content letting things meander along as he had in the past. We have a lot more sophisticated medical care these days which might cure Maya before Hiram sucked all the life out of her. But my gut said no. Unless I stopped Hiram myself, Maya was doomed to join all those other dead teens in the Parsons graveyard.

That night, the coughing began.

CHAPTER TWENTY-SEVEN

I called Liam early the next morning with my news about the map. He was as excited as I was and promised to come over as soon as he could. As I hung up the phone, I glanced towards the ceiling. I could hear Maya's deep, rattling cough, and I clenched my teeth. Hiram wasn't wasting any time.

Liam showed up about an hour later. When I spotted him coming around the curve of the path, I jumped up from the porch swing and pounded across the yard towards him. He gasped in surprise when I threw myself into his arms.

"Wow!" He grinned as he hugged me. "Guess I was gone longer than I thought!" He then stepped back and studied me. "You okay? I worried about you all night after what happened yesterday."

I nodded impatiently as I stepped back. "Yeah, I'm good, but Liam, we're running out of time. Maya told me she's started having dreams about Hiram. Well, she thinks it's Colin Firth, but you know what that means. Mercy May dreamed about Hiram when she got sick. So did one of her brothers." I grabbed his arm and pulled him over to the picnic table under the big oak tree. I opened the journal and carefully removed the map, laying it out on the table. "We have got to find Hiram's grave as soon as possible."

Liam leaned in and studied the little map. I watched him for any signs of recognition. I figured since he'd grown up around here, he might pick out a landmark or two. I was disappointed when he finally shook his head and sighed. "None of it means anything to me. It could be anywhere."

I cursed under my breath. "Then what are we going to do? I mean, this place on the map has to be fairly close to the original cemetery doesn't it? I wonder how many acres Mercy's father owned. Wouldn't he bury Hiram on his own land?"

Liam nodded slowly. "Yeah, you would think so. And it would have to be someplace that no one would want to farm in the future. If we could find a map of the original property, we would know where the borders and stuff were located; that should narrow down the search. Your map might make a lot more sense then."

I nodded eagerly. "But where could we find such a map?"

Liam shrugged. "I think they have that kind of stuff in the county offices. I could ask my mom."

"Good. But what can we do in the meantime?"

Liam turned and studied the woods behind us. "Well, we could take your map and search again. We might find some of the landmarks." He looked down at the paper again and pointed. "See that rock? It looks like a dog's head. That's pretty distinctive."

"Assuming it's not all covered with brush or someone has removed it." I was feeling less than optimistic despite my growing fear for my sister's safety.

Liam glanced over at me. "You have any better ideas?"

I slumped. "No, but we just keep going over those woods, and never find anything. It seems hopeless."

Liam wrapped his arm around me. "Listen, Sophia, you can't give up now. I know it seems impossible, but every time we hit a dead end, you find another clue. At least with this map, we have something to actually search for. Hiram's grave is probably all covered up, and we'd never recognize it for a grave without these landmarks. We might have walked right over it without knowing it. So, come on. Let's take another shot at it."

I smiled weakly. "Why are you helping me? This whole thing is so weird, and for all you know, I could be just some whacked out girl making all this up for attention. I mean, I am known for my active imagination."

Liam's arm tightened around me. "Sophia, I haven't had this much fun in, well, ever. I spend most of my time working at the lodge catering to those needy tourists. Sure, some of them are really interesting, and I've actually learned a lot over the past few summers, but it's all very routine. Then you arrived with your mysterious man, missing graves, and secret diaries, and I've been having a blast. It's a real mystery and for what it's worth, I don't think you're crazy. I've seen Hiram Parsons. I've at least read some of the diary, and I believe there really is something going on. Plus," now his eyes softened as he moved closer to me. "You are the hottest girl on the lake." He kissed me very softly. I closed my eyes, and all I could hear was the pounding of my heart.

When he finally pulled away, I was breathless. He grinned that electric grin. My pulse jumped another notch. "So, what do you say?" he asked, eyebrows raised. "Ready to hit the trail?"

How could I possibly say no?

So, that's how we spent the rest of the week. Liam asked his mom about the land deed, and she said we'd have to go to the county land office in Lancaster close to two hours away. There was no guarantee there would even be an actual map. There might just be a legal description of the property. That wouldn't help us much. She told Liam that lots of times they just marked property lines with certain rocks. So, we searched. And Maya got sicker.

Late one night, I was awakened by a gentle shake. I opened my eyes to find my father looking down at me, his face was drawn with worry. I quickly sat up.

"What's wrong?"

"Maya's gotten a lot worse," said Dad softly. He rubbed his stubbled chin. "She's having a lot of trouble breathing. We're taking her to the hospital in Berlin. You better get dressed."

I nodded, my stomach churning. Dad squeezed my arm and silently disappeared into the dark hallway. I could hear Maya's labored breathing and deep, rattling cough. It sounded so much worse than just a few hours before. I quickly pulled on my clothes and joined my parents outside. Dad was settling Mom and Maya in the back seat of the car. I fought back tears as I stared at my sister's haggard appearance. She looked like she already had one foot in the grave. I climbed into the front seat beside my father and glanced at him. The stark fear on his face released those tears I'd been fighting so hard to contain. As we pulled away from the house, I glanced out towards the woods. My eyes widened as a shadowy figure stepped out from behind a tree, its arm raised as if in greeting. I felt that sharp pain in my chest for a mere instant, but it was enough to tell me it was Hiram. Angrily, I wiped the tears away. I refused to believe it was too late to save Maya. I would show Hiram that I too, could be a force to be reckoned with.

It was late morning before the doctors were done poking, prodding, and otherwise testing my poor sister. Nothing like a hospital to make a sick person feel worse. While we waited, I mentally reviewed all the places Liam and I had searched. What had we missed? I didn't even notice when the doctor came in to talk to us. Dad had to poke me a few times before I realized we were moving.

The doctor, his nametag indicated he was Dr. Patel, led us to a small office. Mom and Dad stood anxiously watching the doctor. I stood behind them trying to keep myself together, my arms crossed tightly over my chest. The doctor looked down at his chart for just a moment before beginning.

"Mr. and Mrs. Whelan, we've studied the chest x-rays and it would appear your daughter has a rather aggressive form of pneumonia. From what you've told us, she suffered a flu virus a couple of weeks ago which could have weakened her immune system. Fortunately, she's young and pneumonia is treatable. We will immediately start her on antibiotics and breathing treatments. I expect she will respond fairly quickly. However, I am glad you did not wait any longer to bring her in."

"So, she'll be all right?" There was a tremor in Mom's voice.

Dr. Patel smiled his reassuring doctor smile. "I believe so. She will need to remain in the hospital for the time being. How long will depend on how quickly she responds to treatment, but I do not think it will be too long. Perhaps a week if all goes well."

I could feel the relief practically pour off my parents as their grim expressions morphed into smiles. They both were saying all those little things people say when they've been handed a reprieve, but I couldn't share in their joy. I knew the doctor was wrong. Aggressive forms of pneumonic TB often were initially diagnosed as pneumonia. However, I also knew that if I told them to test her for tuberculosis, they'd all think I was crazy, but there was no doubt in my mind. It was like Mercy May all over again.

My parents went in to see Maya, but I said I needed to find the bathroom. Really, I just couldn't bear to see Maya looking so bad. I wandered down the hallway until I found some doors that led out to a sunny courtyard. There was a very old man sitting in a

225

wheelchair enjoying the morning sun. I shuffled past him and settled myself on a bench nearby. Tears slowly trickled down my cheeks. I felt so helpless.

"You all right, sweetheart?"

Startled, I looked up to see the old man peering at me through pale eyes. He looked mildly concerned.

"Um, yeah," I mumbled trying to wipe the tears away without being too obvious.

"You get some bad news?"

I shrugged and looked down at my hands. "They say my sister has pneumonia." I wished I had a handkerchief. My nose was running. "But I think they're wrong."

The man tilted his head and studied me intently. "Why would you think that? You a doctor?" He smiled as he said that.

I didn't return that smile. Why would this old coot believe me any more than anyone else? Still, I just needed to talk to somebody. "I think she has tuberculosis, and if I don't find Hiram's grave, she's going to die."

The man's snowy white eyebrows shot up at that non sequitur. "Excuse me?"

I shook my head in frustration. Nothing I said would sound remotely sane so why not go for the gold? I turned fully to the man and leaned forward. "I think my sister is being killed by some kind of weird vampire-like creature called Hiram. A hundred and sixty years ago, a bunch of kids, all related, died from TB. One right after another, and only after they turned

226

seventeen. A lot of people thought some kind of evil spirit was basically sucking the life out of them even though it looked like tuberculosis. They believed that evil was a guy named Hiram Parsons, the first one to die. Anyway, some thought that if they dug up Hiram's grave, they would find his heart full of fresh blood, proof that this evil thing survived on the lives of others. If they burned the heart and made a potion from the ashes, it would then save whoever currently had the disease." I paused and glanced at my audience. The man was listening and actually appeared interested.

"And?" he asked, leaning forward.

I sighed. "And, I think the same thing is happening to my sister. She just turned seventeen a few weeks ago and has been sick ever since. I've seen this Hiram guy. I *know* it's real but I can't prove it. I need to find Hiram's grave and see for myself, but Hiram's father moved his grave so no one could dig it up." I reached into my pocket and pulled out the copy of the map I had finally made. "I found this map his father left, but it makes no sense to me."

The man said nothing for a long time then held out a thin, gnarled hand. "Let me take a look."

I hesitated then handed him the map. He carefully spread it out across his lap.

"Where is this supposed to be?"

"Parsons Corners. Near Little Loon Lake."

The man's eyes immediately widened in surprise. He gave a short bark of a laugh. "Parsons Corners, eh?

Well, sweetheart, you've come to the right feller. I'm ninety-eight years old, and I spent every one of 'em in Parsons Corners. Well, except for those few I spent in the Pacific back during the war. Anyways, I used to do a lot of huntin' in those parts."

I watched as the man carefully studied the map. I hardly dared to breathe, like I might disrupt his concentration or something. For the first time, I felt a smidgen of hope.

After what seemed like an hour, the man's face brightened, and he looked up at me. I swear his eyes actually twinkled. "I know where this is! You got a pencil or a pen?" I helplessly checked my pockets then ran inside to a nearby nurses' station. When I returned, the man took the pencil and began making some shaky marks on the paper. His old hand shook so much, I could tell it wasn't easy for him, but I let him have at it. Finally, he seemed satisfied and signaled me to move closer.

"Look here," he began and pointed to a square he'd drawn in the lower far-left corner. "This is that old Parsons' family graveyard and this line here," he pointed to one of his squiggles, "is the path into the forest. You know it?"

Know it? Ha! Liam and I had only been up and down that stupid path a million times. I nodded, anxious to hear more.

"Good, well this dog head rock is about two miles from that graveyard as the crow flies. It's on state forest land now but used to be part of the Parsons farm. The path don't go all the way. You'll run into Little Loon Lake, so you'll have to go round it. Probably closer to three or four miles to hike all the way." Now he sat back and studied me. I squirmed.

"I know that story you talked about. Matter of fact, my grandpa was supposed to marry Mercy May Parsons, but she died just before the wedding. In fact, most of them Parsons kids died young. Consumption is what they always said. But my grandpa told me there were rumors that some kind of devil had the Parsons family in its sights. Some wanted to dig up Hiram Parsons; thought he was the root of the family troubles. But like you said, his pa moved the grave and no one ever found it. Then all the Parsons moved away, and the story went with them."

Just then, the doors swung open and a nurse came out. "Sorry, Mr. Hopkins, but it's time for your lunch."

She stepped behind his wheelchair and began to move him indoors. Before leaving, he grabbed my hand and leaned close. "You be real careful, sweetheart," he whispered. "Sometimes there's more than a bit of truth in them old stories." With that, he was gone, and I was left trembling in the noontime sun.

CHAPTER TWENTY-EIGHT

Dad and I drove home after dinner. Mom refused to leave Maya's side and decided to spend the night at the hospital. My mind whirled with all the stuff old Mr. Hopkins had told me. I couldn't believe he was the grandson of Michael Hopkins, Mercy's fiancé. It boggled the mind. Even more importantly, he pinpointed the location of Hiram's grave. I would call Liam as soon as I got home. We had to find that grave quickly. Unfortunately, it would take us hours to hike out there. I wondered if there were any roads into the area, but I wasn't counting on it.

The clock chimed ten by the time we pulled into the driveway and eager as I was to talk to Liam, I decided his parents might not appreciate me calling so late. I didn't sleep much that night as I considered what finding Hiram's grave would entail. Was I capable of digging up a grave? And what if I really found a bloody heart? The idea made me queasy. But what worried me most was Hiram. What would he do? He'd warned me away once, but until now, the chances of me actually finding his grave had been slim to none. Now, armed with my new knowledge, thanks to old Mr. Hopkins, I could be a real threat. Hiram didn't know that though. At least I hoped he didn't. Hiram was one spooky dude.

The next morning, I called the lodge as early as I dared, but I was too late. Liam's sister told me he'd taken a group out fishing that morning and wouldn't be back until dinnertime. I cursed softly as I hung up the phone. What should I do now? I tapped my fingers on the table. If I went by myself, would I be able to dig up the grave without help? I paced the room. For a moment, I considered asking Dad to come with me, but how would I explain that I wanted to dig up an old grave? He might be a paleontologist who loved nothing more than excavating dinosaur bones, but I doubted he'd be quite so keen on human grave robbing.

Dad appeared as I continued to ponder my dilemma. "I'm heading out to the hospital after breakfast," he said pouring cornflakes into a bowl. "Do you want to come?"

I hesitated before answering. "I don't know. There's nothing I can do there. I figured I'd just stay here and work on my history project."

Dad nodded but his thoughts seemed far away. "That's fine. I'll call you if there is any change in Maya's condition. I expect for now, it's just a waiting game." He gulped down his breakfast, gave me a quick hug, and disappeared out the door.

In the stillness of the empty kitchen, I pulled out the map and peered at Mr. Hopkin's marks, then frowned. I needed more information. I thought for a moment, then hurried up to Dad's study. I dug through the piles of paper on his desk until I finally located the topographical map Dad had purchased last spring. One of my homeschool projects last year had been all about map reading, so I knew what I was looking at. Marking the grave, I traced the route from the house to the site. It looked pretty straightforward. I'd follow the path to Little Loon Lake, then go along the shoreline until it joined one of the state park trails marked on my map. One seemed to head pretty close to where Mr. Hopkins suspected the grave would be. I figured the distance at a little over seven miles. I considered trying to hike all that way by myself, but I have to say, the idea didn't appeal to me. I'm not exactly Daniel Boone, and if I got lost, I'd probably never be heard from again. I sighed. Best if I just waited for Liam.

Trouble was I hadn't counted on Eloise ruining all my plans. Hurricane Eloise was roaring up the coast and that night, the storm slammed into New Hampshire with a vengeance. I should have been more aware of it, but with everything going on, weather reports seemed of little importance. It rained and rained and rained like someone had turned the shower on high and left it running. Dad called from the hospital and told me they had to stay in Berlin because of flooded roads. I assured him I would be fine, but Dad's voice was strained.

"You okay, Dad?"

For a moment, he said nothing. "I didn't want to say anything yet or worry you, but Maya doesn't seem to be responding to the treatment."

I frowned. "Well, it's only been a day, right? I mean, maybe it takes a while."

"Yeah, yeah, you're probably right." The words were reassuring, but the tone of his voice said

232

otherwise. He was worried, and that scared me. "Listen, kiddo, are you sure you'll be all right by yourself tonight? I hate leaving you alone in this storm. They say Parsons Corner is getting hit harder than here in Berlin."

"I'm fine, Dad." I flinched as the lights dimmed for a moment. Not a good sign. "If anything happens, I'll call the lodge. Don't worry. You guys just take care of Maya."

"Your mom is really worried. She keeps telling me you might be in serious danger." Dad hesitated a moment. "I should have made you come with me."

I swallowed. Most of the time, I blew Mom's predictions off, but her words sent a chill through me all the same. I reassured Dad I would be extra careful and double check all the doors and windows. He wasn't happy about the situation, but there was no choice. I experienced a slight sense of abandonment when he finally hung up.

I closed my eyes and took a deep breath. I didn't like being stuck here alone in the middle of nowhere in a big storm with Hiram creeping around. I didn't like the fact that Maya wasn't getting better. He didn't actually come right out and say it, but I was sure Dad meant she was worse. Hiram wasn't wasting time. It had taken weeks for Mercy May and the others to succumb, but maybe Hiram didn't really need weeks. That meant Maya could die at any time.

I paced the room again, my arms crossed tightly across my chest. I stopped at the window and stared at the monsoon outside. The winds had picked up, whipping the trees around in a kind of spastic dance. Although still early, it was as dark as midnight out there. I chewed my nails. Helplessness didn't suit me. I needed to do *something*.

I jumped as the sound of the phone jangled my already frayed nerves. I snatched up the receiver. "Hello?"

"Sophia? Is that you? Are you all right?"

My body went limp with relief. It was Liam. "Yeah, I'm fine. You guys okay?"

Liam chuckled. "Yeah, we're good. The tourists are ticked though. Guess they didn't count on a hurricane ruining their vacation."

I laughed briefly. His voice reassured me for a moment until the lights flickered again. I gripped the phone more tightly. "Listen, Liam, we've got problems. Maya is in the hospital. The doctor said it's pneumonia and treatable, but Dad called me a little while ago and said she's not getting any better." I hesitated, peering around as if someone might be listening. "I don't think it's pneumonia at all, and if I'm right, we're running out of time."

Liam swore. "So, what do we do? We've spent hours searching for that stupid grave. I have no idea where else to look."

"I do." I briefly explained to him about meeting Mr. Hopkins in the hospital and how he identified the place marked on the old map. "Trouble is, it's about seven miles from here somewhere in the state park."

I could almost hear Liam's thoughts whirring in his head. "Well, we certainly can't go tonight. We'd be lost in no time. If it keeps raining, I'm sure I can convince Mom to let me come over tomorrow, but I have to warn you, it won't be fun hiking in the rain and could be dangerous."

I rubbed my aching head and glanced down at the map spread out across the table. "We don't have any choice. Maya's life is on the line. I'm not going to let Hiram kill her."

"Would your parents really let you go hiking off into the woods in the middle of a hurricane?"

I shrugged even though he couldn't see it. "They're stuck in Berlin at the hospital. No telling when they'll get home." I didn't want to add that if Maya continued to get worse, they might not be home tomorrow either.

"Wait... you're there all alone?" Liam's voice sharpened. I felt a warm rush.

"I'll be fine. I've locked all the doors and windows."

Liam grunted. "I don't like it. Who knows where Hiram is? He could be hiding in your garage or something."

I decided not to mention seeing Hiram near our house the previous day. Part of me desperately wanted Liam to come over and protect me, but I didn't want him to risk his life in this weather. "Listen," I began, "I'll be perfectly safe. Earlier I checked the whole house, including the attic, just to be sure. I'll sleep by the phone, and you can call me at any time if you get worried."

Liam sighed. "Okay. Stay near the phone. If it takes you more than a few rings to pick up, I'm heading over there, even if I have to row a boat to get there. I don't like you all alone in a bad storm like this. If the lake rises, you could get flooded out or a tree could fall on your house, or..."

"I get the idea!" Jeeze, he was worse than my father. "Liam, don't worry. Trees aren't going to fall on me, and we have a boat here if the water rises." I didn't bother mentioning that I didn't have a clue how to use a boat, but why bother trouble as my grandma always said.

"Fine." Liam must have figured out he wasn't going to win this one. "But I will be out there first thing in the morning, and if you suspect anything isn't right, no matter how little or stupid it seems, you will call me regardless of the time. Okay?"

"Okay." I got that warm fuzzy feeling again. It was kind of nice knowing a guy worried about you. My knight in shining armor. I smiled at the image of Liam in armor. "If I suspect anything is wrong, I will call you immediately. Now, I better go. I want to check the windows again."

"All right, but I'll call you again in a couple of hours just to make sure you're okay. Be careful, Sophia."

After he hung up, I quickly rechecked all the windows. After making the circuit of the place, I settled down at the kitchen table and pulled out my laptop. I frowned. No internet. Figures. It was iffy at the best of times, so I don't know why I thought it would work in the middle of a hurricane. I sighed and put the computer away. Now what? The lights flickered and then went out.

With a curse, I stumbled to the drawer where emergency candles, lighter, and a flashlight were kept. I pulled out a couple of tapers along with a pair of small candlesticks and quickly lit the wicks. It was surprising how much light two little candles created. I stuck the lighter in my pocket in case I needed it again.

I wandered to the front window and watched the storm, mesmerized by its savagery. As much as I wanted my family home with me, I was glad they weren't out driving in this mess.

As I turned away from the windows, something caught my eye. I froze for a second then moved closer to the glass, trying to peer through the curtain of blowing rain. I could have sworn I'd seen a figure out there, just at the edge of the drive. I rubbed my eyes, a sour taste filling my mouth. Just as I had about convinced myself there was nothing there, I saw it again. The silhouette of a human figure, like a shadow in the throes of the storm, stood staring towards the house. I inhaled sharply.

He was here.

CHAPTER TWENTY-NINE

I dashed to the phone and frantically pushed the buttons with numb and clumsy fingers. It took me a moment before I finally realized there was no dial tone. Breathing fast, I moaned as my eyes darted around the room looking for some kind of weapon. Surely Liam would realize the phone was dead and come over, right? But who knew when that might be? In the meantime, Hiram could break in and... and what? I paused, rubbing my head. He wasn't after me. He was after Maya, but what if he discovered I had the map and came to steal it? I spotted the small paper still lying on the kitchen table beside a flickering candle. Perhaps if I left it there, he'd just take it and leave. I had a couple of copies now, so even if he stole the original, I'd still be good.

A loud bang from the kitchen shook the house. Stifling a scream, I darted to the front door, thinking I could make a break for it.

"Hello, Sophia."

I spun, my throat so tight, I couldn't make a sound. Looming in the kitchen doorway was Hiram. Water dripped from his dark-clad figure, but the fire in his eyes burned as brightly as ever in his pale face. I backed up against the front door as all thoughts of escape fled. I gasped at the sharp pain cutting across my chest. A slow smile curled across Hiram's face.

Never taking his eyes from me, Hiram sauntered over to the table and picked up the small map with Mr. Hopkins' marks. He glanced at it, eyebrow arched in surprise. His piercing gaze returned and skewered me to the spot.

"Very clever. Wherever did you find this? I knew Father had drawn a map of my final resting place, but I thought it long gone." He held it over the candle letting the edge catch fire, then dropped it into the nearby sink. He watched it burn before turning his attention back to me.

I couldn't speak, it was like my mouth was filled with sand.

"You have been far more resourceful than I would have ever believed, Sophia," continued Hiram, sauntering towards me. The sound of my name in his deep velvety voice sent a shiver down my spine. Now but a mere foot away, he lifted my chin with his cold, clammy hand, forcing my gaze to meet his. I struggled to look away, but it proved impossible. He leaned in, bringing his mouth close to my ear. The reek of his fetid breath made me want to puke.

"Sophia," he breathed, "You cannot stop me. Your sister's life is mine." His gentle caress filled me with revulsion.

"No!" I barked, finally breaking through my fear. "You can't have her! I *will* stop you!"

Hiram stepped back and laughed, a bone-chilling sound. "Oh Sophia, you are so young. So naïve." Genuine amusement filled his dark eyes. Even though I knew he was a slimy creep, he was still disarmingly handsome, and somehow, that made it worse. He regarded me for some time, tapping his chin with a long, slender finger. My heart pounded in my chest like it wanted to burst free. "I cannot express to you my delight upon learning that long-lost relatives had moved into this house." He turned and studied the room. "It has been a long time since any Parsons have lived here. Because of that, I have aged over time, but with your sister's life, I can renew my life energies and slow the process." He smiled. It looked ghastly. I took a step back. He sighed and shook his head.

"Dear Sophia, I am afraid that I cannot allow you to continue your activities. Although I have little fear of you locating my body, you could draw unwanted attention to me."

The threat in his voice made my knees go weak. I didn't like the way this conversation was going. A loud crack of thunder caused me to jump, breaking the weird spell Hiram had over me. Instinctively, I darted to one side, hoping to escape through the dark kitchen. As I glimpsed Hiram reaching for me, I shoved a small end table into his path. He stumbled over it with a curse. One point for me.

The kitchen door stood wide open, puddles of rainwater pooled on the floor. Slipping and sliding, I fled out into the wild night.

I gasped as the strength of the wind threatened to topple me while sharp pellets of sleet and rain slashed at my exposed skin. I had no idea where to go, so I sprinted towards the woods. I guess I figured I could evade Hiram in the trees, but the absolute blackness of the night made it impossible for me to see more than a few feet ahead.

I ran faster than I'd ever run in my life. Who knew I had such speed in me? All I heard was the roar of the rain and shrieking wind. I glanced back seeing nothing but rain and shadows. Hiram could be five feet behind me, and I'd be clueless. My breath came in tortured gasps as I struggled to get air into my lungs. But I ran. I ran for all I was worth.

When I reached the cover of the forest, I scrambled behind a tree, panting. I peeked around the trunk hoping to spot my pursuer. *Where was he?*

Suddenly, a heavy hand clamped down on my shoulder. I screamed. Twisting around, I found Hiram glaring down at me, his face hard with menace. I was caught.

With a cry, I struggled to escape. "Let me go!"

Hiram's jaw tightened, then he sighed as if exasperated. He deftly switched his grip from my shoulder to my arm and began pulling me deeper into the woods. I cried out in pain as I tripped over roots and dead branches. Hiram simply ignored me, continuing his unrelenting march into the dark, dripping forest.

My brain whirred as he dragged me along. What was I going to do? He could kill me and leave me out here in the woods for bears to eat. Suddenly, my heart gave a little flip. I'd left the big topo map marked with the gravesite sitting on Dad's desk. When Liam didn't hear from me, surely he'd go to the house and with luck, find the map. I assumed Hiram was taking me to his grave. But it was so far, by the time Liam got there, I'd probably be dead. My ankle twisted on a rock causing me to stumble. Hiram gave my arm a hard jerk. *Dead?* For the first time, I fully appreciated the gravity of my situation.

Hiram had no reason to keep me alive. I didn't know if there was truly an age limit for his victims, but I suspected I was too young. He'd died at seventeen, so maybe that determined who was eligible. Anyway, at the very least, he considered me a pain in his butt, so I needed to go.

I wiped the water from my face and coughed. An odd smell filled the air. Sort of a combination of ozone and rotting vegetation. Nausea washed over me.

Hiram moved surefooted through the inky black forest, towing me along with little effort. I fought to slip from his grasp, but he tightened his grip making my hand go numb. Once he yanked my arm so hard, I feared he'd pulled it out of its socket. My cry of agony didn't faze him. He was a man on a mission, and he couldn't have cared less how I fared.

I quickly lost track of time and was soon completely disoriented. Hiram was not using any path I could see. He just charged ahead like a bull moose. He must have been working on some internal GPS system because he never hesitated.

On and on we went. I gritted my teeth against the pain of the innumerable bumps, scrapes, and bruises I endured as he dragged me through the underbrush and over stony hills. A sharp gust of wind flung a small tree branch into the back of my head so hard, black spots formed at the edges of my already limited vision. The sting of the driving rain burned my skin. I flinched as a jagged streak of lightning surged across the churning clouds. The farther we went, the deeper my hope of rescue plummeted. How would anyone know where he'd taken me? The downpour would eliminate signs of our passage. Yet, a part of me refused to give up.

Finally, after what seemed like hours, Hiram jerked me to a halt. I gasped for breath, muscles aching as my trembling legs threatened to collapse. My captor wasn't even winded. We stood at the edge of a small clearing surrounded by trees and large boulders but strangely devoid of other vegetation. Oddly, the darkness had receded here, and I could make out my surroundings with relative ease, almost as if a full moon shone only in this spot.

I also noticed that the storm had abated, at least for the moment. Although the wind still whipped the trees, the rain had lessened to a drizzle. However, I don't think I'd ever been more thoroughly soaked in my entire life. I was freezing.

As my teeth chattered uncontrollably, I glanced at my captor. Hiram's narrow face radiated a disturbing intensity as he stared avidly at a small depression in the center of the clearing. With a wild gleam in his eyes, he turned his feral gaze upon me and released my wrist. Still trying to catch my breath, I firmly massaged it, hoping to restore the circulation.

"Since you were unable to find my grave, I thought perhaps it was time to offer you my assistance." Hiram's eyes continued to burn into me. Suddenly, my windpipe spasmed, cutting off my air. My hands scrabbled vainly at my throat, trying to free myself from the invisible assailant. Hiram's thin lips curled into a slow leering smile as he reached up and gently ran the back of his hand against my wet cheek. Abruptly, my air passage reopened. I coughed and wheezed, trying to suck air into my starved lungs. A low chuckle resonated through my brain.

I attempted to pull away, but my muscles refused to respond. I wanted to scream, run, anything to escape this monster, but it was impossible. I whimpered softly.

"You cannot escape me. Remember that." Hiram stepped back and shook his head. "I regret you are yet too young for me, dearest Sophia. Still, I may draw upon your energies to replenish some I have lost, as I did earlier. Not enough to sustain me like your sister's but it will help. I apologize for the pain you will have to endure."

He gazed past me into the clearing. "I think the time has come for you to meet me face to face."

I blinked away the icy rainwater that dripped down my face, my heartbeat throbbing in my ears. I didn't like the idea of meeting him face-to-face, and I really didn't like the whole *I can draw upon your energies* and *sorry for the pain* thing. Frantically, my eyes swept across the hollow looking for a way out, but saw nothing. Hiram seized my wrist again and forced me down the slope into the depression. He stopped where an old rusted shovel lay partially buried beneath a layer of dead leaves. Hiram picked it up and thrust it into my numb hands.

"Dig."

"Dig?" I stared at the heavy shovel in confusion then at the soggy ground. "Where?"

Hiram pointed at my feet. "There."

I started to protest, but before I could even open my mouth, I thrust the dull edge of the shovel into the waterlogged soil, unable to control my actions. It had been close to two hundred years since his father had interred Hiram in this remote forest hollow, so I figured removing the wet and heavily compacted soil would be beyond my strength. But it wasn't. The soil was oddly loose and crumbly like they had filled the grave with potting soil and peat moss. Don't get me wrong, it was still hard, dirty work, but it could have been a lot worse.

I had excavated a hole about six feet long, three feet wide and four feet deep when I paused to catch my breath. I'd been pretty much working on auto-pilot; my brain blank of everything beyond digging that blasted hole. I glanced up to find Hiram watching me, an amused smirk on his chiseled face.

"You are almost there," he said, his grin widening. "Don't stop now."

Instantly, I resumed my task. I had no choice. My body ignored my pleas to stop. Hiram was running this show, and I had no say in any of it. I continued to dig. My sodden clothes clung to my body, and wet, sticky mud covered every inch of me. My muscles burned with fatigue, but still I dug. Suddenly, my shovel thudded against something solid.

"Stop."

I halted immediately, panting from exertion. Wiping my matted hair from my face, I peered up at my captor. Hiram's glittering eyes narrowed. Backlit by another fiery flash of lightning, his body created a monstrous silhouette above me. I cringed at the booming crash of thunder that followed in its wake.

"Can you not feel it?" He squatted down at the edge of the grave, his voice low and intense. "Can you not *feel* the energy being drawn from you?"

My stomach churned with nausea. Slowly, I lowered my gaze to the dark, wet wood just visible beneath my muddy feet. Hiram's coffin. Abruptly, a blanket of crippling exhaustion engulfed me. The shovel, now unbearably heavy, slipped from my weakened grasp. I heard Hiram laugh as I collapsed to my knees.

"Give me your hand."

Gritting my teeth, I lifted my shaking hand. Hiram seized it in his icy grip, hauled me out of the hole and flung me into the mound of mud and debris that now surrounded his open grave. The acrid stench of mold and death filled my nostrils. My leaden body lacked the strength to even consider escape. I watched listlessly as Hiram hopped into the grave and completed the job of exposing the coffin. It wasn't long before he returned to my side, pulling the lid of the coffin out of the hole behind him. He tossed it beside me.

"Look, Sophia," Hiram whispered seductively into my ear. "And see at last what you have been searching for."

I didn't want to look. I didn't want to see a horrible moldering corpse. I fought the urge to throw up and kept my eyes firmly shut.

"Look, Sophia. *Now.*" Hiram's deep commanding voice could not be ignored. Believe me, I tried. Slowly, I turned my head and opened my eyes to stare into the open grave.

CHAPTER THIRTY

The coffin should have been invisible in the impenetrable shadows of the moonless night, even with the odd glow of the hollow, but I saw it plainly at the bottom of the hole. My mouth dropped open.

No rotting corpse lay there. No bundle of bones or zombie-like creature. It was simply Hiram himself, albeit a much younger version. It looked like the seventeen-year-old boy in Grace's drawing. I blinked, thinking I must be hallucinating, but the image didn't change. Confused, I turned back to the Hiram crouched beside me.

He laughed, then shook his head. "My father should have listened to his brothers. Sadly, I *was* the source of all their pain." For a moment, I could have sworn a shadow of grief passed over his features, but it quickly disappeared. "I did not wish to harm my family," he shrugged. "But I had no choice."

My body shook violently with convulsive chills. There was no doubt in my mind that I was going to die out here and be tossed into that grave to spend eternity with the earthly remains of Hiram Parsons.

"I… I don't understand," I stuttered, wrapping my arms tightly around my body. "Why are you doing this?"

For a long moment, Hiram said nothing, his gaze fixed upon the figure in the coffin. "I have no choice," he whispered. "When I was seventeen, I went with my father to help a neighbor whose only son was dying. The man had no other family and was in poor health himself. While my father assisted the farmer with his chores, I went inside to take the food my mother had sent to the boy. I knew him from school, but although we were of an age, we were not particular friends."

I listened numbly, surprised he would reveal so much, but maybe he figured it didn't matter since it was obvious, I wasn't going to leave here alive.

Hiram turned, his face rigid. Another shudder ran through my body. "The boy, his name was Peter, had consumption. It was obvious by his flushed cheeks, sunken eyes, and bloody cough. I'll admit, his intense gaze frightened me. As I neared him with a bowl of soup, he grabbed my arm, and his eyes…" Hiram's voice trailed off for a moment. He gave himself a little shake and continued.

"His eyes were not his own. *Something* was looking at me through him; something… evil. There was a hunger there. Peter tightened his grip, and I felt a shock run down my arm. I pulled away and the next thing I knew, Peter was dead. His father died a few weeks later."

I licked my lips, shifting my eyes down to the corpse. "Then you got sick."

Hiram nodded. "Night after night, I dreamt of Peter and every morning, I was worse. My strength ebbed with each passing day. The evil that had resided in his soul, now grew within mine. Peter had no other family, so the demon transferred itself to me. It *drives* me. It wants to survive, and that will only happen if I drain the life from others. Members of my own family are the most powerful and rejuvenate me, or should I say us." He looked away again. "I am not strong enough to fight it. As long as there is even one Parsons from my family line alive, it will continue to possess me."

I opened my mouth, then closed it again. In a way, I felt sorry for him. Being forced to kill your relatives one by one over the years must be an like an endless nightmare for Hiram. However, that didn't mean I was going to let him kill my sister. I had to stop him somehow.

"I'm sure you have figured out what will happen next." Hiram sighed and rested his hand gently on my head. "I am sorry, Sophia. I cannot gradually siphon off the energies of a younger person such as yourself, but I promise, the pain will be short-lived. Your sister, however, is the same age as I when was taken over by the accursed spirit. For whatever reason, the energies of those who have reached their seventeenth year are the most nourishing. Yours will be like consuming a bar of chocolate. The energy will not sustain me for long. I would prefer to wait until you are of age, but you have left me little choice."

"Please!" I croaked, clutching at his arm. "You don't have to do this. I won't tell anyone. Just leave Maya alone, and we'll leave. No one has to know about you. Really!"

He shook his head sadly. "I am sorry, but the process has begun. Your sister's energies have already begun to restore me. And the demon. Over the years, I learned to survive on fewer victims, but as I said, only those with whom I share blood can turn back the clock. It has been a very long time since anyone directly related to me has lived in Parsons Corners. I cannot waste this opportunity."

I didn't know what to do. My thoughts were jumbled, and I hadn't the strength to fight. Hiram lifted me from the mud, cradling me in his powerful arms. His handsome face smiled down into mine as he carefully pushed my matted hair from my eyes. "You would have grown into a beautiful woman, Sophia. Again, I am sorry." He then gently placed his hand over my heart. I felt a sharp pain, stiffened, and went limp. This was it.

"Stop!" A voice rang out through the clearing followed by the distinct crack of a gunshot. My captor flinched.

With a snarl, Hiram whirled, flinging me into the open grave. I cried in horror as I landed on the cold, wet corpse. The stench of mud and rotting vegetation filled my nostrils as I cringed in the suffocating darkness, unable to escape the confined space. I struggled to hear what went on above me and gasped recognizing the second voice. Liam!

Instantly, the storm exploded back into the clearing, and heavy rain cascaded over me and down the sides of the grave.

What should I do? I shuddered glancing down at the waxen face of the young Hiram. Then it hit me; if I wanted to stop Hiram, I had to listen to the stories. That meant cutting out his heart and burning it. I dug into my pockets for my faithful Swiss army knife. Would it be enough? I snapped open the blade as I pulled away the rotting fabric of Hiram's shirt exposing his pale chest.

With a soft moan, I lifted the knife, but my arm froze above the corpse. I couldn't do it. This Hiram looked too young, too lifelike. And what if there were maggots or blood? I would throw up for sure. Liam's distant voice called out again followed by another gunshot. I bit my lip. There was no choice. I *had* to do it. Too many people depended on me. I took a deep breath, squeezed my eyes shut, and with a shaking hand, plunged the blade into the center of the chest. Above me, I heard Hiram roar in what sounded like pain.

Breathing hard and fighting back nausea, I sawed through the dry skin. Water ran into my eyes and was collecting in the coffin and grave. I had to hurry.

Dead Hiram's face might have looked almost normal, but he was still an old corpse. Desperation driving me on, I pulled the tissue and brittle ribs apart with a sickening crunch, then slashed away at rope-like tendons with short, frantic strokes. Fear for Liam gave me the strength to yank open the chest to expose Hiram's heart.

I bit back a cry of revulsion and recoiled against the corner of the grave. Inside the ravaged cavity, Hiram's heart spasmed with a horrifying regularity as dark red blood oozed through it. The surface was mottled with seeping patches of decay, as if it rotted from within. My breath came faster and faster as I fought down my panic. Once exposed, a cloud of noxious fumes emanated from around the heart. Vomit rose in my throat.

"Sophia!" It was Liam, his voice high with desperation.

I had to act, but couldn't make myself grab the oozing malevolent thing with my bare hand. I wanted to jump out of that black hole and escape its obscene presence. A cry of pain sounded in the night. *Liam!*

I didn't let myself think. I thrust my hand into the chest cavity, my fingers enclosing the soft, pulsating mass. An excruciating bolt of agony surged up my arm, but I refused to let go. With a moan of disgust and pain, I yanked the heart from its resting place, averting my eyes. It was all I could do to keep from puking all over the grave. Things were bad enough without that.

Something warm and wet trickled down my arm, and I jerked with horror at the dark trails of liquid dripping from my hand. A scream fought for release as my fist convulsed around the cold mass. The rich iron scent of blood filled my nostrils. That was the final straw. I turned my head and threw up all over dead Hiram's stomach. I had to get out of there.

I stumbled to my feet, struggling for balance in the muddy, water-filled hole. My foot crunched through the corpse's rib cage. I shrieked, fighting to stay erect. This was a nightmare straight out of a Stephen King novel. Still clutching the pulsing heart, I struggled up the slick sides of the grave. I had to get far enough away to destroy the heart. Why couldn't Hiram have been a regular run-of-the-mill vampire? A simple stake to the heart would have ended the whole ordeal. But no, I had to *burn* the damned thing!

I shimmied on my stomach over the top of the muddy grave, my head whipping around, desperate for any sign of Hiram or Liam. The rain came down in sheets now, and the hollow might as well have been inside a cave, the otherworldly light having disappeared. I heard some shouting and another shot, but the roar of the rain made it impossible for me to tell where it was coming from. The heart throbbed frantically against my fingers like it knew what was coming. I had to move.

I struggled to my feet and swayed as a wave of dizziness washed over me, another sharp pain piercing my chest. Time must be running out. I turned and staggered back up the hill. Although I wanted to look for Liam, our only hope was for me to destroy the heart. There had to be some place protected from the rain where I could start a fire. Another earsplitting clap of thunder nearly caused me to drop my hideous cargo.

With a cry, I suddenly tripped and sprawled onto the wet forest floor. Spitting out a couple of dead leaves, I turned my head and made out the top of a lichen-covered log. Then an idea came to me. I crawled along the remains of the dead tree, ignoring the pain of the sticks and stones that dug into my knees and hands and inhaled sharply as I reached the end and found the log was hollow. I inhaled deeply, praying nothing was living in there and thrust my hand inside the log. Yes! Protected from the rain, the interior of the log was dry and crumbling. Pushing deeper, I felt a pile of leaves and twigs farther back, obviously, the remains of some animal's old den.

Clenching my teeth, I shoved the oozing heart into the log. Its spasms had become even more frenzied, and my own heart seemed to match its wild beat.

My bloodstained hand dug frantically in my pocket for the lighter I had taken from the house. Desperation made me clumsy and the small square lighter slipped from my stiff fingers. With a sob, my hands clawed back and forth through the forest debris. Where was it? After what seemed like an hour, my fingers grasped the cold metal and quickly snatched it up. I gave a short sigh of relief.

I snapped open the lighter's lid, the distinctive snick reassuring me, and flicked the little wheel, fighting to control my trembling hands. Immediately, a bright yellow flame erupted and illuminated the interior of the log. The knot in my stomach loosened just a fraction. I quickly scraped together the pile of brittle leaves and dead wood around the heart, trying to not look at the disgusting mass where it now stood pulsing in a pool of shiny blood. I paused. Would it even burn? Hiram would undoubtedly come looking for me at any moment, especially if he realized I had the heart. I needed more flammable stuff.

Frantically, I tossed more leaves haphazardly over the heart and carefully lit a few of the driest. Despite the damp, they caught. I fed more and more leaves into the growing flame. My hands shook even harder as I listened for any approaching sounds, certain that Hiram could feel the heat surrounding his heart. I fed the flame more leaves and hunks of dead wood I scraped off the log's interior, but the fire wasn't growing fast enough. Tears mixed with rain on my cold face as I tried to think. Brows furrowed, I looked at the lighter. It was an old Zippo, not a cheap disposable kind. Didn't it contain some kind of fluid? I pulled off the outer casing like I'd seen my grandpa do and looked at the bottom of the lighter. There was a fluid-soaked pad inside. Using my knife, I cut out the pad and dropped it on top of the squirming heart.

Instantly the pad flared, and I fed larger twigs into the hungry fire as fast as I could. For a moment, I didn't think they'd catch. I used my body to protect the blaze from the howling wind and rain, praying the fire wouldn't go out. I scrabbled around for more fuel. The flames burned brighter now, igniting the dry wood inside the log. The heart writhed as if in agony.

"NO!"

I whirled around and screamed as Hiram's wild-eyed figured came sprinting out of the woods. Behind me, I swear the heart answered his furious cry. I turned back to my fire and added more sticks. *Please, please, please.* My throat was so tight, I never could have spoken the words aloud. The fire grew. I tossed on more debris. It grew hotter and engulfed the heart. Yes!

My sense of triumph was short-lived. Shocked, I was yanked by the collar of my shirt and hurled against a tree with a bone-crunching force. For a moment I lay there dazed, then I heard Hiram scream. I lifted my head and watched in disbelief as the flames flared higher and higher engulfing the entire log in flames. How could that be? All I'd had were some sticks and leaves. Now it looked like a veritable bonfire. A strange, sickly green mass writhed in the center of the conflagration while Hiram's roar of agonized fury drowned out all other sounds.

He stood motionless before finally turning to face me. I gasped. He had grown noticeably older, but there was a fiery hatred in his eyes that made my blood freeze. He took a shambling step toward me, followed by another, then another. Again, I could not move, staring into his mesmerizing glare as his fury consumed my soul. He seized me roughly by the front of my mud-stained shirt, pulling me up from the muck.

"*Damn you!*" he hissed, his handsome face contorted by pain and anger. "*Damn you to hell!*"

I feebly struggled against his iron grip. With a snarl, Hiram struck me violently just above my heart. I screamed, a poker of red-hot agony piercing my chest as I felt the remainder of my strength drain from my body. Black spots formed in the corners of my vision, and the last thing I remembered was the sound of a distant gunshot as the world faded to nothing.

CHAPTER THIRTY-ONE

"Sophia! Sophia, wake up. C'mon, can you hear me? Oh, please don't be dead. Sophia!"

Far away, someone called my name. My brain was confused, unable to figure out what was happening. I struggled to open my eyes. It was dark. And wet. And very cold. My body shook with uncontrollable spasms. I closed my eyes again and felt something draped over me.

"C'mon, Sophia," pleaded the voice again. "Wake up. Please!"

Again, my eyes fluttered open. This time I made out a blurred shape hovering above me. I blinked. It was just so dark. Made it hard to focus.

"That's it! C'mon, Sophia. Keep them open. It's me, Liam."

My eyes widened. Liam? I gradually became more aware of my surroundings. I was lying on something very cold and wet. Must be the ground. The air had the unmistakable musty smell of wet vegetation, but there was something else. Some unpleasant, burnt smell. I couldn't quite place it.

"Sophia? Can you hear me?"

I turned my attention back to what I now clearly identified as Liam's face floating in the darkness. I tried to smile. "You're not dead." I was proud of myself for making that deduction.

Liam's broad smile didn't mask his relief. "Neither are you." He licked his lips and looked around for a moment. "Can you sit up? We need to get out of here."

I didn't want to sit up. I wanted to go to sleep. I don't think I had ever felt so completely exhausted in my entire life. Not one single muscle seemed willing to cooperate. However, Liam's voice carried a sense of urgency that even I picked up on in my muddled state.

"Maybe. Give me a hand."

Liam got behind me, wrapped his arm around my shoulders and gently assisted me into a sitting position. I groaned as I pulled Liam's jacket closer around me. Every muscle and bone in my body screamed in protest. My skull throbbed as I took several deep breaths and lifted my head. I froze. It all came back. All the horror of the night. Frantically, I turned to Liam, clutching his arm.

"Hiram! He's here. We've got to go!"

"He won't hurt you anymore." Liam's voice quivered but spoke with a finality that caused me to fully focus on him. The dark shadows of the forest began to mute into a misty gray as sunrise approached. The merciless rain had stopped, but the woods were alive with the sound of dripping water and swaying branches. In the hazy light, I studied the bruises and cuts that marred Liam's handsome face. I willed my hand to reach up and gently touch a nasty gash across his brow.

"Oh Liam," I whispered, fighting a sudden urge to cry. "He hurt you."

Liam shrugged but wrapped his arm more tightly around me. "Not as much as you," he replied with a catch in his voice. He remained silent for a long moment. "I thought he'd killed you." The last was so faint I almost missed it. I did cry then.

"Sophia." He turned to look at me. "Hiram is dead. I mean, really dead. We don't have time to talk about it right now. We need to get you out of here."

I nodded. I was having a hard time focusing. Then, I gripped Liam's arm. "We need some of the ashes of Hiram's heart," I rasped. "The story says the only way to save Maya is to have her eat some."

Liam frowned at me. I thought at first, he was going to refuse, but shaking his head, he got to his feet. My burning eyes followed him as he limped over to the smoldering fire; gray tendrils of smoke trailed into the sky. I winced in sympathy. It killed me to think he'd been injured because of me. Liam reached into his pocket, knelt down for a few moments, then hurried back to me carrying a small bundle.

"Is this enough?" With a slight grin, he handed me a long, narrow baggy full of ashes. "Hope you don't mind. All I had was a bag for picking up my dog's poop." He glanced back over his shoulder, and ran his hand through his wet hair. "It was weird, but all the ashes in the center were completely cold and kind of a weird reddish color. I took some of those. There were some smoldering remains of a log, but that's it."

I stared at the small plastic bag decorated with colorful cartoon puppies. It felt like it weighed ten pounds although I realized it was only a few ounces. I nodded and carefully shoved the bundle into my pocket trying not to picture the squirming bloody mass that had created those ashes. I prayed the story was true, and they would cure Maya.

Liam took a firm grip my arm. "Okay, you need to try and stand up. I have a four-wheeler up the hill on the other side of the rocks, but I don't think I can carry you over there. You're going to need to help."

I nodded and gritted my teeth as Liam clumsily pulled me to my feet. Immediately, the world spun around me as my stomach gave an answering lurch. I was sure I was going to barf again. Liam's deep voice steadied me. I couldn't tell you what he said, but the sound alone worked wonders calming my jangled nerves.

Slowly and awkwardly, he helped me up the rocky hill to where his ATV waited. He grunted in pain a few times, so I knew the trip wasn't any easier on him. Finally, we reached the top and his blessed vehicle. Liam assisted me onto the rear seat and fastened a helmet on my aching head.

"Do you think you'll be able to hold on?" he asked, brow furrowed.

I grimaced as pain shot through my chest. "Yeah, sure. But what about you?"

Liam gave me one of his best heart-throb grins. "Of course. I was born on one of these. I never fall off."

I had my doubts, but we both needed to get someplace dry and warm. I shook more violently than ever, chilled to the bone. Even Liam was shaking. I could only imagine what he had gone through with Hiram. It was then I spotted the rifle fastened to the side of the ATV. That explained the gunshots. I eyed Liam with new respect and concern.

I don't remember a lot about the trip back through the woods. I concentrated on staying awake and not falling off the ATV. Liam frequently checked on me, but as time went on, I became less and less aware of my surroundings. All I know is the trip seemed endless.

"Oh my God, Liam! What happened?"

My eyes snapped open. I had drifted off and didn't realize we'd come to a stop. I tried to sit up but found I barely had the strength to remain upright. I heard several strange voices and a pair of strong arms lifted me up. The next thing I knew, I lay in a soft, warm bed in soft, warm pajamas while a worried looking woman tried to get me to drink some hot cocoa.

I blinked at her. All this waking up in strange situations was beginning to get to me. "Mrs. MacKenzie?"

Liam's mother smiled at me. Like the bed and pjs, her smile was also soft and warm. I immediately felt better.

"How do you feel, sweetheart?"

I moved a little and winced. Everything still hurt as if someone had been using me for a party piñata. But it wasn't just the pain; it was the leaden feel of my body as if the simplest movements took more energy than I possessed. Hiram's face popped into my head. Had he sucked out too much of my life force or whatever? I didn't understand what he had done to me or what it might mean for my future. It scared me.

"Do you remember what happened?" Liam's mom eyed me carefully.

I hesitated. I couldn't just say I got lost in the woods. I glanced at my wrist. A distinct ring of bruises stood out against my pale skin where Hiram had held me. I bit my lip.

"I... I was kidnapped."

Liam's mom nodded and gently stroked my hair. "That's what Liam said, but he wasn't too clear on the details. Your parents are trying to get home. Last night's rain caused a lot of flooding, but Liam's dad has taken one of our boats and will hopefully get them here soon. The police will want to talk to you as well."

I nodded. I had to figure out exactly what to tell everyone. Obviously, I couldn't tell them about Hiram's otherworldly nature, or my burning up his heart so I could feed it to my sick sister, but there were enough details I could share. Hiram had kidnapped me, and Liam had come to my rescue. A warmth spread through me as I considered that. I could just say Hiram was going to murder me and bury me in the grave. I closed my eyes. swallowing down a surge of panic as the uncontrollable trembling returned.

Liam's mom held my hand. "It's okay, Sophia. It's all over now and you're safe."

I stared at the ceiling and nodded weakly. Tears leaked from the corners of my eyes as the exhaustion weighed me down. I didn't want to think about it anymore. I closed my eyes and allowed myself to drift off.

A doctor staying at the lodge looked me over and claimed, other than some nasty bumps and bruises, I was physically all right but definitely suffering from hypothermia and severe shock. Ha. That was an understatement. Liam, I learned later, had a few bruised ribs as well as a variety of bumps and contusions. The verdict was we would both live.

The local police chief came by to see me, and I told him my edited version of events. I couldn't tell him what had happened to Hiram, however since I had no idea. I hoped Liam could fill me in on that part of the story.

He came by to see me right after the chief left. I fought back tears as I studied his bruised and battered face. I didn't know what to say.

He sat on the edge of my bed and took my hand. I smiled at him. He leaned forward and gently kissed me. I threw my arms around his neck and burst into sobs as the reality of the night's events came crashing down on me. He simply held me and let me cry myself out.

Finally, with no tears left, I collapsed back onto the pillows. I looked away in embarrassment. Liam turned my face towards his, gave me another kiss, and handed me a wad of Kleenex with a sympathetic grin. I suddenly laughed.

"You really are always prepared, aren't you?"

Liam laughed and squeezed my hand. "Remember, I have to be prepared for all kinds of emergencies from lost children to hundred-year-old killer zombies."

The smile fell from my face. "How did you find me? What happened to Hiram?"

Now it was Liam's turn to look away. A curtain of pain covered his smile. "When I couldn't reach you by phone, I knew something was wrong. I took my ATV and got to your house as fast as possible. I figured out what had happened when I got there and found you missing and the door wide open." He paused and absently fidgeted with his watch.

"I feared the worst; that Hiram had taken and killed you. Trouble was, I had no idea where to even look. I searched your house and found the map in the study with the gravesite marked. I didn't have any other ideas, so I headed there."

The images of those dark dense woods, the rain pouring down in the howling gale, and the gut-wrenching fear, came rushing back. I clutched Liam's hand. He smiled again, but it didn't reach his eyes.

"I didn't want to warn him of my presence, so I parked a ways from where you'd marked the grave spot and hiked in. That's when I saw you." Liam's voice broke. I stared at him. He looked away and wiped his eyes.

"It was the most horrifying thing I've ever seen," Liam whispered, his voice hoarse. "It should have been pitch black out there, but that clearing seemed to have some kind of weird light of its own; I could see everything clearly. You were lying on the ground, and I saw Hiram pick you up in his arms. Then he... he placed his hand on your chest and your whole body went rigid. I just knew he'd killed you." Liam paused again and ran his hand through his blonde hair.

"I took my rifle and shot at him. I swore I'd hit him, but he came at me." Liam gave a short, pained laugh. "I really hadn't considered what to do if he came after me, so I just ran, hoping to draw him away from you in case you were still alive. I guess that part of the plan worked at least."

I nodded. "It gave me time to retrieve his heart."

Liam tilted his head, eyes wide. "So, you really did burn it? That's truly what those ashes were?"

"Yeah." I shuddered, putting the experience out of my mind. No doubt that little episode would provide fodder for nightmares for years to come.

Now Liam nodded as if in understanding. "That explains why he finally left me and came after you. I'm sure I hit him a couple of times, but it didn't faze him. But then something changed, and I could tell he was hurting. I don't think the bullets bothered him until you started to destroy his heart. As long as his heart was intact, he was okay."

"He was really pissed." I gave a small painful smile recalling Hiram's reaction. I swallowed. The guy had tried to kill me. Twice.

"I lost Hiram for a few minutes, and as I came up the hill, I saw he had you again. That's when you screamed." Liam's bruises stood out even more vividly as what little color he'd had drained from his face. "I've never heard anything like that before, and I hope to God, I never do again. Then… well, then I shot him again. He dropped you, and just stood there for a second, like he couldn't believe it. I was trying to figure out if I should shoot him one more time when he collapsed to the ground and… and disappeared."

I stared at Liam. "Disappeared? Like poof? He was gone?"

Liam nodded slowly, staring off into space. "Yeah, just like that. Poof. I guess by destroying his heart, you destroyed whatever kept him here." Liam shuddered and closed his eyes. "You were so still. Your face was totally white. I… I thought for sure he'd really killed you this time."

We both sat in silence for several long seconds reliving those final moments. I'd been so frightened for Liam that I hadn't considered what he must be thinking about me. I turned to him.

"Are you okay?" I bit my lip. "You actually shot somebody. That can't be easy to deal with."

Liam stared at the floor for a moment. "I should be upset, but it wasn't like shooting a real person. More like being in a video game, especially after his body disappeared. Game over."

I digested this for a moment. The last thing I wanted was for Liam to be traumatized by killing someone, even if that someone was technically already dead. I sighed.

"What did you tell the cops?"

Liam shrugged. "I told them pretty much everything I just told you, except I left out the part about him disappearing. I said he'd run off, and that I wasn't sure I'd actually hit him. I mean, how could I explain he'd simply vanished?"

I gave a small laugh. "Yeah, I left out the part about how Hiram enjoyed sucking the life out of teenagers and the entertaining bit about digging out his heart and setting it on fire."

Liam shook his head. "Well, even if you did tell them that, I'm guessing they'd attribute it to shock. You were in pretty bad shape when we got back."

I squeezed Liam's hand. "Thank you. Thank you for saving my life." My voice was husky and didn't even sound like mine.

Liam smiled his simple god-like smile. "You're welcome."

CHAPTER THIRTY-TWO

"Sophia!"

I looked up from the beef barley soup Liam's mom had forced on me. My father rushed forward, arms out and face white. I don't think I'd ever seen him look more frightened. I was just able to set the tray aside when he embraced me in a powerful bear hug.

"Sophia, are you all right? Did he hurt you? I am so sorry we weren't here for you. I should never have left you up here alone!" Dad's words tumbled out so quickly, I barely made out what he was saying. It didn't matter. I just hugged him back, not wanting to let go. The mere scent of his aftershave made me feel safe.

"I'm fine. Really." My voice still sounded weak to me. I figured it would take a few days for me to get back up to speed.

Dad finally released me from his death grip and sat down on the edge of my bed. He reached out and gently caressed my cheek. "We should have taken your fears concerning Hiram Parsons more seriously."

"It's okay, Dad." I squeezed his hand.

He smiled, but still looked deeply troubled. "No, it's not okay. No one knows where that nutcase disappeared to. The police are searching for him, but so far there's been no sign of him. He might come looking for you again. He might hurt some other girl. This is very serious."

I nodded, but I knew I was safe. I totally believed Hiram's soul sucking days were over.

Dad continued to study me. "Your mom stayed at the hospital with Maya. She wanted to come, but somebody had to stay with your sister."

"How... how is she?" I wasn't sure if I wanted to know or not.

Dad sighed and ran a hand across his stubbled jaw. "She seems to have stabilized for the moment, but still isn't responding to the treatment. The doctors are going to try some other things."

I pushed myself up, grimacing briefly at all aches and pains. I suddenly remembered my little bag of ashes. "Dad, I need to see her."

Dad gave me a sad smile. "You will. Soon. But right now, you need to take care of yourself. The doctor says you were suffering from severe shock and exposure. Besides, the water is still high, and many of the roads are blocked."

I shook my head impatiently. "Dad, you managed to get here. Liam can take us across the flooded area in his boat. But I really need to see her! Please." My voice trailed off as I fought back tears. I was terrified I was going to be too late.

I caught the uncertainty in Dad's eyes. Of course, he was worried about Maya, but he was still dealing with the stress of having almost lost another daughter to a crazed lunatic. He looked away.

"Honestly, Dad, I'm okay. But, I'm just so worried about Maya. Besides, we'd be going to a hospital. If I collapse or something, we'd be in the perfect place. I won't be able to rest until I see her. And you know Mom won't rest until she sees me."

He sighed deeply, and I knew I'd won.

"Let me go talk to Liam's dad and that doctor. If they both agree, we'll go."

I watched as he left the room, shoulders slumped. My heart broke. He looked like he'd aged ten years. Liam reappeared a few moments later.

"You heard?" I asked.

He nodded. "You're really going to try and feed her some of those ashes?" A look of faint disgust crossed his face.

"Yeah. I don't know if it will actually help, but I have to try."

"So far, everything else has fit the story." Liam reached out and took my hand. "But, try not to give up if it doesn't. Doctors have all kinds of new ways to treat tuberculosis, and now that Hiram's gone, I think Maya's got a real chance."

The weight settled on my shoulders a bit more firmly. It really hadn't occurred to me that feeding her the ashes might not work. I had blindly assumed that everything would fall into place once we got rid of Hiram and torched his heart. Still, I wasn't going to back down now.

Dad returned after a while with the doctor in tow.

"I want him to check you over one last time," said Dad, his brow furrowed. "If he says it's okay, then we'll go. Liam's dad said he can take us back across the flood to where I left the car."

It took the doctor just a few minutes to look me over. I still had zero energy but did my best to hide my fatigue. At last the doctor proclaimed me fit to go, but ordered me to rest over the next few days once we reached Berlin.

Before we left, Liam brought me a small plastic bottle half full of apple juice. I dumped in the ashes and shook it up. The concoction looked disgusting, but there was nothing I could do about that. Hopefully, Maya would be so out of it, she wouldn't notice.

It took us twice as long as it should have to reach the hospital in Berlin. As downed trees, flooded roads and debris slowed our progress, my anxiety continued to grow. Would Maya still be alive when we got there? I just had this impression of impending doom.

When we arrived, we learned that to our dismay, Maya had been moved to intensive care. We hurried to the ICU where we found Mom stretched out across several of the hideous waiting room chairs. Seems like the hospital would want to make things more comfortable for people worrying about their loved ones. Mom looked completely done in; her face gray with exhaustion. She woke instantly when Dad touched her shoulder.

The minute she laid eyes on me, she burst into tears and threw her arms around me. It was pretty much a repeat of what I'd gone through with Dad, but at least I stood on my own two feet. Believe me, that wasn't easy either, but I was determined to see Maya no matter what.

After Mom had settled down a little and convinced herself I had survived my ordeal, she told us that Maya's breathing deteriorated overnight and the doctor worried they might have to put her on a respirator. The new medication didn't seem to be having any affect. I felt a tightness in my stomach. If they did that, I wouldn't be able to get her to drink the potion with the ashes in it.

"Can I see her?" I fingered the small bottle of the mixture I held in my pocket, my sense of urgency intensifying.

Mom gently stroked my head. "Let me ask, but I'm sure it will be all right for just a minute."

That's all I would need.

The nurse led me back to the small cubicle that held my sister. She explained about the machines and warned me not to touch anything. I nodded, not really listening.

If I hadn't known that the figure in the bed was Maya, I'm not sure I would have recognized her. She seemed to have lost like thirty pounds since the last time I'd seen her. Her translucent skin stretched painfully across the sharp bones of her face. Tears stung the back of my eyes as I listened to her fight for every breath. The nurse squeezed my shoulder and told me to call her if I needed something.

I slowly approached Maya, my heart beating like a trapped bird. I hovered by her bedside for several long moments shifting from one foot to another. Finally, I reached out and took her hand, careful not to dislodge the IV taped there.

"Maya?" I kept my voice low. "Maya, can you hear me?"

For several long moments, nothing happened. I bit my lip, then sighed with relief as Maya's eyes flickered open. They stared at me, dull with fever. "Hey." I could barely hear her.

I glanced behind me, then leaned forward tightening my grip. "Maya, you need to listen to me. I have something you need to drink. It's probably pretty horrible, but I think it's the only thing that can make you better. Do you understand me?"

I heard nothing except for the horrible rasping noise she made as she breathed. Maya's eyes focused on me for just a second, and she gave a faint nod.

Licking my dry lips, I reached into my pocket and pulled out the small plastic water bottle I'd filled with a mixture of ashes and apple juice. I figured the juice would make it easier to get down. I unscrewed the lid, then gently lifting her head, I gave her a sip of the potion. She made a face but managed to choke down several good swallows. She closed her eyes signaling no more. I prayed it was enough. I replaced the cap and slipped the near-empty bottle back into my pocket.

"Get well, Maya. I love you," I whispered into her ear. She gave my hand a weak squeeze.

I had done all I could.

Later that day, the doctors came to talk to us.

"We've done some further testing," said the old guy my dad called Dr. Frasier. "And it looks like we were wrong with the diagnosis. Has your daughter traveled overseas anytime recently?"

My parents looked at each other in confusion and shook their heads. I held my breath.

The doctor pursed his lips and looked at the clipboard in his hand. "The reason I ask is your daughter has tested positive for a particularly aggressive form of tuberculosis. In the old days, they used to call it 'galloping consumption'. It's extremely rare, especially here in the United States, so I'm wondering where she might have contracted it."

"Tuberculosis?" Dad frowned. "Can you treat it?"

"Oh yes. TB is actually highly treatable as long as the patient takes their medication as prescribed."

I almost fainted with relief. They *knew*. They could finally treat her now and Maya would be okay. The doctor was still talking about how in her weakened state, Maya would have to stay in the hospital for a while, and we'd all need to be treated, blah, blah blah. I have no idea if my ash concoction made the difference but deep down, I believed it had. It was over.

EPILOGUE

Maya never returned to the house in Parsons Corners, although she continued to improve rapidly. It was decided Dad and I would go back and pack up everything then meet Mom and Maya back at our home in Manchester once they released Maya.

I had a couple more meetings with the police about my ordeal in the forest, but Hiram was never found. No surprise there. His fate would always be Liam's and my secret. No more Parsons' descendants need ever worry about losing their lives to that menace. There was some confusion when Liam led the police to where he'd rescued me and they discovered the opened grave. There was nothing in the coffin now but a pile of bones and tattered remains of rotting clothes. The police surmised Hiram planned on murdering me, then burying me in the coffin. I didn't contradict them. It was actually true.

When Dad and I returned to the house by the lake, it felt different. A peaceful air filled the place that hadn't been there before.

During our final day at the house, I went up to my room and pulled out Mercy May's diary, examining the worn black leather for a long time.

"It's over, Mercy," I whispered gripping the book tightly. "Hiram is gone for good. No one else will suffer because of him." I jumped as a chilly breeze

277

blew in through the open window, fluttering the sheer curtains. I smiled. Mercy had heard me.

I took the small book back up to the attic and carefully replaced it in its secret compartment. It didn't belong to me and needed to remain with all the rest of Mercy May's belongings. After closing the tiny drawer, I opened the other and stared down at the small, black watch. My lips pressed tightly together, I reluctantly picked it up, feeling its cold and lifeless weight in my hand. An unexpected chill ran down my back as I opened the case and gasped. An ugly jagged crack now stretched across the face of the crystal; the hands of the watch frozen at 11:47. Was that the time I had destroyed his heart? I didn't know for sure. Taking a deep breath, I opened the other side of the case and shuddered. The once clear portrait of Hiram Parsons had faded to nothing but a blurred shadow. Unnerved, I snapped the case shut and thrust the timepiece back into the drawer, slamming it shut. *Sorry Hiram, but death doesn't necessarily mean immortality.*

"Sophia!" I heard my dad call from downstairs. "Liam is here to say goodbye."

A lump formed in my throat. This part was going to be hardest of all. Liam and I had already said our big goodbyes, but I'd been dreading this final one. I fingered the locket that now hung around my neck, and a rush of warmth flowed through me. We had made lots of plans to keep in touch. No matter what the future held, I would always have a bond with Liam that neither time nor distance could ever erase. He was my first real crush, but more importantly, my first real friend, and I owed him my life. As I got to my feet and brushed off the dust, I took one last look around. Many untold stories were hidden in this attic, but they weren't mine to tell. With a sigh, I flipped off the light and headed downstairs.

❖   ❖   ❖

In the silence of the attic, there was a faint tick followed by a second, then a third as the hands resumed their tireless movement around the face of the old watch.

THE END

AFTERWORD

Tuberculosis is a bacterial disease caused by *Mycobacterium tuberculosis.* Once referred to as consumption as it seemed to consume its victims from within, the disease killed more people in nineteenth century New England than any other disease. It was not uncommon for the infection to kill several members of a single family, and thus was much feared. As odd as it sounds, vampire scares did indeed sweep through rural New England during the 1800s especially when tuberculosis infection was high. The most famous case of a supposed vampire involved a young woman by the name of Mercy "Lena" Brown who lived on a small farm in Exeter, Rhode Island.

In 1882, Lena's mother died of tuberculosis. Less than a year later, Lena's twenty-year-old sister passed away. A few years after that, her brother, Edwin became ill and traveled to Colorado in the hope that the drier climate would improve his health. Finally, in 1892, Lena herself succumbed to the disease, while Edwin, who had recently returned from the west, was fading fast. In a meeting of family and friends, the suggestion was made that perhaps something evil was stalking the Brown family, and, in the end, it was decided that no less than a vampire must be siphoning away the lives of their loved ones. The family was convinced that in order to save Edwin, they must exhume the bodies of Lena, her mother and her sister to check for fresh blood and other signs of vampirism.

Much to everyone's horror, despite being dead for three months, Lena's body was well-preserved and blood was found in her heart. The family immediately burned the organ on a nearby rock and fed the ashes to Edwin, who, unsurprisingly, passed away shortly afterward. Today, many believe that because she died in January, Lena's body had been stored in a crypt until the spring thaw, thus preserving her body and resulting in its life-like appearance.

Lena's father, George Brown, never contracted the disease and lived in Exeter until his death in 1922. He was the only member of the family to survive.

Mercy Lena Brown was eventually buried, without her heart, in the Exeter Baptist church cemetery. Lena was not the only New Englander suspected of being a vampire but was certainly the best documented.

For more information on this fascinating subject, I would suggest readers turn to Michael E. Bell's excellent book, *Food for the Dead: On the trail of New England's Vampires.*

ACKNOWLEDGMENTS

As usual, I must thank my No. 1 Fan, Spencer Keene for being my beta reader and giving me good advice.

I must also thank my family and friends: Tim Reed, Hilary Reed, Margie Faraday, Jan Seavey, and Connie Evans, for reading over the manuscript and finding so many of those little niggling typos and missing commas my eyes refused to see. Thanks also to Amanda Stacey for her wonderful cover design.

ABOUT THE AUTHOR

Ellen Reed lives in Henniker, New Hampshire but was grew up in New Jersey, and has lived in a variety of places, from Jakarta, Indonesia to Eagle River, Alaska. Mom to four and grandmother to three, it has always been her dream to write books for children. While spending a summer in Norway, she wrote and illustrated several stories for her young daughter when they grew bored with the limited number of English language books they had brought along. It took National Novel Writing Month in 2009 for her to finally get up the nerve to try writing an actual novel and she has never looked back.

Made in the USA
Middletown, DE
28 July 2019